CHRISTOPHE

Safe Haven: Vengeance

Christopher Artinian

CHRISTOPHER ARTINIAN

Copyright © 2019 Christopher Artinian

All rights reserved.

ISBN: 9781080966752

CHRISTOPHER ARTINIAN

DEDICATION

To Mike, Emma and Lucy. I will forever be in your debt.

CHRISTOPHER ARTINIAN

ACKNOWLEDGEMENTS

A never-ending fountain of thanks to my wife. Tina never stops working to help get my books to a wider audience. She is next to me every step of the way from the start of a new idea to the last full stop, and I would be lost without her.

As always, a massive thank you to the members of the fan club across on Facebook. The huge wealth of support I receive from them never leaves me anything but flabbergasted.

Big thanks to Sheila Shedd, my editor. A safer catcher's mitt I would struggle to find. I also want to thank my good friend, Christian Bentulan. I love every cover he has done for me and he always manages to amaze.

Last but by no means least, thanks to you for buying this book. This is number five in the series, so I'm guessing you've read the other four at least. I'm so happy you stayed on this journey with me.

CHRISTOPHER ARTINIAN

PROLOGUE

They had lived on the road ever since the day it all went to hell; finding caravans, buses, motorhomes, anything they could to travel around in and stay safe from the RAMs. They had shared a thousand stories beside the campfire, reliving their adventures, their near escapes from reanimated corpses, violent conflicts and difficulty with other groups of travelling bandits. Anything that made a good tale. In their lives before, they had existed in the shadows, making their money in the grey if not the black economy. Life now was not so very different.

Mason's eyes glinted in the flickering flames and the bottle he brought up to his mouth cast an amber filter on his normally ruddy face. He glugged back a couple of mouthfuls of whisky before handing it to the next person in the circle.

"So, it was just me against two of them things," he continued. "I was out of bullets, and I'd dropped my knife on the other side of the wall. Their grey eyes—those devilish pupils locked onto me and they charged," he said, looking around the campfire at the rest of the faces as they all watched, eagerly anticipating his words as well as the bottle being passed their way.

"What happened? What happened then, Mason?" Tanya, the woman who now held the bottle, asked.

Mason exhaled a whisky fumed breath and brought his hands up in front of him, shadow playing the events as he recalled them. "Well, the wall was easily twelve foot, so there was no way I was getting back over that." He looked around again to see everybody hanging on his words. "I had two choices: kill or be killed. I readied myself. They were both lightning-fast, but one was maybe just a foot in front of the other. That's when I knew I had a chance. The first of them dived at me—almost flying it was. It launched through the air like a bird, its arms stretched in front of it, its hands reaching for me, trying to grab me." He paused again as a second bottle made it into the circle, and he took a thirsty drink from it before passing it on.

Tanya closed her fingers around his and the pair looked at each other in a drunken gaze, both knowing instantly that they would have someone to share their bed with tonight. "Then what happened?" Tanya asked, provocatively licking her lips before putting the mouth of the bottle up to them, letting the whisky flow down her throat.

For a moment, Mason forgot himself, transfixed by the woman in front of him, but then he turned back to the rest of his audience. "Well, then it was almost like being back in the boxing ring. In the ring you have to know how to give and take a punch for sure, but you need to duck, weave, and parry too. I saw my opportunity, and I parried," he said, jerking both his arms to the right as if he was fending off the same potential blow that very moment. "Well that thing, it went straight into the wall. I heard the crack—like a coconut smashing. Then it was just me and the other one. It came at me the same way, only I didn't have time to straighten up and bring my body back round, so I ducked and rolled."

Excited gasps went up from around the circle, just as the first bottle was passed back to him. Mason took another drink and looked across to the other fires. At least half a dozen were burning inside the wide camp ring that had been created by the vehicles. At each one, stories like his were being told and the narrators knew only too well that if they weren't entertaining, the audience would soon lose interest and move along. He passed the bottle to Tanya, who repeated the gentle, but barely perceptible, caress of his fingers. "And was it dead? Did its head crack like the other?"

"Nooo. Then I realised what a fool I'd been. These things...they're not like men. They just keep going. The first one, it stood up. *Stood up* I'm telling you."

"No!" a woman from the other side of the fire exclaimed.

"Yes. It stood up. Its skull was cracked alright, but that wasn't the end of it. Its forehead was all caved in, its nose was squashed...an eye was practically out of its socket, but that thing came back towards me, *running* no less."

Another gasp went up from his listeners. "Then what?" Tanya asked.

"Well by then I was really pissed off," a small chuckle went up from around the fire. "It dived at me again, but I had no wall behind me now—nothing that was going to stop it but myself. I waited and waited, and then, right at the last second, I shot it a right hook." He paused for effect, looking around at the faces again before continuing. "I felt its jaw break against my knuckles. The thing went crashing to the floor, and this time it was jarred enough to stay put a while. The other one was just starting to rally itself when I saw a decent-sized rock on the ground next to me." Mason stretched his fingers around an imaginary rock, giving his audience a clue as to the size of stone he was talking about. He hefted it up and down, indicating its weight. "Before the thing got fully straightened up, I was on it, pounding and pounding until there was a hole in its skull the size of my fist." The imaginary rock was squeezed away to nothingness as he clenched his fingers tight.

"Did it fight back?" Tanya asked.

"They always try to fight back," he said, "but I didn't let up, and the thing went down for good. Well. The other thing was still stunned; it didn't have the same spring in its step, and when it climbed to its feet this time, its bottom jaw had dropped right open, *unhinged*. Well I knew there and then that thing wouldn't be biting anything ever again, but that's not to say it wouldn't try. It came towards me. It didn't dive, but it ran full steam. I dodged at the last second, pulling back fast enough to grab the back of its head. Then, using its own momentum, I pushed it with all my strength towards the wall. There was an almighty pop, and it slid down, leaving a bloody stripe against the brickwork. And that was it. Neither of them bothered me again."

The story finished right on cue as the second bottle was passed from his left once again. He felt a pat on the back and some *yeahs* and small cheers went up for a fireside tale well told. It was getting late, and nobody started with a new story. As the first, then the second bottle bled dry, people began to drift from the group and stagger towards their homes-on-wheels until it was just Mason and Tanya left to watch the flickering flames.

Tanya looked at her watch in the orange glow. "It's not even midnight; there's plenty of fun to be had before morning yet," she said, clamping her hand around Mason's thigh.

"That there is," Mason said with a leery smile. In the shadows and with the benefit of so much whisky, he did not see the ravages of time or life on the road etched on Tanya's features; he just saw a woman who wanted him. He stood up and extended his hand. Tanya grabbed it and climbed to her feet.

"You're a gentleman," she said.

"Don't you believe it for a second," Mason replied, smiling down at her.

They moved a little closer and their lips met in a whisky flavoured kiss that seemed to last an age. Mason moved his hand round and gently squeezed Tanya's left buttock. "How about you and me go back to yours and have a little fun?" she said.

He placed his other hand on her right buttock and pulled her into him. She could feel the excitement rising in both of them and he gave her another kiss, more forceful this time. "You read my mind," he said, and led her by the wrist back to his caravan.

*

The next morning, Tanya woke first. She lay on her side watching Mason sleep. His greasy blonde hair was flecked with grey and his red complexion gave him a look as if he was permanently in a rage, but it was a look she liked. She could do a lot worse than hook up with him. He was one of the group's leaders, no small feat when they were over sixty strong. It would give her position if she was his woman. *It would give me perks*, she thought as she looked around the spacious caravan.

"What are you thinking?" Mason asked.

"I thought you were asleep. You know how to scare a girl."

"Didn't you say the same thing last night?" he replied, and they both laughed.

"I was thinking this place could do with a woman's touch."

Mason eased himself onto his side to look at her. In the morning light, her little flaws were more apparent than they were by the glow of the fire, but she was a good-looking woman, all the same. "I see. And if you were to move into this luxury abode, how would you intend to pay the rather steep rent?"

"Hmm, let me think." Tanya's lips curled into a smile and her head slowly disappeared under the covers. She pressed her mouth against Mason's hairy chest, then flicked her tongue against his left nipple before continuing her journey downwards. He lay back and placed his hands behind his head, smiling broadly as Tanya's lips kissed and nibbled his lower torso.

"Y'know what? I could see this tenancy working out. I'll get the papers drawn up." He closed his eyes and his breathing began to get heavier. All the while, the smile broadened on his face.

Tat tat tat, came the rapping against the caravan door. "Mason? You there?" came the voice.

The smile quickly disappeared from Mason's face. He whipped back the quilt, revealing Tanya naked and curled up halfway down the bed. She had not heard the first tapping on the door, but she heard the second. She looked at Mason, then at the bedside clock.

Mason climbed out of bed angrily, stood to one side of the caravan door and opened it a crack, shielding himself behind it, but showing Tanya in her full glory quickly trying to cover herself up. "A man can't even get a blow job in peace around here. What the fuck is it?"

The man at the door looked towards Tanya for a moment, then looked up towards Mason. "They're back," was all he said before turning and leaving.

Mason shut the door and walked straight across to his side of the bed where he began to put his clothes on. "I thought we were going to have a little more fun," Tanya said.

"We will later. Got some business to take care of first. Make yourself a drink, and don't you dare think about putting any clothes on," he said smiling. He bent down and gave her a long kiss. Their breath still carried the heavy fumes of whisky from the night before, but that was just part of life on the road for this merry troop. "Don't go away now."

"I have no intention," she said, and dragged the quilt back over her.

Mason pulled his t-shirt on and walked to the door, looking back one last time before heading out into the cool morning air. He headed off towards the noise. It was six-thirty in the morning; many were still sleeping off the effects of the drink from the night before, but this was urgent business. This was the reason they had been parked up in this tree-lined meadow for the last ten days.

"Good to see you, Mason," said a woman with long, curly red hair. She had a pale, freckled complexion that made her look younger than she was, innocent almost, though Mason knew she was anything but.

"Carol, you old whore," he said, leaning in and giving her a rough kiss, "What have you and your lads brought back for us?" He nudged his chin towards two teenage boys with similar colouring. "You were gone long enough."

"Well if you want a job doing, you do it properly," she said smiling.

"And?"

"Do you mind if I have my fucking cup of tea first?"

"Yes, as a matter of fact, I fucking do. I was just about to get my end away and I got broken off for this, so your fucking tea can wait." Everybody laughed, and for the first time, Mason noticed the other elder statesmen of the convoy were in attendance. He looked around and nodded.

"What's that you say? You just got your end broken off? Sounds painful," Carol said, and they all laughed again. Another man arrived with a tray of steaming drinks. Carol took one, as did the rest of the group. They gathered around the entrance to one of the motorhomes, and Carol sat down on the step.

"So come on then," said one of the other men, "don't leave us in fucking suspense."

"Right," she said. "They've got a big fucking campsite. Bloody thing goes on for miles. That's where they've put us up. Even gave us our own caravan. They give you a breakfast and evening meal at the village hall. At the site itself, you can get a lunch if you want one, all gratis. Got themselves a bottomless foodbank. There's a scavenger group what goes out quite regular. Now there are three trained soldiers and a few others I've seen walking around with guns. Apparently, when they go on a scavenge, quite a lot of them go out at the same time, so that would be the best time to strike."

"Strike? They've got food; is that all we're going in for?" Mason said.

"I haven't finished yet y'impatient bastard. They've got a hospital. As soon as you arrive, you get escorted there and you have to have a full medical exam. They've got a qualified doctor and loads of meds. I managed to have look when I went to take a piss. They've got cupboards of the stuff, enough to keep us trading for a year. But that's not all," she said, taking a drink of her tea.

"Well go on," Mason said.

"There's a pub. They've got their own microbrewery and distillery. They have a currency system where you can trade batteries, fruit, veg, all sorts for drink. The owner says the proceeds go 'back to the community,'" she said, a mocking smile on her face.

"Proper little socialists then?" Mason added, and the others laughed.

"Anyone passing through can trade. I even heard they go to the islands and trade with them. This place is a goldmine."

"Okay, so what do you suggest?".

"We're there now. We're helping out in the village hall; Davey even went out on one of the fishing boats yesterday. I say, get another couple of families in for a few days, y'know, speak to different people, have a look around; they might be able to find out a bit of stuff I haven't. Then the next time the place empties for a scavenger trip, we hit them."

"Hit them?"

"Take 'em for everything we can grab quick. There's over five hundred up and down the coastline; we don't want to get into a full-scale battle. We hit the pub, the village hall, the hospital and we're on our way. We'll be set up for a long time to come, and the great thing about these bleeding-heart dopes is we'll be able to do it all again next year. Send a couple of different faces in there and bam," she said, breaking out into a wide grin.

"So, you mentioned guns?" said one of the men.

"I've seen three of the soldiers with them, and when they go out on scavenger missions a couple more people carry, so there must be a small cache somewhere, but nothing like what we've got. There are lookouts to the north and west—"

"West?" Mason said. "West is in the fucking sea."

"East then. I always get those two mixed up."

"Filling me with fucking confidence you are," he replied and a small ripple of laughter travelled around the circle.

"Anyway, as I was saying, I think the lookouts have them, and that's it."

"Sweet," Mason said, scratching his stubbled chin. "And you've drawn the maps like I asked?"

Carol handed over a tatty looking piece of paper with a pencil drawing on one side and writing on the other. "There you go."

"No expense spared eh?"

"It's not like there's a stationary store there."

"Right well, let me wake the fuck up and we'll put a plan together."

"You wake up as much as you want, me and the kids need to head back."

"You can just come and go as you please?"

"Not quite. We have to have the physical done again."

"And it won't raise suspicions you heading back in there?"

"I told a few people last night that we didn't know what to expect from the place, that we buried a stash of supplies in case we needed to make a quick escape. So when

I return with some tins and a few bits and pieces, they won't think anything of it," Carol said.

"Smart thinking. Better make it look like it was worth the trouble."

"Don't worry—I can be very convincing when I want to be."

"Oh I know you can," Mason said with a grin. "Right, don't forget to take the radio; it's band eight. We'll see you soon."

Carol nodded and left.

"Well then, looks like we've got some work to do. We'll meet back here in an hour and iron out the details," Mason said, putting the empty mug on the tray and walking back to his caravan.

1

It was cold enough to snow outside, but the worst of the weather was behind them now. The night was closing in and the sign for the Haven Arms swung gently in the breeze as Mike crossed the small carpark. He could see the orange glow of the fire and lanterns in the main saloon bar, and applause started as another song from the guitarist came to an end.

Mike watched proudly as his friend Beth placed her fingers back on the fretboard and immediately began to play another piece. Sat in front of her was her beloved, Barney, looking at her as if she was some megastar performing at Wembley Stadium. When Mike had first met these two, the world had fallen apart, and but for their shared fight and determination, none of them would be here now.

Mike opened the door and a wall of heat hit him as he walked inside. A few heads turned, but most continued to watch Beth on the small stage in the corner.

"Mikey!" called Kirsty, coming from around the bar to greet him with a huge kiss on his cheek.

"Hi Kirsty," he replied, squeezing her tightly. "Sorry I've not been around for a while."

"Never mind that; it's lovely to see you now," she said, gently brushing a lock of hair from his forehead. "What can I get you to drink, darling?"

Mike smiled. Kirsty was an awful lot like the pub's owner, Jenny, and had an incredible way of making everyone feel like the most important person in the world. She had arrived a few months ago, and she and Jenny had hit it off straight away. She was in her early fifties, and even now managed to wear enough makeup to cover the wall of a small room. "I can't really stop. Luce asked me to come over and pick up the alcohol, whatever that means."

Kirsty walked back to the bar. "Come on, you can stay for one," she said, taking the top off a brown bottle and pouring the contents into a glass for him.

"You're a terrible influence; has anyone ever told you that?"

"Everybody tells me that," she said, grinning broadly. "You enjoy that my darling, and I'll go get the booze."

Mike picked up his glass and took a drink. It was room temperature, but the beer tasted good. He turned and leaned his back against the bar as he watched Beth sing. She smiled as she saw him and Mike waved. There were familiar faces and unfamiliar ones, too. Safe Haven was still growing.

There was a crowd sat over in one corner. They looked like they'd been there for some time, and the volume of their conversation was getting louder by the second. Laughter erupted from the table, drowning out Beth's singing for a moment, but then her gentle voice became the focus of the room once more.

"Here we go," Kirsty said, plonking down a crate full of bottles containing clear fluid.

Mike turned back around and picked one of the bottles up. "What is this?"

"Alcohol. Lucy wants it for the hospital."

"This beer's good," he said, replacing the bottle carefully into the crate.

"The microbrewery's doing really well, and we've got all sorts being made here now. Spirits, wines, the lot," she said, smiling and grabbing another bottle of beer for herself. "You and Lucy will have to come across for a proper booze-up one night."

"We will, I promise."

Raucous laughter came from the table in the corner again. "They've been here half the day," she said before taking a drink.

"They causing you any trouble?" Mike asked.

"No, they're just...noisy."

Mike took another drink as the door to the pub opened again and a man and a woman walked up to the bar.

"Evening," they said, as a younger, assistant bartender went across to serve them. The man pulled a heavy rucksack from his shoulders and removed two large bags of freshly picked potatoes from it. The bartender carried them across to a set of scales and weighed them.

"Ten kilos. That's ten bottles of beer or ten shots," the bartender said. The couple nodded gratefully and the bartender returned to them to take their order.

"How's the bartering thing working out? As the first commercial enterprise in Safe Haven, you're our guinea pig," Mike said, smiling.

"So far so good," Kirsty responded pointing up to a blackboard with a list of commonly bartered goods listed. "People seem to be taking to it pretty well."

Mike looked up at the board. "Remind me to bring a wheelbarrow of carrots with me the next time I come."

"Your drinks will always be on the house," she said.

"How come?" asked an older man who was sat at the bar, cradling a glass of whisky.

Suddenly there was a yelp from in front of the fire, followed by raucous laughter from the table in the corner again. One of the men had stamped on the tail of Jenny's dog, Meg, to get it to move so he could feel the heat of the fire unobstructed. Meg headed over to the bar with her tail between her legs and Kirsty rushed around to comfort the gentle creature.

Mike took a drink from his bottle, placed it down on the bar, and walked over to the table. He bent down to talk into the man's ear so he'd be heard over the sound of Beth's song. "You won't be laughing in a minute when you're trying to pick your teeth off the floor with broken fingers."

The man stood up; the effects of the alcohol made him stagger a little. He was a good six inches taller than Mike, but Mike moved in closer to him. "What did you say to me?" the man asked, a drunken glint in his eyes.

"What, are you deaf as well as stupid and ugly? You really did get a raw fucking deal didn't you."

All the men and women at the table burst out laughing. "He's got your number," one of them said.

"I eat and shit out little bastards like you for breakfast," the man said, becoming increasingly enraged.

Mike smiled. "Come on then. Give it a go. Your mates can run a sweepstake on what day next week you'll wake up," he said, not breaking his gaze for a second.

The party behind him laughed again and the man began to shake with anger. A hand reached out from one of the women at the table and grabbed the man's arm. "We're guests here. Don't be an idiot, Colm." The man's breathing remained heavy for a while, but now Beth had stopped playing and he realised all the eyes in the pub were looking towards him.

Colm blinked as if coming to his senses. "I...I don't want to fight you," he mumbled.

"Then you'll apologise to my friend at the bar, and you're going to make it up to Meg there." Mike looked at the table to see an assortment of currency. "I tell you what. Two packets of batteries will buy Meg a fish supper. That's the least she deserves."

The man turned and picked up two packs of AA batteries from the table. He shoved them into Mike's hand

and looked over to the bar. "I'm sorry," he said. "I'm sorry for what I did to your dog." He looked back at Mike, who gave him a curt nod before walking back to the bar.

The man sat down and Beth began to play again. Kirsty smiled as Mike picked up his bottle to take another drink. She turned to the old man cradling his whisky. "That's why he'll never pay for a drink," she said.

*

The village hall had been host to more meetings in the last few months than any other time in its history. The population of Safe Haven was growing and sensible decisions had to be made regarding everything from food and housing to health and policing.

Nine members were on the council to ensure that there was never a tied vote in the process. They took it in turns to chair the meetings, and if any member of the township wanted to raise an issue, they had the opportunity to do so via one of the representatives.

There were four tables pushed together and arranged in a large rectangle, with another one placed horizontally across the end. Lucy was chairing today's meeting, and the members of the council were making small talk while Emma and Sarah prepared drinks and brought them over.

When everyone was seated, the conversation died down and they looked towards Lucy.

"Okay, we've got quite a bit to get through this evening," she said in her soft New England accent. "I'm chairing tonight, so I'll get my stuff out of the way first. Thanks to the incredibly hard work of Mr Hughes and Mr Shaw over there," she said, nodding towards the two soldiers, "I'm happy to tell you that our hospital is back up and running at full capacity. We have two brand new units that replaced the ones burnt out in the fire and they've been kitted out exactly the same way the old ones were. Our stock of pharms and other medical supplies are steadily building, and since Mike took that group back into Inverness to raid the chemist, we've probably got enough antibiotics to see us through next winter, even at the rate the population is continuing to grow."

"That is truly excellent news," Raj said, and the others mumbled their happy approval.

"The recruitment drive is ongoing, but I've got Stephanie, who is a qualified nurse, Lisa, who's a midwife, and twelve trainee medical staff, in addition to the vital help Raj and Talikha provide. We're already in a much stronger position than we were before the winter and if we were hit by another outbreak, I'm confident we could deal with it this time.

"That's fantastic news, Lucy," Hughes said.

"Well, this is what we're about isn't it?" she said, gesturing to the people around the table. "It's about making the community stronger, about overcoming problems, about building something better. And on that note, Jenny, over to you." Lucy sat down, and the always glamorously dressed, fifty-something ex-hotelier stood up.

"As you know, the Haven Arms began a barter system last week as a kind of experiment. It's still developing like everything is here, but so far it's working well." Jenny reached under the desk and pulled out a blackboard.

1 KG OF FRUIT - 1 BOTTLE OR SHOT
1 PACK OF 4 AA OR AAA BATTERIES - 1 BOTTLE OR SHOT
2 KG OF VEG - 1 BOTTLE OR SHOT
5 BOOKS (NO MORE BIBLES THANKS) - 1 BOTTLE OR SHOT
1 PACK OF C OR D BATTERIES - 2 BOTTLES OR SHOTS
3 TINS OF FOOD (IN DATE) – 1 BOTTLE OR SHOT
2 PACKETS PASTA/RICE/NOODLES/GRAINS – 1 BOTTLE OR SHOT
1 LITRE OF DIESEL - 2 BOTTLES OR SHOTS

(BOTTLE – BEER/CIDER. SHOT – WHISKEY or VODKA)

Everybody examined it for a moment. "So nobody can buy a drink unless they come in with those items?" Emma asked.

"Well, yes and no; this is just a guide. We're almost like a trading post now. I've been working closely with Ruth and Jules," Jenny said, smiling towards her friends, "and obviously, George too. There are some things that are worth much more than just one or two drinks that would be of benefit for the community, and for those things, I'll write up a chit that the trader can use across the course of a few visits."

"I'm not sure I understand," Sarah said.

"Right, I'll give you an example. The other day, someone came in with a professional woodworking kit. Now, George had actually asked me to keep a lookout for specialist tools of any sort. This set looked like it had never been used and I knew it would have cost a pretty penny back in the day. The man was one of the new arrivals who we've got across at the campsite at the moment. They weren't his; he'd found them, and thought they might be good for trade. I gave him a chit for fifty drinks. Each time he uses it, it gets marked off and signed by me or a member of the bar staff until it's down to zero."

"I see. And how much mark-up do you make selling it on to George?" Sarah asked.

Jenny burst out laughing. "Oh darling, these aren't like the old days. We've got a microbrewery and small distillery working, in addition to the stuff that gets scavenged when Mike or the boys head out. Everything goes back into the community now. The fruit and veg, I keep some to live on and trade, some goes to produce the booze, but the rest goes to the community pot. There were over a hundred people in here tonight," she said, gesturing around the room. "They all left with full bellies. There can never be an equilibrium in society because there will always be some who strive and some who don't, but there shouldn't be people who starve and there shouldn't be people who don't have shelter and there shouldn't be people who don't have healthcare. The pub is the focal point for this community, it's supported by the community and in turn, it's supporting the community."

"Here, here," Ruth said. "Jenny has done an amazing job. She's helped the library grow no end. David, Richard and myself have been inundated, and we've started lending. We're in the process of setting up the Dewey Decimal system for the books to keep tabs on everything before it gets too big. We've nearly filled one of the static caravans with shelves already."

"You're really setting up a card catalogue?" Emma asked, trying to hold back a laugh.

"Yes," Ruth said in all seriousness.

"Erm, that's great," Emma replied, looking across at Hughes and Shaw who were also trying to suppress grins.

"If I could just add," Lucy interjected, "Jenny has been supplying us with something that borders on the strength of surgical alcohol for the hospital." Lucy looked towards her. "You're doing a terrific job, my friend."

Jenny blushed. "Well, I'm not sure about that. Now, I want to extend this to all of you around this table. If there is anything you think the community could benefit from, if there's anything you need me to look out for, just let me know."

Jenny sat down and Lucy took the floor again. "Thank you for that, Jen. Okay, next on the agenda, the Dig for Victory Campaign. Em, over to you."

Lucy sat down and Emma stood. "Well, as you know, we've had teams going up and down the coast these last few weeks, helping people get at least one plot on their land ready for crops. In some cases, this had been a front or back garden; in other cases, it's been an entire croft. We've got a number of polytunnels assembled and they're already producing. On some of Mike's scavenging missions, he's brought a substantial amount of seed back, and come harvest time, not only will we be gathering enough to see us through to spring, but we should have plenty to trade with some of the islands, too."

"And what about our present situation?" Lucy asked.

"Well, like I said, the polytunnels are producing at present. We've got a couple of potato crops almost ready, and we've got a really healthy supply of dried and tinned foods, thanks to the scavenger teams. But Sarah will be able to give you a fuller picture of where we stand food-wise," Emma said, sitting down.

Sarah shuffled some papers in front of her and stood up. "We've got three working fishing boats that are currently going out once a week, fuel permitting. We've got some smaller sailboats that seem to be fairing pretty well too. In addition, we've got two teams of foragers. One does the coastline collecting seaweed, mussels, scallops—anything that can be used for food. The other does the woods and forests, picking mushrooms, berries, wild herbs and so on. They alternate, and the teams are getting bigger all the time, so they're sharing knowledge. As well as that, we've set up a smokehouse, and we're distilling seawater so we're not going to run out of salt any time soon."

The council meeting went on for some time. Each person took a turn to speak until the floor opened up to any other business. Jules was the only one who put her hand up.

"Okay Jules, you have the floor," Lucy said.

Jules stood up. "Thanks, Lucy. George asked me to bring this up for a vote." The faces around the table looked at each other. George rarely had anything to do with the council. He was a workhorse and an old-fashioned gentleman who rarely asked for anything. "Fry's army. They came from a place called Loch Uig. George thinks there's a chance his other granddaughter might be there. He wanted to know if we could send a group out to see if the encampment was still there."

The room fell silent. Fry was a madman who had nearly destroyed Safe Haven. He led a huge army of raiders who went through villages and towns stealing, raping, kidnapping, destroying. That army was the stuff of nightmares. Everyone around the tables had fought and won the war they waged against Fry and his men, and none of them ever thought they would hear that name again.

After over a minute of nobody saying anything, Hughes spoke up. "How does he know Fry's camp was in Loch Uig?"

"Turns out Wren came across them," Jules replied.

"How come we're only finding out about this now?" Shaw asked.

"Look," Jules said, "You're two battle-hardened soldiers. Even before all this shite you'd dealt with death and destruction," she replied in her Belfast twang. "Wren's sixteen years old; she hadn't told George much about anything from her time on the road. Little bits came out here and there, but that was it. The other night, George started talking about the weapons he'd built for the battle. Wren asked what battle, and they got into it from there."

"Okay," Hughes said, "and what makes him think that his other granddaughter might be there?"

"Wren and Robyn had holed up in a house, did alright for a little while. Then one night they heard cars pull up. They both ran, but they got split up. The next day, Wren went back to the house; the place had been ransacked and there was no sign of Robyn. Poor kid stayed in the woods nearby for a few days to see if her sister would return, but she never did. Turns out they'd had run-ins with Fry's men before and had managed to escape them each time. Wren knew it was hopeless; that if she went to Loch Uig she'd end up captured, that there was no way she'd be able to rescue her sister by herself. Her only hope was that Robyn might escape. They'd made a pact that if ever they got separated, they'd continue on to Inverness, to George's place, and meet up there. Well, as you know, where George lived was overrun with RAMs, so Wren found that old place out in the woods. She went into Inverness on a regular basis for food, spending hours on the rooftops, watching the streets below, hoping one day she might see her sister walking up one of them, but she never did."

"Poor kid," Lucy said, "but this must have been some time ago that they were separated?"

"Well, yeah, a few months at least," Jules replied.

"So, let me get this right," Sarah said. "George wants us to send a group across a zombie-infested wasteland to scope out a place that's likely to be deserted now, on the off chance that the bastards that used to be there might have taken his granddaughter?"

"Erm, yeah, pretty much," Jules admitted.

"Okay," Lucy said. "Let's put this to a vote, all in favour, raise your hand." Lucy paused and looked around the table. Jules's was the only hand that went up. "All opposed?" The other eight hands went up.

"Sorry, Jules," Lucy said. "If George gives us something more concrete, maybe we'd have a different result. But it's a long way across dangerous country, and say there is still a camp there. Our group could get caught, they could end up in a fight. Hell, there could be an army there as big as the one that came here. We don't know what the situation is."

"But surely that's why it would be worth sending a group down. At the very least, we'd know who else is out there."

"Sorry Jules, we can't risk it. I know how close you are to George; I'll tell him if you don't want to," Lucy said.

"No. No, it would be better coming from me," Jules said sadly. "If there's nothing else to talk about, I'll head up there and let him and Wren know."

Lucy looked around the table. "No sweetie, there's nothing else. Please tell George...please just tell him..."

"Don't worry. I understand," Jules said, heading out of the hall. The walk from the hall to the carpark gave her a few moments to think. *What am I going to tell George?* He was family to her. When she had led the group at the Home and Garden Depot, back in Inverness, he had been like the father she never had growing up. He was always there for her, always supportive. He had asked her for something important when he never asked her or anyone for anything, and now she was going to let him down.

Jules was so preoccupied that she did not hear her name being called at first. "Jules...Jules...Oy! Y'deaf old bag!"

She turned around to see Mike. "Oh, hi Mike. Sorry. I was in a world of my own."

Mike smiled as he approached her but then saw the sadness in her face. "Jules? What's wrong?"

"Nothing. I'm okay."

"No you're not; I can tell when there's something wrong. For a start you're not swearing like a drunken navvy," he said, trying to raise a smile from her and failing.

They had become good friends soon after they had met. They constantly threw insults at one another, but it was all in good humour. "It's nothing, Mike, honestly."

"Jules. This is me you're talking to. Remember? The guy you continually groped when we were making our escape from Inverness on the bike. The guy who's still got three of your fingernails stuck in my neck from when you dragged me back onto my arse at the dock last winter."

A thin smile finally broke on her face. "You wish. I was holding on for my bloody life. I didn't realise when I climbed onto the back of that thing what a complete fucking psycho you were. And quit whining, if I hadn't have grabbed you on that dock, those things would have turned you into mincemeat."

"So come on, tell me." Jules just looked down to the floor. "Hang on. It was the council meeting, wasn't it?

Did somebody say something to you? What's going on? If you don't tell me, I'll get the answer from one of the others."

Jules's shoulders sagged and she gave in, relaying the entire story to Mike, who just stood there, shocked. "So that's where I'm heading now, to tell George."

"Wait a minute," Mike said. "Nine people, and you were the only one to vote yes?"

"Yeah!"

"Emma and Lucy?"

"Nope. I was all alone on this one."

"Are they still across there?"

"Mike, don't."

"Are they still across there?" he asked more firmly.

"Mike, leave it alone. This is why we have a council...to make the tough decisions."

"Yeah, bollocks to that. I'm going to go talk to them."

"Mike...Mike!" Jules said, running after him as he stormed across to the village hall.

Mike burst through the doors just as the rest of the committee was stacking the chairs and moving the tables back to position. He did not need to say a word for everyone in the hall to know what was on his mind, but that did not stop him.

"Here we go," Hughes said under his breath.

"Seriously?" Mike said as he stormed towards them. "What the fuck is wrong with you people?"

"Mike!" yelled Lucy.

"Who do you think you're talking to?" shouted Emma.

"Honestly? I haven't a fucking clue. I'm looking around at these faces, and I thought I knew who the people were behind them, but I was wrong."

Lucy, Emma and Sarah all looked at Jules. "Don't stare at me," she said. "I was trying to stop the mad fucker from coming in here."

"This is why you're not on the council," Emma said, "You just react. If you don't like something, you just go off on one. We need to make decisions that are best for the community. How would sending a group halfway across the country purely on an off chance be good for anyone? This is you all over. You don't think things through properly."

Mike upended a table. "How fucking dare you? After everything we've been through, how can you say that?"

Emma shook her head. "I can say it because it's true. We're trying to build something here. We're trying to build a future."

"And Luce, you voted no too?" Mike said, staring a virtual hole through her.

"Yes, Mike. I voted no. If there was anything more definite, something else to go on, then I might have voted differently, but to put people's lives at risk for something that isn't more substantive than a hopeful hunch would be irresponsible."

Mike shook his head. "I don't know you people. I thought I did, but I don't."

"You are so out of order speaking to us like this," Emma snapped.

The rest of the committee just looked on, agog, not wanting to get in the middle of a family argument. "I'm out of order?" Mike spat. "*I'm out of order?*"

"Is there an echo in here?" Emma asked.

"George is one of us. Wren is one of us. If this was you we were talking about, Em, I'd be heading down there with less than this to go on." Emma opened her mouth to answer him, but words failed her. "I'm going to check where this place is on a map, load up a car, and set off first thing tomorrow. The very least Wren and George deserve is to know that they're worth the effort."

"Mike, it's not that simple," Lucy said.

"No Luce, it is that simple. I've got a lot of faults, I know

I have," he said, looking at Lucy, then Emma, and then at the circle of rapt faces. "But I admit when I'm wrong. I told everyone that this committee would always do the right thing, the decent thing. Well, I was really wrong about that, wasn't I?"

2

Jules ran out of the village hall after Mike, desperate to try and calm him down. "Please stop, Mike," she said as he reached the opposite side of the road. "This is all my fault. I shouldn't have said anything."

"No, you were right to, Jules. You've got nothing to be sorry about," he said looking back towards the hall. "They're the ones who should be apologising."

"Look, I don't want you heading down there by yourself. I'll come with you. It's the least I can do."

"I'm not intending to take them on by myself, Jules. I'm literally just going on a reccy. Seeing if this place is still occupied."

"I know that, but it's a long way. Forgetting about what you might find when you get there, there's a lot of dangerous ground to cover. It would be stupid to head out alone, and trust me, living with my brothers, I know stupid."

Mike smiled. "This is my decision, Jules. I don't want to put anyone else at risk."

"Yeah well. It's my decision to come with. I'm going to head up to George's place and tell him the news."

Mike and Jules continued to the pub carpark. He looked across at the Land Rover. "I'm surprised George lets you drive around in that after what you did to his other pride and joy."

Jules smiled. "You roll one car into a ditch and nobody ever lets you forget about it."

"It makes sense for us to take that tomorrow if it's okay with you."

"It's fine by me. So what time?"

"Let's start early. You okay to pick me up at six?"

"Jeysus! You're not kidding, are you?"

"We can make it a bit—"

"No, no, six o'clock it is. I'll see you then." She threw her arms around Mike and kissed him on the cheek. "You're a good soul, Mike…even if you do get on my tits most of the time."

*

Jules walked straight into George's kitchen; knocking was for strangers. She smelt the peat burning from the fire in the living room and headed in. George was sat up, but fast asleep, and Wren had a lantern by her side. She was reading a book about basket weaving, while Wolf lazed at her feet.

"Hi," Jules whispered as she sat down in one of the armchairs.

Wren's face lit up to see her, and she put the book down. "Hi," she whispered back, briefly looking towards her grandad before giving her full attention to Jules. "So, what did they say?"

"They said no."

"Oh," Wren said, her shoulders sagging.

"Yeah, but Mike and I are going," Jules said, smiling.

Wren looked at her for a few seconds. "What do you mean?"

"I met Mike in the carpark afterwards and told him…"

"And?"

"And he went back into the meeting, tore a strip off all of them and announced he was going to go anyway."

Wren smiled. "And you?"

"I was the only one who voted to go. You and George are family to me. If there's a chance your sister's down there then it's a chance worth taking."

"I'm going to come too," Wren said.

"Erm excuse me young lady, but no way. It's way too dangerous."

"Jules, I appreciate what you're saying, but I was living out there alone for months. I know how dangerous it is, and this is my sister. She'd be doing the same for me."

"But Wren, your grandad needs you. You've got to think about him in all of this as well."

"I am thinking of him, and if you refuse to take me then I'll make my own way."

Jules laughed. "Can I ask you something, Wren?"

"Course you can."

"Why have you only just brought this up? You've been here a few months? Why have you only just raised this? Your sister could have been there all this time: why'd you wait so long to tell us?"

"I don't talk to Grandad much about life out there, about what happened before I got here. I tell him the odd bits, but there are some things that I just don't touch on. I told him Robyn and I got split up, but I didn't tell him the rest of it, because if she was taken captive, then I can only imagine the horror she's had to go through. It makes me feel ill thinking about it."

"Okay, but I still don't understand. Why now?"

"Grandad told me about the battle. He told me about how you defeated Fry's huge army. That made me think; there might be virtually no one left to defend Loch Uig. Before Grandad told me about that, it was a pipe dream, but hearing what happened that night, it became a reality. Look, I'm not an idiot, Jules. I know a thousand different things could have happened, but her being taken by those men was always the most likely option. If this was one of your brothers, wouldn't you want to check it out?"

Jules nodded. "Yeah...yeah, I would."

"All I'm asking is we go have a look."

Jules let out a long sigh. "Well, I'm picking Mike up at six tomorrow morning. Make sure you're ready soon after that."

"I will be," Wren said, climbing out of her chair and giving Jules a big hug and kiss on the cheek. "Thank you."

"Don't thank me darlin', it's Mike you want to be thanking."

"It's both of you," she said, returning to her seat.

"Huh? What? What's both of who?" George said, waking up a little confused.

"I'll go make us a pot of tea," Jules said. "You can tell him the news."

*

Hughes, Emma, Sarah and Lucy sat in one corner of the pub. It had closed for the evening and they were now the only patrons. Jenny brought a tray of drinks over, and the logs crackled in the fire as Meg nestled down in front of its warm glow once more. The well-positioned lanterns cast enough light for the assembled group to see the grim looks on one another's faces. Jenny sat down and handed out the glasses to her friends.

"Well, we can always rely on Mike to liven things up can't we," she said taking a sip from her glass.

"I feel like shit," Lucy said.

"So do I," Emma added.

"You know what he said was true. If it had been you or me who was missing, he'd be heading there with less than this to go on," Lucy said.

"I know. Why do you think I was so pissed off?"

"So what do we do?" Lucy asked.

"What's there to do?" Hughes said. "It's not like anybody can stop him when he's got an idea in his head, is it?"

"That's not what I meant. I mean do we go with him?"

"No," Sarah said, placing her hand into Emma's. "Look, Mike's heart's in the right place; that doesn't mean his decision is well thought out. The whole point of the council is to reason things, not just go on impulse. We have to make decisions based on fact and there were no facts to back up the case to go down there."

Lucy picked up her glass and took a drink. "Screw it, I'm going."

"What?" Emma said.

"Love, think about this," Hughes replied.

"I have thought about this."

"No, you haven't. You've let him guilt you into it," Sarah said.

"No, I haven't. I've guilted myself into this. I mean, how selfish am I? He's right. If this was one of you, we'd all be heading down there."

Hughes was the one to let out a sigh now. "You stay here. I'll go with Soft Lad. The place can last without me for a few days; it can't last without its only doctor," he said standing up and knocking back his drink in one go.

"No, I'm going regardless. I want to. The hospital can manage. Raj can handle things there."

"Where are you going?" Jenny asked.

"I'm going to see if I can persuade Barney to come with us."

"What about Shaw?" Lucy asked.

"Shaw's better keeping an eye on things here. He's good in a firefight, but if we need to move fast, his leg gives him problems ever since that accident."

"No need to see Barney; I'm going too," Emma said.

"No you're bloody not," Sarah replied.

Emma turned to look at her. "This council. It's what Safe Haven needs, but it needs people who act, as well. It wasn't committee meetings that beat Fry's army, it was action. It wasn't the council that saved my little brother and sister, it was action. And we can reason and talk and argue until we're blue in the face, but at some point, we just have to act, because action is what makes the difference. Action is what saves lives. I'm going with my brother tomorrow."

Sarah pulled her hand away. "I don't want you to go."

"Sarah, I—"

"This is madness. *It's madness.* Your brother will be the death of you. He'll guilt you into something like he always does. Like he always does with all of you," she said, looking around the table.

Lucy answered sharply, "He's the purest person I've ever met, and if people end up feeling guilty, it's because he's doing the right thing and they're not." She stood up and looked at Hughes. "I'm glad you're going, but I'm going too."

Emma took hold of Sarah's hand again. "I'm sorry, Sarah…I am going."

Sarah stood up, tears of frustration in her eyes. "Fine, go. I'll even look after Sammy and Jake while you're away. Then the second you're back, I'm moving out," she said and stormed out of the pub.

Emma just sat there looking towards the door.

Jenny took another drink from her glass. "Like I said, you can always rely on Mike to liven things up."

*

"Are you okay there?" Lucy asked Wren, looking over the back seat of the Land Rover Discovery to the boot compartment.

"I'm fine. These sleeping bags make good seats when they're all squished together."

"Well if you need a break to stretch your legs, just let us know."

"Will do."

Mike turned around from the front passenger seat to look at Emma. "You okay, sis?"

Emma just carried on looking out the side window. "I don't want to talk about it, Mike."

"Look, she was just upset; we'll be back before you know it and everything—"

"Jesus! What is it about I don't want to talk about it that you don't understand?"

Mike angled round to look at Lucy, then Jules, who both gave barely perceptible shakes of their heads as if to say, *leave it alone.*

"Well this is nice…we haven't all been on a jaunt together in a long time," Mike said with a smirk on his face. "Heard any good jokes lately, Bruiser?" he asked Hughes.

"You know the one about the little pissant from Yorkshire who never knew when to put a sock in it?" he asked with a thin smile as he steered the car around a bend, revealing a long straight stretch of road in front of them.

"Once or twice," Mike said, grinning.

"I've got a question," Wren piped up from the back. "Why do you call Hughes 'Bruiser?'"

"When I got to Candleton, he was the first person I met," Mike said. "He was guarding the entrance to the village and he came across as a right hard man. Of course, this was before I realised what a little pussycat he really is."

"Screw you, veggie boy," Hughes replied

"Anyway, I thought I might have had to get physical, and I was sussing out the other guards and Hughes looked the most threatening. I said to myself, 'he looks like a right Bruiser,' and the name stuck."

Hughes laughed. "You're a mad bastard."

"Why?"

"We were all bloody armed. We were trained soldiers, and you were thinking about taking us on."

"I didn't care if you had tanks behind you, I was looking for my family. Nothing was going to stop me."

Hughes thought for a moment. "True enough."

Emma broke her gaze from the window and looked towards Mike, whose eyes were now firmly fixed on the road ahead once again. She delved into her pocket and found a pen top which she flicked towards him, hitting the back of his neck.

"Ow!" he cried, turning back around quickly. Lucy and Jules were both smiling, Emma was staring out of the window with a smirk on her face. "Was that you?" he asked, looking at his sister.

She turned her head to look at him. "Was what me?"

Mike broke into a smile, and Emma did too, and that was it. They were friends again.

"I don't ever remember seeing any of this before when we've headed out," Jules said.

"That's because we've never come this way before. It's pretty much the same distance as if we went via Inverness, and if memory serves, there's a bloody big combine harvester that we'd have to take apart blocking the road over there at the moment," Hughes said. "I've packed a blow torch in case we need to head back that way, but given a choice, I'd prefer not to."

"It's pretty," Jules said as they drove through the picturesque highland landscape.

"Yeah, well, that was the other reason I decided we'd take this route," Hughes said with a smile on his face.

"Funny bastard aren't you?" Jules replied.

"I do my best," Hughes said, looking at her in the rearview mirror.

"How long do you think it will take us to get there?" Emma asked.

"Who knows? In the olden days, you'd be looking at about three and a half to four hours. Thing is though, we don't know what the roads are like, we don't know what the RAM situation is or anything," Hughes replied.

"So wouldn't it have been better to take the combine harvester apart and head that way?" Jules asked.

"Well, we haven't really been south of Inverness since all this began. I mean, yeah, you and Soft Lad went down the A9 a bit that day on the bike, but you didn't get that far. 'Course, we've got no idea what the roads are like that way either, so it's broad as it is long," Hughes said.

"Fair enough," Jules replied.

*

Sarah was just about to set off to the beach to pick mussels from the rocks when there was a knock at the door. She opened it to find George standing there. He looked at the large bag she had over her shoulder and then stared at her grey Minnie Mouse sweatshirt. "I like your top," he said, desperately trying to thaw the icy look that greeted him. "Just wanted to see if you needed anything."

Sarah looked angry for a second, but mellowed quickly, realising none of this was actually George's fault. "No...no I'm fine. Thanks, George."

"Can I come in for a second?"

"I was just about to head down to the beach."

"I won't keep you long," he replied.

Sarah stepped aside and George walked into the hall. "Let's go into the kitchen."

They sat down at the table. "Jules told me how the vote went last night. I understand. I don't hold any ill will towards anyone for it. I mean, that's the whole point of having a committee isn't it?"

"I thought it was," Sarah replied.

"Look, I'm sorry things have turned out this way, I didn't want—"

"Wait, George; it's not that people didn't want to help. It's just that there was no real evidence we could do any good, just hunches and hope. If we knew for sure, there wouldn't be a scouting party, there'd be a whole army heading down there. But instead, we've got six people, including my partner and your granddaughter, heading into god knows what, on nothing more than a teenager's gut feeling."

George sat there for a moment not saying a word and looked down at his hands. "I did it for Wren. I expected it to get voted down, and to be honest, I would have voted it down myself. She had given up hope of ever seeing her sister again, and then...I wish I could turn back time. Why did I tell her about Fry? What possessed me?"

Sarah leaned forward. "You weren't to know, George."

He shook his head. "What I wouldn't give to take it back. But once it was out, it was out and she started obsessing about it. I could tell the way her mind was working that she was thinking about heading out herself." He looked up from his hands towards Sarah. "I couldn't lose her, not again. So I said I'd ask Jules. Sure enough the next time Jules visited I asked her, and I was sure...I was sure nothing would come of it. Wren has nothing but respect for the council; I felt if they voted it down then she'd begin to see sense, but now…"

"Yeah, you can always rely on Mike to screw your plans up."

"I feel sick to my stomach. I tried to forbid her to go, but Wren will always do what Wren wants to do. I came here to say sorry. This is all my fault."

"You tried to do the right thing, George. You've got nothing to be sorry about." Sarah stood up, went to the kitchen sink and opened the cupboard underneath, pulling out another large canvas supermarket bag. "C'mon, I'm heading down to the bay to pick shellfish. You can keep me company. Is Wolf in the car? He can come too."

"No, I've left him at home. The workshop door's open so he can come and go as he pleases. It's what he's used to."

"Okay then, it'll just be the two of us."

*

"These roads seem to be in great nick considering the winter we had. I thought there'd be potholes everywhere," Hughes said.

"Well, it's not like they get a lot of traffic now is it," Mike replied.

"True enough."

The Land Rover followed the long winding road through the forests, hills and mountains. The sun kept breaking through the clouds, making the lochs shimmer. "Wow!" Lucy said. "You forget how beautiful this country is."

"It's something else isn't it?" Jules replied.

Hughes narrowed his eyes and began to apply the brake. "Erm, can you pass me the binoculars?" he asked.

Mike reached into the glove compartment. "What is—" Suddenly he saw it too.

Hughes brought the car to a stop and the pair of them climbed out. The soldier brought the binoculars up to his eyes. His face went pale but he did not say a word. He looked towards Mike and handed him the glasses.

"You're worrying me, Bruiser. What is it?" Mike stared through the lenses for just a few seconds before bringing them back down. "Oh shit!"

3

The cars were parked end-to-end, blocking the whole road ahead. Woodland lay on either side making it impossible to bypass by vehicle. "What do you think?" Hughes said.

"About what?" Mike replied.

"Funny boy."

"We need to get through; that's the end of it."

"Yeah, but we don't have a clue what that is. Is it a community trying to protect themselves? Is it a bunch of bandits trying to collect a toll? Is it a family of fucking cannibals wanting to make ornaments out of our bones?"

Mike gave Hughes a long look. "Don't take this the wrong way, Bruiser, but you really need to stop reading those horror books, mate."

"You can mock me."

"I thought I was."

"Look, let's just get a bit closer and see what the score is."

The pair of them walked back to the car and climbed in. "What is it?" Lucy asked as the car set off once again.

"A roadblock," Mike said as he reached down to his rucksack in the footwell, making sure he had easy access to the shotgun. He grabbed a handful of shells and put them in his pocket. His faithful machetes were in their familiar crisscrossed position, ready for action if needed.

Lucy turned to Wren. "If anything starts happening, keep your head down." She pulled her Glock 17 from the holster underneath her jacket as the Land Rover slowed to a stop once more.

Hughes checked his weapon. "Okay ladies, keep your eyes peeled. Me and Mikey will head up there first."

"Screw that. I'm coming with you," Lucy replied.

"Luce, we don't know what this is. We don't want to go in heavy, just in case."

"Fine. Let me and Emma go then. That's not going in heavy."

"Hey keep me out of this," Emma replied. "I'm more than happy to hang back and let my brother the diplomat go greet the strangers. If they're not enemies now, they will be by the time he's finished with them."

Mike turned in his seat. "Look—"

"What is it?" Lucy asked, seeing the sudden look of horror on his face.

"Where the hell is Wren?"

The rest of them turned to see the hatchback slightly raised and no sign of the sixteen-year-old. Mike, Hughes and Lucy all jumped out of the car. They scoped the woodland on both sides of the road but could see no sign of her. "This is just brilliant," Hughes said, pulling his SA80 rifle from the back.

"Wren!" Jules shouted, joining them on the road.

"Subtle, Jules. That's great. There goes our chance of a quiet entrance," Mike said.

"Wren!" she shouted again ignoring Mike.

"She can't have gone far," Emma said, climbing out of the car and heading towards the trees.

"Where do you think you're going?" Mike asked.

"To look for her."

"Jesus, what's wrong with you people? We're not splitting up. Stay here. One thing at once. Let's suss out what this roadblock is first; we might have bloody guns trained on us for all we know."

Suddenly there was the familiar clunk of a magazine being pushed into the housing of a rifle and the charging handle being engaged. "Nobody move," said a gruff voice from behind the group.

Mike's immediate impulse was to turn, but he had no way of knowing whom the owner of the voice had his weapon trained on. He could not risk his family or friends. "What do you want?" he asked instead.

"Drop your weapons and your bags now," said the voice.

There was a pause and Hughes looked at Mike as if to say *shall we rush him?* The thought was only fleeting, though, and Mike gave a barely perceptible shake of his head. He slipped the rucksack from his back, and he and Hughes placed their weapons on the ground before straightening once again with their hands raised. Lucy did the same with her Glock, and the other two just raised their hands, their weapons still left in the car. "Can you at least tell us—" Mike began.

"I'm asking the questions here. Now—"

"Put the gun down," Wren demanded, her voice coming from the trees behind them.

"You sound a little too young to be aiming a gun on me, missy," said the gruff-voiced man.

Wren fired a bolt from one of her two pistol crossbows. It whistled past the man's head and cracked through the bark of a pine tree on the other side of the road. "Guns aren't really my thing, and that was a left-handed shot. Wait until you see what I can do with my right."

The man wavered for a moment, but then placed his rifle down on the ground and put his hands up. "Okay, I guess you win this one."

Mike immediately picked up his rucksack and shotgun then turned to confront the man who had held them at gunpoint just a few seconds earlier. The figure stood there with a look of bitter frustration on his face. Wren circled him, keeping her pistol crossbow carefully aimed while joining the others.

Mike regarded the man for a moment before speaking. The would-be captor was in his sixties, tall and lean, but with a powerful looking upper body. His craggy brown face suggested he spent a lot of time outside. "Where are the others?" Mike said, bending down to pick up the man's rifle before backing away to a safe distance.

"What others?"

"The rest of your group."

"What group?"

Mike smiled. "Okay old man. Protecting your people, I can respect that."

"Who are you calling old man? You cheeky little twat. There aren't any others, so just fucking get on with it. Kill me and get it over with."

"At least he's got your number, if nothing else," Hughes said with a smirk.

"Look," Lucy said. "We don't want any trouble. We just want to pass through your roadblock."

A confused look swept over the man's face. "You just looking to be on your way?"

"Yeah. That's all we want. If we can just move the cars you'll never have to see us again," Lucy replied.

"Who are you people?" the man asked.

"We're just people trying to get to the other side of this roadblock. We don't want anything from you. We don't want to harm you. We just want to get to where we're going," Lucy responded.

"You're the first people I've seen in months," he said.

"Well at least it's not affected any of your social skills," Jules said.

The man gave her a long look before speaking again. "I'll get them moved. But there's another bunch about a quarter of a mile down the track."

"Why are you blockading the road?" Jules asked.

"Looking for people," he replied.

"Well, you found some."

"Not you."

"Who then?" Jules replied.

"How old are you?" the man said, looking at Wren.

"Sixteen. Why?"

"She yours?"

"Yes and no."

"You're just passing through?"

"That's all we're doing sir," Lucy replied.

"My village is the next turn. A few months ago an army came through here. They took everything. Took all the women, including my niece, Deb. They took anything of value: food, fuel, everything. They shot me and left me for dead. An old-timer who'd been out hunting for a couple of days came back around and found me. Saved my life. Winter got him, though, flu. Then it was just me. Been hoping they'd head back through this way so I could have a crack at taking a few of them out at least."

"This army. Buses with metal sidings? Motorbike scouts?" Mike asked.

The man's eyes narrowed. "What do you know about them?"

"Plenty," Lucy said.

"They've got my sister," Wren blurted.

"Might have," Emma said.

The tension in the man's shoulders relaxed. "I'm sorry," he said to Wren.

"We're heading there now," Wren said, immediately causing the others to give each other exasperated looks.

"Heading where? You know where these people are?" the man asked.

Lucy placed a gentle hand on Wren's shoulder and took over. "Look, we *think* we know where they *used to be* based. This trip is nothing more than a scouting trip. We're going to find out if the base is still there, and if it is, how big a force is guarding it."

The man looked from Lucy to Wren, to Hughes and finally to Mike. "I'd like to join you," he said.

"Listen, I don't mean to sound unkind, but we might need to move quickly," Jules said.

"Yeah well, I might look old but I'm fitter than most," he replied, "and if we get into a scrape, I've had my fair share of fights."

"There won't be any fights," Lucy said. "This is just surveillance, and I'm sorry, but I agree with Jules. We don't know you; we don't know what you'd be like in a pressure situation. We've all been together a long time. We've lived together, worked together and fought together. Bringing along somebody new, somebody who, a few minutes ago, had a gun pointed at us, wouldn't be a good idea."

The man took a step towards Lucy and Wren went on high alert again, raising the pistol crossbow a little. "I've been by myself for months. These men took everything from me. Now you tell me not only do you know them, but you know where they're based. My niece might still be there. I know it's a longshot, I'm not a fool. But you've given me something when just a few moments ago I had nothing. Please...Please let me come. I'll take my own vehicle. I've got my own weapon. I can fight."

"Y'see that's the problem," Emma said. "You're looking for a fight, and a fight could get us all killed. We're just going to check it out for the time being."

"Okay, look, I understand. I'll leave my rifle. I'll do whatever you ask, but please, I'd like to go with you."

"How old was your niece?" Mike asked.

"Thirty, and she was more like a daughter than a niece."

"Our car's cramped as it is. Get your stuff together," Mike said handing him the rifle. "We need to move out as soon as we can."

The man's face lit up into a smile. He slung the rifle over his shoulder and extended his hand towards Mike. "Thank you. Thank you. I'm William; Will for short."

"I'm Mike."

"Thank you. I'll get the cars moved so you can get through. I'll meet you at the other roadblock in a few minutes. Thank you again," he said, almost running towards the barricade.

"What the fuck is wrong with you?" Emma demanded as Will started the engine of the first vehicle.

"Erm…yeah, what Emma said," Jules replied.

"This guy's family was taken by these people. Trust me, I know how that feels and it's pretty shit. Don't worry—I'll keep an eye on him, but he deserves to come along with us," Mike replied.

"This is just you all over. You make these rash bloody decisions without thinking anything through, putting the rest of us at risk. He's a loose cannon," Emma said.

"I don't think he'll cause any trouble, and if he does, I'll take care of him," Mike replied.

Will parked the first car then climbed into the second and manoeuvred it out of the way before driving it along the road. They all watched as it disappeared around a corner.

"I have to agree with Jules and Emma, Mike. This is a bad idea," Lucy said heading back towards the Land Rover. Jules, Emma and Hughes all gave him stern looks before following her, leaving Mike and Wren alone.

"What's that look?" Mike asked.

"What look?"

"That one."

"You did the right thing."

"Really? I thought you were going to give me hell too."

"You know what it's like to feel hopeless then suddenly be given hope again. He deserved that. Everybody deserves that."

4

Jenny was wiping the tables down from the previous night when a frantic banging sounded at the front door. Meg roused from the warm hearth and began to bark.

Jenny rushed to open the door to see Stephanie, Lucy's head nurse. Tears were streaming down her face and her clothes were torn. She was bleeding across the top of her chest from what appeared to be scratch marks.

"Oh my god, Stephanie! What happened?" Jenny asked, guiding the distraught young woman into the pub and closing the door behind them. Meg continued to bark but eventually settled back down in front of the fire, keeping a close watch on the visitor.

Stephanie sat there sobbing for a moment before calming down enough to talk. "Two men attacked me."

"What? What two men?" Jenny asked, outraged.

"I think they came in the other day. They were part of a bigger group. They're staying across at the campsite."

"Did they...hurt you?" Jenny asked.

"They tried. I struggled free and ran here straight away. I looked to see if they were following me but when I looked back they were gone."

"Who's at the hospital now?" Jenny asked.

"It was just due to be me and Lucy this morning, but with Lucy gone, it's just me," Stephanie said, starting to cry again.

"Okay love, it's okay," Jenny said placing a comforting arm around the young woman and giving a squeeze. She got to her feet and strode to the bar where she poured two glasses of brandy, grabbed the handheld radio and headed back to the table. "Sip this," Jenny said, "It will help." She handed Stephanie the glass and took a big drink from her own then hit the talk button on the handset. "Shaw, this is Jenny."

The radio hissed for a moment and then eventually crackled to life. "Go ahead, Jenny."

"Shaw, I need you at the pub as soon as possible. It's an emergency."

"Emergency? What kind of emergency?"

"I'll tell you when you get here."

"I'm on my way."

Jenny sat down again and took hold of Stephanie's hand. "It's alright, love, we'll get this sorted.

*

Hughes kept checking in the rearview mirror to make sure Will was keeping up behind them. Dark clouds loomed in the distance and the occupants of the car began to regret not packing rain gear. They passed a sign saying Fort Armadale, and Hughes slowed the car down as the road weaved around.

"Holy shit!" Mike said, as they entered the village.

The car came to a complete stop and Hughes and Mike climbed out. It looked like it had been invaded by demons. Some of the houses were completely burnt out. The rotting corpses of decapitated men were strewn along the paths; the minister of the local church had been tied to the towering, cross-shaped stone war memorial in the centre of the village green.

"Fuuuck!!!" Hughes said as Will's car pulled up behind them.

Mike felt a presence by his side; he shifted his gaze to see Lucy, then Emma, Jules and Wren. "These people are animals," Jules said.

"No, they're not, Jules. Animals aren't capable of this kind of horror," Mike replied.

"Wren. I think you should go and sit back in the car, darlin'," Jules said.

"You think I've not seen stuff worse than this?"

"Dear God!" Will said as he joined them. "Who in Christ's name could do something like this?"

"These are the people we're looking for," Lucy said. "Judging by the decomposition of the bodies, this all happened some time ago. A few months at least."

They looked around at the houses. Nearly all of them had damage, broken windows, doors, fences.

"Come on," Emma said, "this place is giving me the willies." They all viewed the devastation one last time before heading back to their vehicles.

Hughes started the engine and they were on their way once more. The car was silent; Mike turned to look back. Emma stared out one window, Jules the other, while Lucy looked grimly straight ahead, all of them lost in thought. He looked over the top of the back seat towards Wren. Her head was bowed and she was silently sobbing. He gently reached back and tapped Lucy on the knee. She looked at him as if waking from a dream. Mike nodded his head towards the teenager and Lucy angled round to see Wren crying.

"Wren, what is it?" she asked, swivelling in her seat and kneeling up so she could see the girl properly.

"I was just thinking about Bobbi."

"Is that what you used to call Robyn?"

Wren nodded. "If she's in Loch Uig, these last few months are going to have been worse than hell for her."

Lucy extended her arm over the back of the seat and took one of Wren's hands. "Don't torture yourself, Wren."

Wren wiped her eyes. "I suppose you're right. It's just when you see things like that, it's hard not to start thinking the worst."

"I know, it's only natural. You're a special girl, Wren. If your sister is half as special as you then she'll have found a way to get through it."

Wren smiled, wiping away the last of her tears. "She's twice the person I am. It's funny; we never really got on that well…but then when this happened…she turned into my best friend. I couldn't have survived this without her. I'm really happy I found you and my grandad, but I've been very lonely without her."

*

Shaw, Barnes, and Jules's three brothers: Andy, Rob and Jon all appeared from behind the bar. They had come in through the kitchen of the pub, and rather than barking, Meg, tail wagging happily, went up to greet them. "Hello girl," Shaw said, stiffly crouching down to make a fuss of her.

"Thank god you're here," Jenny said, "and you've brought back-up."

"What is this, Jen?" Shaw asked, standing up. He suddenly saw Stephanie and his blood ran cold. "W...what happened?"

"She was attacked by two men over at the hospital. She was the only one there, so right this second, there are no staff on duty." Shaw looked towards Barnes.

"I'm on it," Barnes replied and headed out.

"Did you know the men, Stephanie?" Shaw asked.

"Not by name, but they were part of the group that arrived the other day. They're on the campsite. Pale, red hair, freckles."

"Okay. We don't have the luxury of one-way mirrors and police line-ups. Do you think you're okay to come across with us and point them out?"

Stephanie looked towards Jenny. "Would you come with me?"

"Of course I will, love," Jenny said. She looked down at Stephanie's clothing. Let me just get you a jacket to cover yourself up."

"Shaw, this is Barnes. Over," the radio crackled.

Shaw picked up the handset, "Go ahead Barney, over."

"You need to get over here quick. I'm in ward one. All the meds have gone. I've got two confused patients here who are scared witless. I've not checked the rest of the place yet, but I'm guessing it's going to be the same story. Over."

"We'll be there in five. Over and out," Shaw said and placed the handset down.

Within a couple of seconds, it crackled again. "Shaw, this is North Ridge, over."

He picked the radio up and pressed the talk button. "This is Shaw, go ahead. Over."

"Shaw, we've got four caravans, two motorhomes and a bus that have just gone straight through the checkpoint without stopping, over." Shaw looked at the radio in his hand. "Shaw! Shaw!"

"Understood. Standby. Over!"

"What are you thinking?" Jenny asked, seeing the shock on Shaw's face.

He looked towards Jenny then at Stephanie. "I'm putting us in lockdown. He picked up the radio, "North Ridge, East Ridge, this is Shaw. We're implementing lockdown. Put up the barricades. Repeat: put up the barricades. Over."

"Message received and understood. This is North Ridge, over and out."

"Roger that, Shaw. East Ridge, over and out."

Shaw looked towards Andy, Rob and John. "We're going to get the arms stash in the village hall," he said as he stood and turned towards Jenny and Stephanie. "You two stay here and keep the doors locked."

"Do you really think we're under attack?" Jenny asked.

"I'm not going to take any risks."

*

The group went through several more villages that had all suffered the same level of devastation. There was not a soul left alive, not a house or building left unblemished. The dark clouds that had been threatening to burst open all morning fulfilled their promise as torrents of rain began to fall from the skies.

Hughes put the windscreen wipers on full but still had to slow right down, as he could barely see beyond the end of the car bonnet. They were just about to leave the village limits when Wren shouted: "Stop!"

Hughes jammed on the brakes. "What? What is it?" he asked, frowning into the mirror.

"That house. That last house—I saw someone."

Hughes put the car into reverse, hoping Will would see the lights and do the same. All six occupants looked towards the large, brick-built detached building with its overgrown garden.

"Where did you see them, Wren?" Lucy asked.

"The bedroom window. Top right."

"Are you sure? In this rain it's pretty difficult to see anything."

"I'm sure," she replied.

Mike turned to look at her. "If she thinks she saw something it's worth checking out."

"Why?" Emma asked. "So what if someone's in the house? How does that help us?"

"We won't know until we find out, will we?" Mike replied.

"This is mental," Emma said. "We can't just stop every time we see movement; it will take us a lifetime to get there."

"Hey, look. If somebody managed to survive through this, they might be able to tell us something useful."

"Like what, Mike? What could someone possibly tell us that we don't already know? We've been through a load of villages now and they all tell the same story. It's a grim, shitty story, but it's the same one. Fry and his army are maniacs, and everyone they ran into had a pretty bad day."

Mike looked at his sister, opened the car door and stepped out into the pouring rain.

"Your boyfriend's a dick," Emma said to Lucy.

"Hey, he was your brother before he was my boyfriend," Lucy replied. Their heads felt a draft and they looked back to see the hatchback had opened once again.

"I didn't dream it," Wren said, joining Mike.

"I didn't say anything."

"I can tell what's going through your mind."

"Jesus. What is it about women? They all think they're bloody mind readers," he said opening the gate and walking down the path. "Would I be out here getting soaked if I thought you'd imagined it?"

Wren followed and had caught up to him by the time he reached the door. "Shall we break a window?" Mike just looked at her and tried the handle, The uPVC door swung inwards, and Mike took the shotgun from his rucksack. Tapping on the frame as loudly as he could, he called, "Hello?"

The two of them waited a few seconds for a response, but none came. "Hello?" Wren shouted, battering against the door with her homemade spear.

Mike smirked. "Nice weapon. They show you how to make those on Blue Peter?"

"That's funny," Wren replied. "It'll be even funnier when I shove this up your arse."

"You've been hanging around with Jules and my sister way too much. You were such a quiet girl before you met them." They both smiled and entered the house.

The two of them cleared the ground floor before heading upstairs. They went from room to room as the water continued to drip from their hair and faces. "This was the room," Wren said. "This was the room I saw them in. I did see them; I'm not making it up."

"I believe you, I believe someone was here."

"Why?"

"A, because you said you saw something, and B, because when we went into the kitchen, there was a slightly darker patch on the welcome mat, like the door had been opened and rain had come in."

Wren looked at him. "Oh," she said, as they both headed back downstairs to the kitchen.

Mike opened the back door and looked out into the garden. Once it would have been a little slice of paradise, as beautiful bushes and trees surrounded the lawn, but now, nature had been left to flourish untethered. The lawn was overgrown, spreading dandelions and weeds erupted from the grass, and a line of footprints had trampled a hasty exit as widening strides disappeared beyond the garden. Mike and Wren stepped out into the downpour once more. They headed to the back fence and looked over to see a shallow embankment leading to a stream at the bottom and beyond that, a wooded area.

"Should we go after them?" Wren asked.

"Whoever it is really doesn't want to see anyone if they're prepared to head out in weather like this. After what happened to this place, I can't really say I blame them. Maybe we can check again on our way back, but who's to say they haven't just legged it. They might never come back. We can't just wait on the off chance."

"I suppose you're right," Wren said, and they headed back to the car.

"Well?" Emma asked as they climbed back in.

"There was someone there, but they scarpered before we got to see them," Mike said, placing his rucksack back in the footwell.

"Can't think why," Emma said. "Nothing says 'we come in peace' like a bloke with a shotgun and a girl carrying a spear."

Hughes engaged first gear and they moved off once again. The woodland gave way to hills, rocks and cliffs, and ahead, the road waned through a narrow valley. They had been travelling for just a few minutes when Hughes stopped again.

The rain was still pouring down, and this time it was Hughes and Mike who climbed out of the car. The passage had been carved between almost vertical rock faces on each side and they both just stood there with their hands on their hips, looking at the landslide that had blocked the road ahead of them.

"There's no other way around. This is the only road to Loch Uig," Hughes said.

"How far do you think it is?" Mike asked.

Hughes wiped the rain from his face, "Can't remember exactly, but not that far."

"Looks like we're on foot then," Mike replied.

"Yep. Looks like we're on foot."

5

Shaw and Jules's brothers—Andy, Rob and Jon—arrived at the village hall. Breakfast had been cleared away long since and now lessons were underway, but today they would be cut short. Ruth and Beth looked towards the door as the men entered, and Shaw quickly guided the two women out of earshot of the children.

"We're under attack," he said.

Panic-stricken looks swept over their faces. "What? From who?" Beth said.

"Not sure. There's been some trouble at the hospital. Stephanie was attacked, our med supplies have been stolen and a convoy of vehicles just swept through the North checkpoint without stopping."

"Oh shit," Beth said.

"Yeah. It's not safe for the kids here," he said, looking at the group of thirty young faces. Can you get them to the East ridge on the bus?" he asked.

"Stuff that. If we've got a fight on our hands, I'm stopping here," Beth replied.

"Ruth, I know it's asking a lot, but can you take them?" Shaw asked.

"Of course."

"Snap to it. Right, we need to sound the siren," Shaw said.

"The siren?" Beth brought her hand to her heart. "Oh my god, this really is it. Do you think it's the rest of Fry's army?"

"I've got no idea who it is, Beth, but hesitation could cost us lives. Forgetting everything else, the convoy that broke through the barrier hasn't been checked. If there are any bite or scratch victims among them, that could be it for us and it's not worth the risk."

"Mike and Hughes picked a great day for a trip."

"Yeah, tell me about it. Now when that alarm sounds, everybody knows what they need to do," Shaw said.

The children filed out behind Ruth. Worried looks adorned their faces despite the assurances from the librarian, and now headteacher, that it was all right.

Annie and John, Beth's younger siblings, ran up to her, breaking rank from the procession. Annie was almost in tears as the tension in the air became more palpable. Beth knelt and hugged them both. "It's okay. Go with Ruth."

"I don't want to leave you," Annie said as Sammy and Jake, Mike's younger siblings, came up to join them.

"What's happening?" Sammy asked Shaw.

Shaw couldn't help but smile. Sammy was nine going on fifty-nine. "Look, it's going to be okay," he replied. "You just need to help Ruth look after the other children while we take care of things here."

Sammy pursed her lips in thought for a moment before nodding, taking hold of her younger brother's hand, and walking away.

"I promise I'll see you soon. Now go with Ruth," Beth said, kissing both her siblings before ushering them away.

"It's ready. I've got the generator running," Rob said, coming back into the hall.

"Okay, listen—change of plan. I'd like you, Andy and Jon to go with the kids and Ruth."

"What? No way. If we're in trouble, we want to help here."

"I understand that, but I'm sending that school bus out to the East Ridge. There are two men at that checkpoint. What if it gets attacked and there is a busload of thirty kids across there with no one to defend them? I need soldiers I can rely on," Shaw replied.

Rob nodded. "Okay, I understand. I'll go get my brothers."

"Thanks, I appreciate it," he said, watching him go.

"I'd be happier with someone else guarding the kids," Beth said when he was out of earshot.

"The East Ridge is the safest place by far and away. It's got a much greater line of sight and, if this was a coordinated attack, they'd have seen something long before now. I need those three out of the way, cos I don't want to get my one good leg blown off by one of those gangly fuckwits trying to unjam their weapon."

"Fair point," Beth replied.

Within a minute, the bus was loaded and on its way. It pulled out of the carpark, leaving Shaw and Beth alone, looking at the World War II Carter air raid siren that George had restored for just such an occasion. "Well, here goes nothing," Shaw said, starting it up.

The two blades of the chopper began to turn, and for a moment, the only sound either of them heard was a low *whooshing* as the air passed through the portholes of the stator, but gradually the whooshing gave way to something else. The rising hum became a huge wall of sound that made their very bones vibrate as the warning that Safe Haven was under attack went up.

"Holy shit!" Beth shouted, flattening her palms against her ears to block out as much sound as she could.

Shaw let it run for over a minute, then disconnected the power. They both watched as the blades slowed down and the reverberations diminished. Even when all sound had stopped, the air felt electrified.

"Now we hope," Shaw said.

"What?" Beth replied.

"I said: now we hope!"

"Hope? Everybody should know what they're doing, we've drilled enough times."

"There's a world of difference between drills and somebody springing to action when the shit hits the fan," Shaw said, heading back inside the village hall.

"You're not filling me with confidence."

"Yeah, there's a reason for that."

*

The landslide was steep, but not impassable. Mike climbed it first. The rain had turned the earth covering the rocks into slushy mud, and by the time he reached the summit, his face and clothes were caked in clay-coloured residue. He turned to help the next member of the group up, and all of them began to laugh. For a moment he didn't understand why, but then he looked down at himself and got the joke. "Glad you find this funny," he said.

"Here you go, Mikey boy," Hughes said, throwing up a tow rope. Mike looked around. There was nothing solid to attach it to, so he tied it around his waist, dug his feet in and lowered the other end. Lucy climbed up next, followed by Wren, Emma and Jules. When Will started to climb, Hughes had to help him, and he cast a knowing glance to Mike.

Hughes reached the summit and Mike extended his arm to pull him up the last few feet. The group walked across to the other side of the landslide, and the drop seemed far steeper, except for one, narrow slide of earth to the left. Mike kept the rope around his waist and lowered the rest of the group down one by one. Will had as much difficulty going down as he did on the way up, and this time it was Emma who caught Mike's eye to express concern.

Mike untied the rope from his waist and dropped it down before lowering himself onto the steep, thin slip of earth wedged between the cliff face and the rest of the landslide. He shot down like a child in a playground, springing back to his feet at the bottom.

"It's going to be a laugh getting back up there," Hughes said as they stepped back from the fallen boulders, earth, and shrubbery.

"Don't worry, we'll find a—" Mike cut off and edged back a little further.

"What is it?" Lucy asked, seeing the puzzled look on Mike's face.

"Erm, give me a minute." He walked several metres away, then looked at the large roadblock once more. "There's something weird about this," he said, returning to the side of the others. He brought the rucksack around from his shoulders and pulled out his hatchet, then walked up to the steep, muddy face of the landslide and began hacking and digging at the slippy orange earth.

"Well it was bound to come eventually; I suppose it was just a matter of time. He's finally gone round the twist," Emma said.

"Yeah, I always thought it was going to be a violent killing spree kind of mad, though, not the 'Richard Dreyfus building a mud mountain in his living room' mad," Jules replied.

"In fairness, he's not in his living room," Wren said.

"Fair point," Jules replied.

Mike dug away a bucket's worth of debris before a metallic *clunk* made everyone fall silent. He raised the hatchet again, then brought it down in the same spot, making the same sound. He burrowed his hand into the narrow gap and dragged it out, pulling a big lump of clay with it, and finally revealing a dirty, white space in the hole he had made.

"Pass me some water," he said, and Lucy immediately gave him a bottle out of her backpack.

"What is it, Mikey?" she asked.

He took the top off the bottle and sprayed a little against the dirty white surface, hardly making it shine, but certainly making it more easily identifiable. He returned the bottle to Lucy.

"Mike!" Emma said. "You're starting to freak us out. What the hell is it?"

He turned to look at her. "It's a lorry. This isn't a natural landslide. Somebody put it here hoping we'd believe it's a natural roadblock."

"Who? Who would put it here?" Emma demanded.

"You asked me what it was. I didn't say I knew why it was here."

"So what do we do?"

"We keep our eyes open."

"For what?"

"For everything."

*

"Oh my god!" Sarah screamed as she shot a frightened glance towards George.

George took a deep breath. "Well, I hoped we'd never hear that again," he said, immediately beginning to head back up the beach.

"What the hell do you think it could be?" Sarah asked.

"I brought my radio in the car, we'll find out. I know they swapped a few duties round; do you remember where you're going?"

"I'm helping to load the mangonels."

"That's handy; you're with me then," George replied. The two of them scrambled back up the rocks as quickly as they could. When they reached the top, George headed to the car for the radio and Sarah went straight into the house.

There were weapons caches up and down the Safe Haven coastline, and one of them was at their house. She ran up the stairs, pulled the loft ladder string, and the steps magically emerged from the ceiling. Sarah stumbled on the second rung, as panic began to take hold of her, but gathered herself before continuing. She climbed to the top and reached into the darkness, feeling around for the heavy holdall. It took everything she had to lift it onto her shoulders before climbing back down the aluminium steps.

"Sarah?" George called as he entered the house.

"Up here."

George climbed the stairs and relieved Sarah of the bag, making it look much lighter than it was. He carried it downstairs and placed it on the kitchen table. It fell open, revealing rifles, shotguns, pistols and ammunition.

"A convoy shot through the checkpoint without stopping, and there was a raid on the hospital. Stephanie got attacked," George said.

"Oh shit! It's real then?"

"It's real," George replied.

Sarah hated guns; she hated the sound of them, she hated using them, but she hated the thought of someone using them against people she loved even more.

She removed a Glock 17 from the bag and placed it in the back of her jeans before putting two extra magazines in her pocket. "Take whatever you want," she said.

"I've got mine in my car," he said, lifting the holdall back onto his shoulder.

"I've got butterflies in my stomach," Sarah said.

George reached out and took her hand. "It's okay poppet; you'll be fine."

The pair of them headed out of the house, and Sarah cast one more longing glance towards it before leaving the garden.

*

Humphrey was still barking long after the siren had fallen silent. Raj and Talikha both knew their roles. If the emergency alarm ever went up, they were to head to the hospital to help Lucy receive casualties, and now more than ever, in Lucy's absence, it was essential they made haste.

Humphrey jumped down from the diving platform into the dinghy. He knew when they were getting ready to go ashore and he did not need a command. Raj and Talikha joined him in the boat and Raj immediately started the motor.

The pair of them had heard the last broadcast. Safe Haven was under attack; more than that they did not need to know. Everyone had their part to play and this was theirs.

It did not take more than a few minutes for them to reach the dock. The waters of the small harbour were too shallow for their yacht, still, they rarely strayed far from shore.

Talikha tied the rope around the cleat, and Raj lifted Humphrey up onto the wooden pier before climbing up himself.

"Are you alright, my love?" he asked.

"We have drilled for this. Everything will go as it should," she said, with a less-than-confident smile. They both began to jog along the jetty and towards the campsite.

"Thank Christ you've arrived," Barnes said as Raj, Talikha and Humphrey all bounded through the door of the first static caravan, which constituted Ward One. The campsite was spread over a wide area, and the hospital was set back in one corner. "Look, there's a problem on site, too. I'm going across to get Shaw now—hopefully, we can scramble a small squad together to deal with this before we face the rest of what's coming our way."

"What happened here?" Talikha asked, looking around the ransacked cupboards.

"Someone stole all the meds and attacked Stephanie. We don't know if it's to do with the convoy or not, but it's an awfully big coincidence." Barnes handed Raj his Glock and spare magazine. "The rest of the hospital staff should be arriving soon. Keep the doors locked, keep your eyes peeled. I'll see you when this is all over."

*

Richard and David had led very dull lives down in Skelton, but the day they met Mike, all that changed. As librarians with their friend Ruth, they had always been outsiders watching quietly from the edges, but now they played a vital part in this new society. They were working from home, coding some of the books the library had acquired the previous week, when they heard the siren.

They shot each other urgent glances, and without pause, placed the books down and ran out of the room like firemen responding to a bell.

Richard grabbed the car keys from the telephone table. "What do you think it is?" he asked.

"That siren only means one thing: We're under attack," David replied.

"Should we find a weapon?"

"We've drilled for this. Don't tell me you've forgotten everything already."

"No, but this time it's actually for real."

"It doesn't change anything. We go to the blockade and do what we trained to do."

They headed out of the door and climbed into the car. Richard tried to put the key in the ignition, but his hand was shaking too badly. He put the key in his lap for a moment and placed both hands firmly on the steering wheel. David did not say a word; he was feeling the same thing and a rebuke would be hypocritical. Richard picked up the keys and tried again, this time he found the ignition slot and started the car. "I really have a bad feeling about this," he said as he pulled the gear stick into reverse.

The vehicle backed out of the drive and straightened up onto the road. Richard changed to first gear and looked across towards his friend. "Me too," David replied.

6

Rockfall netting adorned the cliffs on both sides of the road suggesting that landslides had been an issue in the past, but for the time being, the only issue was *who had created that barrier?*

The group advanced cautiously; there was not much to see but tarmac and paint as they walked down the broken white line in the centre. The road curved around and they continued down the increasingly steep gradient, seeing at the bottom of the incline that the rock on both sides finally gave way to thick forest.

Mike and Hughes walked in front, while Lucy and Wren brought up the rear. The more distance they covered, the more they relaxed, as no threats confronted them. "Tell me about your sister," Lucy said.

Wren smiled. "Where would I begin?"

"Well, did she look like you?"

"Erm, kind of. We both look a lot like Mum, but Bobbi has this rock chick thing going on where she dyes her hair black, wears black leather, and generally tries to look like a badass."

Lucy laughed. "So, she's a seventeen-year-old Joan Jett?"

"Eighteen. She was eighteen the day before yesterday," Wren said quietly, and Lucy put a comforting arm around her shoulder. "Who's Joan Jett?"

"Oh man. Well, she was a little before my time too, but she was like the ultimate badass rocker. Wore black leather and broke all the rules."

"Yeah then, that sounds like Bobbi. Other than the being a rocker part…she's tone-deaf." They both laughed.

"Is she like you in other ways?" Lucy asked.

Wren nodded then shrugged. "We never used to be. In fact, we didn't get on at all. She was into boys and going out and having a good time. I was training most of the time and when I wasn't, I was doing schoolwork or had my head buried in books. But when all this happened, things changed."

"Well, yeah, I get that."

"No, I mean, we grew closer than ever. I suppose it must have been hard for her when I was getting all the attention. There was rarely a weekend where Mum and Dad weren't driving me to an athletics meeting or taking me to training, so she just went and did her own thing. She seemed to try less and less and we just ended up worlds apart." Wren looked into the distance, remembering. "But then…I guess she realised it was just me and her and the only way we were going to make it was if we both pulled together."

"So how did you?"

"How did we what?"

"How did you pull together?"

The grey clouds parted and a small crack of sunlight broke through, bathing them in a sliver of warmth. "Bobbi gave up giving up," Wren said with a small laugh.

"Gave up giving up?"

"Yeah. When we left home, she gradually got better and better; she started working with me rather than against me, and then one day, she picked up a bow."

Lucy looked confused. "What, like a violin bow?"

Wren laughed. "No...I'm not explaining this very well. I made her go with me to an archery range I'd read about; I thought it would be useful if I learnt how to use one. Bobbi thought it was a dumb idea, but she came along to keep me company. I sat down at the range with a beginner's guide book—now Bobbi has never been big on reading, so she just picked up the bow and started figuring it all out for herself. I hadn't got through the first page before she'd fired an arrow."

"And?"

"And it wasn't a million miles away from the bullseye. She fired another, then another and another and...turns out she's a natural. In the meantime, I could barely hit the target, let alone the bull. I found the crossbows in a locker and I decided they were more my thing. We both practised every day. Now, you really have to know Bobbi to realise what a big deal that was. Bobbi never practised anything, but something changed. She became disciplined, and it spread to other stuff. When something was difficult, she didn't give up like she once had, she persevered. I wouldn't have lasted those first few weeks without her."

"Somehow, I think you would have, Wren. You're a special girl. Everyone who meets you can see it."

"Well that's kind of you to say, but—"

Mike and Hughes came to a sudden stop, and Emma, Jules and Will nearly walked into the back of them.

"What is it?" Lucy asked as she and Wren joined them.

"Can you hear that?" Hughes asked.

"Hear what?" Lucy replied.

"It sounds like music."

Lucy and Wren listened, then they could hear it too. It was quiet at first but was gradually getting louder and louder.

"It must be a car with the stereo on or something," Jules said.

They all readied their weapons. It was not the most civil way to greet a stranger, but they had no idea who they were up against and experience had taught them not to take any risks.

"What's that other sound?" Wren said.

"I don't hear anything," Mike replied.

Wren got down onto her hands and knees and placed her ear to the tarmac. "We need to go. We need to go now."

"What are you talking about?" Lucy asked as the music continued to get louder.

"Run! We need to run, now!"

"Wren," Emma said turning and grabbing hold of the teenager's shoulders. "Start making sense, what are you talking about."

Wren's chest was heaving up and down with panic. "There's a horde, a big one heading this way."

"A horde of what?"

"RAMs, zombies, the living dead—call them what you like but they're headed this way and we need to get the hell out of here now."

The music continued to grow louder and all their attention was suddenly drawn above them as a drone with a loudspeaker attached came into view above the trees.

"That's Pink Floyd," Mike said.

"What?" Wren asked, becoming incensed by the lack of willingness to listen to her.

"That's Pink Floyd, 'Run Like Hell.'"

"I'm telling you, we need to go now!"

"Fuuuck!!!" cried Mike as the drone continued towards them and the first few RAMs appeared from around the bend at the bottom of the hill.

"Oh Fuck!" Emma said.

"That's what I've been trying to tell you," Wren cried.

They all turned immediately and began to run back up the hill. For the time being, there was a gap of about one hundred and fifty metres between them and the marauding army of beasts, but Mike realised immediately that his decision to bring Will along was not going to end well. They had run fifty metres uphill, and Will was already trailing behind by about fifteen. Mike reached into his bag and handed the tow rope to Hughes, then dropped back and took the older man's arm. "Come on Will," he said.

Will shuffled his arm free, but continued running with his rifle still over his shoulder. "There's no way I'm getting out of this and don't pretend there is," he said between laboured breaths, "but I need you to promise me something. I need you to get to that place and free those women." He slowed down. "At least in my head then, I can die knowing my niece won't have to live the horrors I've pictured anymore."

Mike looked back and the horde, which seemed to number at least a hundred, was gaining speed. He looked towards Will, who had already resigned himself to dying, then up the hill to his family and friends. "I shouldn't have said yes to you," Mike said.

"You granted an old man a dying wish."

"It wasn't meant to be a bloody dying wish—that's the point."

Will smiled. "Go, make sure you get those girls out. Thank you, Mike…now go, I've got an idea," he said, slowing even more and extending his hand. Mike shook it then turned and sprinted as fast as he could.

Will ran to the side of the road, glancing back towards the army of flesh-crazed beasts that were no longer interested in the drone which was now just hovering, like some flying mechanical overlord. The only thing the creatures were interested in was prey: the living, moving bodies ahead of them.

Mike looked back to see Will beginning to climb the rockfall netting like an old soldier on an assault course. It was working, the beasts started to veer towards him. Mike turned back to his direction of travel and watched the rest of the group as they continued up the steep incline. He increased his pace to try and catch them.

Will had climbed out of reach of the grabbing hands, looping one arm through the netting, while holding his rifle with the other.

"Come on then y'bastards," he yelled at the top of his voice, trying to rile them up to keep their attention while the others made their escape.

The music was still playing from the drone, but it was barely audible over the sound of the creatures' growls now as they clambered to get their fingers on the old man's foot or trouser leg.

Mike stopped running and looked back. Another noise had joined the commotion. He looked up to see a second drone appear. It was smaller and seemed more like a child's toy; something that looked like a jar of water was attached to the front of it.

Will noticed it too and looked back towards Mike, mirroring the younger man's confusion. The second drone flew under the first then began to head towards Will like a guided missile.

"What the fuck?" Mike said as the Mechano set with blades shot towards the older man.

Seeing what was happening, Will dropped his rifle into the crowd and turned to face the wall, gripping the netting with all he had. The small drone smashed against him and the rock face at the same time. Will managed to hold on through the impact, but he could feel shards of metal rip through his flesh. The drone dropped into the crowd of creatures, whose excitement had been piqued further now as blood began to drip onto their hands and faces. Then Will heard, smelled, and finally felt something else. For a few seconds, he did not understand what was happening, then he remembered the jar the drone was carrying. His flesh was sizzling; his clothes were melting before his very eyes, and a white smoke-like gas was rising from the side of his rib cage.

"Acid," he said in a hoarse whisper.

Will's left arm slid out of the netting and his body began to skid down the cliff face until his feet were low enough to be grabbed by the waiting creatures. He disappeared in a flash like an injured seal being dragged beneath the waves by a hungry shark—or a hundred hungry sharks. Mike looked towards Lucy then began to sprint once more, taking her arm and urging her to move faster. Will's heroics had bought them only a few seconds, but seconds could mean the difference between life and death.

Will's disappearance into the throng of bodies made the creatures who were trailing immediately lose interest. Their heads turned towards the rest of the group and their pace increased despite the gradient of the incline, which was beginning to tell on Hughes, Emma, Lucy and Jules as each stride began to strain a little more than the last.

Wren fell back, realising the rest of the group was struggling, and grabbed the rope from Hughes. As she continued to run, she tied one end of it around her waist just as she had seen Mike do.

The landslide barricade was in sight now, but Mike knew it would not be a simple task to mount it. It had been designed specifically to ensnare, and the one narrow slide that they had descended would require more time than they had to climb. He ran to the wall and leapt as high as he could, clawing at the netting before falling back to the ground. His right-hand snagged the thick wire, giving him the briefest of seconds to pause and aim his other hand higher up. He grabbed another rung, then another.

It happened in a flash and by the time Lucy realised what was going on, it was too late. "Nooo!" she screamed.

"Keep going, Luce! Keep going, and take out the drones if they come near you."

"Mike!" she yelled again, her voice breaking.

"Ruuunnn!" he shouted back.

Jules, seeing what was happening, grabbed Lucy's arm and forced her to carry on running while Mike continued to climb. The beasts began to converge below him. He stayed deliberately low, his boots tantalisingly close to their fingertips as they clawed upwards. A small handful continued after the others, but it was Mike most of them were interested in now; he was trapped.

He looped his arm through one of the holes in the netting. The pain and discomfort of the wire digging into him were nothing compared to the anguish he felt as he watched the dozen or so creatures that had not joined the horde below continue their sprint in pursuit of the others. He pulled the shotgun from his rucksack, clamped onto it with the hand he had weaved through the netting then pumped the forend before taking it in his left hand once again and firing. The recoil nearly dislocated his shoulder and his foot slid a little, but there was a bloody explosion below him and the sound rallied his audience into a heightened state of frenzy.

Wren was the first to approach the barricade; she veered left before turning to get a running start at the slide which married the cliff face to the blockade. The rain had ended, but the steep clay surface was still treacherously slippy. Everything depended on the first jump. If she could get high enough, the gradient was a little less severe and she might be able to scramble further up.

Wren flung her spear over the top and grabbed her hunting knife in her fist. Everything was silent to her now as she started her final run-up. She glanced quickly towards the others, then to Mike, then to the small band of vicious creatures who were heading towards them. It was all down to these next few seconds.

She charged then launched into the air. Her body jarred against the slippery red-brown clay surface, and before she began to slide down once again, she jammed in the hunting knife as hard as she could. She brought up her left hand and plunged her fingers into the thick, gooey clay, expecting it to break away any second, but it did not. Wren kicked the toes of her feet into it, then edged up further and further. Now her senses came back to her and she could hear the panicked shouts of the others, the pounding feet of the creatures, and the guttural growls that she'd hoped she would never have to hear again.

7

The lead vehicle in the convoy was a motorhome that had metal shutters fitted over the windows, but not the windscreen. It roared along the clifftop road, blazing a trail for the vehicles behind it.

"I'm getting a bad feeling about this," Tanya said, looking across towards Mason. "Maybe we should forget about this one, just head on down the coast."

Mason smiled. "What are you talking about? The fun's just about to start."

"That siren…that didn't strike me as something a group of badly organised local yokels would have."

"So they've got a fucking siren. They'll be telling everybody to get indoors and hide under the tables, which suits me fine. Last thing we want is to get involved in a street fight. This oughta be a straightforward in and out. If they've got sense, they'll keep their heads down until we're gone and nobody will get hurt."

"And if they're not smart?"

Mason looked across at her. "What? Say what's on your mind."

"I don't want to face another Brondaig," she said and turned from Mason's gaze.

Mason let out a long breath and returned his eyes to the road. "Look, we fend for ourselves. These are different times now, but we do what we've always done."

"There were children in that crowd."

"Going all maternal all of a sudden? You never struck me as the type."

Her head shot back around to look at him and where there had been sadness in her eyes before, now there was anger. "You don't know me. You think because we've been on the road together and shared a bed you know me. I had a family, before all this. I wasn't a saint, and they weren't saints, but they were family, and to think of what happened back in Brondaig, that was just…"

The cockiness had gone from Mason's voice as he continued. "Look, some of the lads got out of hand. They were high on those mushrooms and they just went too far."

"Went too far? They massacred that village. We'd got everything we'd gone in there for. We had all their food, their booze, their meds—we even got vehicles and diesel. They didn't put up a fight and they were still murdered."

Mason continued to stare at the road ahead as he spoke. "That won't happen again. Those men were spoken to."

"Spoken to?"

"I'm not happy about what went on there. We do what we need to survive and occasionally that means killing, but it's not good business to wipe out a fucking village."

"Good business?"

"That's what I said. You take out a village, that's it, they stop producing, there's no chance you can head back there in a few months to restock. It's business."

"Jesus Christ, is that all not killing people means to you?"

There was a pause before he answered. "Yes."

*

Hughes and Lucy stopped running about ten metres before the blockade and turned. Wren was nearly at the top of the slide, but she needed more time. They raised their weapons and began to fire, taking down RAM after RAM in quick succession.

Fountains of blood and brain tissue spewed from the back of the creatures' heads as bullet after bullet brought them down. Within a few seconds, the group of RAMs that had broken away from the horde around Mike's feet were down, and Lucy and Hughes slowly backed up, keeping their weapons raised, ready to fire on anything else that came towards them.

Wren was almost there. She reached over and dug her fingers into the thick layer of earthy clay that lined the top of the lorry's roof, then took a breath. She heaved herself up and across, praying that she would not slide back down. Her upper torso hit the top of the barricade hard, winding her, but she immediately sank the knife into the thick earth coating. Jules and Emma held their breath as they watched Wren's legs dangle over the side of the landslip barrier.

Wren scrambled to her feet and saw Mike was shouting and kicking out, trying everything he could to keep the attention of the beasts as they swarmed around him. She looked down and unravelled the rope, lowering it to the ground.

"Emma first," shouted Wren, "she's a bit lighter."

"You cheeky little shite," Jules responded.

"I didn't mean it like that," Wren said.

Emma grabbed hold of the rope, and Wren sunk both her feet into the earth, leaning back, using what weight she had as well as all her strength. Emma began to climb, looping the rope around her left arm while using her right to dig and scramble up the incline. Wren continued to pull, but she could feel her feet starting to slide.

*

Another two jar-carrying drones appeared, while the larger one still hovered, blaring a morbid soundtrack above all the unfolding action.

"Oh shit," Lucy said, looking towards them. "Mike said we need to take the drones out."

Hughes looked towards Lucy, then towards the creatures, and finally towards the drones. "Okay, you concentrate on the RAMs, I'll take care of the drones."

Just like the first, these two smaller drones flew below the larger one. The first headed towards Mike while the other dove towards Hughes. Mike would get hit first, so Hughes forgot about the one coming at him for the time being and raised his SA80. The trajectory of the craft was straight and predictable. Hughes fired a burst of shots. One of the propellers became detached, scuttling into the blades of another, and the drone descended like a super-powered spinning top. The jar smashed on the tarmac and clouds of white gas rose while the ground sizzled.

Realising what was in the jars now, Hughes quickly diverted his attention to the other drone, which was heading straight towards him. He unleashed another long volley and hit the drone several times, but it kept coming. At the last second, he dove to the right, taking Lucy with him. The drone crashed to the ground, the jar exploding into a hundred pieces as the liquid bubbled its acidic destruction against the road.

"Fuck me!" Hughes said.

"Jesus," Lucy replied, looking towards the hissing mess.

Hughes realised this was no time for reflection. He sprang back to his feet. "Come on, let's get moving," he shouted.

"How many bullets do we have?" Lucy asked.

"Not enough to make that many headshots from this distance."

"What the hell was Mike thinking?"

"We are talking about the same guy here, aren't we? When did he ever think about anything?"

"Good point," Lucy replied, taking aim at another beast as it started towards them.

"Look, we'll get on top of that barricade, then figure out what we're going to do next—but one thing at a time." Hughes stopped again and this time looked towards the drone that was still blasting out music. He raised his rifle once again and took careful aim before firing four shots. There was a small burst of flames from the body of the hovering construction before it too went into a dive and smashed against the road with a crunch.

"We've blinded the enemy for the time being, but we'd better keep our wits about us," said Hughes. "Whoever these people are, they're not just your average thugs."

*

The wire from the rockfall fencing dug into Mike's arm and everything from his elbow down was starting to go numb. "Oh shit," he cried, but he could not even hear his own words over the din of the creatures.

Over the last few months, since all this had begun, he had been in close quarters with these creatures more times than he could count. The black windows of their pupils housed a malevolence; even he struggled to fathom its depths. As he stared into them a familiar chill ran through him.

It was not looking towards these creatures that caused his blood to run cold…it was something else. Something he had not dared confess to anyone, not even to Lucy or Emma, the two people closest to him in this world. He dragged his eyes from the horde and their grasping hands and he looked across to the opposite cliff. There he was, sat with his legs dangling over the edge, looking down, watching. "Not now," Mike said to himself and squeezed his eyes shut.

He opened them again and the apparition was gone, but he felt his heart racing. He looked down at the sea of faces once again, and there was Fry, looking up at him now, right in the middle: a red face and ginger beard amidst the jostling rabble of grey. He barged the creatures out of the way until he was stood directly below Mike. The growls had deafened Mike to everything, but he could hear Fry's voice clearly as he spoke.

"It won't be long now, Mike. You'll be joining me soon. I've saved you a seat in Hell, right next to mine," Fry said, and a wide, yellow-toothed grin broke onto his face.

"You're not real!" Mike whispered, closing his eyes. He opened them again, but Fry was still stood there looking up at him. The fiery-haired Glaswegian reached into his pocket and pulled out a cigar, biting the cap off and spitting it at the face of the beast to the side of him. It bounced off the creature's cheek and to the ground, and Fry's grin grew wider. He placed the cigar between his teeth, pulled out a book of matches and lit the end, taking a long suck and blowing a plume of blue smoke up at Mike's face.

"You do realise this is all your fault? The old man dying, your family being in danger. Look at them," Fry said, angling his head around to view the barricade. *"If it wasn't for your recklessness, they'd all be home safe, but nooo. Mike wants to play hero, as usual. Tell me, how's that working out for you?"* Fry asked, laughing and taking another drag on the cigar.

"Leave me the fuck alone," Mike yelled. The loud report of a gun cut through the noise of the beasts and he looked towards the sound. Lucy had brought down another creature abandoning the herd. Mike looked back down and now's Fry's red, mocking face had been replaced with the familiar pallid hue of a RAM. It stared up at him with its arms reaching and clawing at the rock beneath his feet.

"See you soon, Mikey boy," came the whisper.

Mike looked around frantically to find the source of the voice, but there was nothing. He looked towards the barricade once more and saw Emma was now up there with Wren, and together they were hauling Jules up. Not much longer to hold on, then they'd be safe. The numbness in his arm gave way to pins and needles and he knew it would not be long before he'd lose control of it completely.

*

The second Jules was on top of the barricade, Hughes ushered Lucy towards the slide. She placed the Glock in the back of her jeans and now, with three people heaving on the rope, her ascent was much faster and smoother than the others. Finally, it was Hughes's turn. He was not as nimble and weighed considerably more than each of the women. Lucy knelt down and covered the horde as the other girls pulled hard on the rope. She fired just once as a creature broke free, but the remainder were still transfixed with Mike as he continued to do whatever it took to keep their attention.

"So what now?" Emma asked, as Hughes dragged himself to his feet.

"We need to get above Mike," Wren said.

"What?" Emma asked.

"It's the only way. We don't have enough bullets to take all those things out, we need to get to him from above and lower the rope down."

"Erm, okay. And how do you propose we get up there?"

"I can do it," Wren said.

"What?" Emma asked. "It wasn't exactly easy for you to get the few feet up to here."

"Yeah, that was wet clay. This is rock we're talking about now. I can rock climb; I've done it before."

"Wren, you don't have any equipment, the rock surface is wet, it's way too dangerous," Lucy said.

"How about we take out as many as we can with the guns, then fight the rest hand to hand?" Jules asked.

"We've got rid of a fair few, but there must be still about eighty there," Hughes said, looking towards the creatures. "We'd need headshots every time; we'll use up everything we have and then what will happen if we run into more trouble?"

"Well, I think we can safely say this expedition is over now," Emma replied, "so what does it matter?"

"It might be worth a try," Lucy added. "I can't think what other options we have."

Hughes let out a long sigh. "You're right. We'll call it a day on this and come out better prepared next time. I'm sorry love," he said, turning to look at Wren. "I promise you we'll—Oh shit!"

Wren was already a quarter of the way up the cliff face with the rope looped over her shoulder. Even at this distance, Hughes could see her white knuckles as she held on with everything she had.

"Oh shit!" Lucy echoed as she watched the teenager struggle to find firm footing on the craggy rock face.

Wren looked to her right. The rockfall netting was two metres away at the most. She suddenly had a new plan, and her muscles flexed as she gripped onto a small overhanging piece of rock, pivoted and reached like a monkey in a tree to another small ledge. The netting was just at the end of her fingertips now. She hung there for a moment, her legs unable to catch on to anything solid. She began to swing, slowly picking up momentum until she pushed hard and let go at the same time.

Hughes, Jules, Emma and Lucy all gasped like members of the audience at a circus as they watched a trapeze artist fly through the air. Wren's fingers missed the netting at first, and Jules and Emma screamed at the same time as they had visions of her falling to the tarmac below. But then Wren hooked onto a section of thick wire and her body smashed painfully against the side of the cliff face. She remained there for a moment to catch her breath. She looked across to see Mike watching her and then realised she had caught the attention of a number of the creatures herself. She clutched the wire with all her might as hungry growls began to rise into the air around her.

8

Kirsty had arrived at the pub shortly before the siren had sounded, and taken Stephanie upstairs to clean the scratch marks with some of the surgical alcohol that Jenny's still produced for the hospital. She gave the young nurse a fresh top of Jenny's to put on. It reeked of perfume, but it made Stephanie feel less exposed, less violated.

"Thank you," Stephanie said, stroking Meg's coat.

"You're alright, sweetheart."

"I need to be getting back to the hospital."

"Just sit awhile. You can give yourself a few minutes just to catch your breath."

Jenny appeared at the door. "That top looks better on you than it ever did on me."

Stephanie smiled. "Thank you. Thank you both for looking after me."

"Don't be silly. You had a nasty shock. It's the very least we could do."

Suddenly, there was the sound of breaking glass from downstairs.

"That sounded like the front door. I've only just locked everything up," Jenny said. Meg started to growl, but Stephanie comforted her until she calmed down.

"Where's the radio?" Kirsty asked.

"Damn it. I left it behind the bar."

"Have you got any weapons, Jen?" Kirsty asked.

"No. I like leaving the fighting to people who can fight," she replied.

"Okay, you must have something," Kirsty said, heading out of the bedroom. She went into the kitchen and straight to the knife block, pulling the three largest kitchen knives from the marble slots.

She started back out when she saw the red, dry powder fire extinguisher. She'd just pulled it from the wall mount and headed back into the bedroom when she heard multiple male voices downstairs. Kirsty walked back into the bedroom and handed the other two women a knife each; their faces took on a new level of seriousness. Whether they liked fighting or not, they were in it up to their elbows now.

"What do we do?" Jenny whispered,

Kirsty pushed the door to a little, but did not close it entirely. "We stay quiet. They might not come up here. Anything down there can be replaced; we can't. They're probably after the booze and the trade items."

The voices began to get louder as the men began to climb the stairs.

"You were saying?" Jenny said, nervously clutching the kitchen knife in both hands.

The crack of a rifle sounded from outside in the carpark and the feet on the stairs paused for a moment before tearing back down. Jenny ran towards Meg to prevent her from barking, while Kirsty and Stephanie rushed to the window, to see an armed man they didn't recognise lying on the floor as blood pooled beside him. Three men and two women rushed from the pub into the carpark with their guns raised. Kirsty immediately recognised one of them. "Bastards were in here yesterday. They must have been casing everything out."

Jenny joined them at the window as three more shots sounded. Two of the women and one of the men dropped to the ground; the remaining two darted back towards the entrance to the pub. Another shot was fired and a man screamed just as the pub door burst open once again.

"They got me in the fucking shoulder," came the cry as two pairs of feet began to ascend the staircase.

"We'll get to one of the bedrooms—we'll be able to see where the bastards are from up there," the other said.

"Okay," Kirsty said, beginning to breathe heavily, "remember: it's them or us. We didn't ask for this." She removed the plastic safety tie and pulled the pin from the extinguisher, as Jenny rushed to comfort Meg once again.

They heard the familiar creak of the floorboards then footsteps as the men walked across the landing. The door flew open; the man whom Mike had confronted the previous evening just stood there for a second, his mouth gaping. Kirsty looked back at him then brought the extinguisher up in front of her and pulled the trigger.

A powerful fan of white powder hit the man in the face like a sandstorm. He fell back onto his wounded friend, choking, and Kirsty edged the door open a little further. She moved out onto the landing, continuing to direct the jet towards the two intruders. Within a few seconds, they were both on the floor, spluttering and gasping for breath. Their eyes were stinging, their lungs hurt, and any thoughts of putting up a fight were gone.

They writhed on the carpet, incapacitated, as more feet climbed the stairs. Kirsty removed her fingers from the trigger and brought the extinguisher up, ready to aim the powerful jet at anyone who came around the corner. There was a pause on the last step and Kirsty's heart jumped into her mouth; she expected to see another group of marauding scum appear.

Barnes shot a quick glance down the hallway and looked at the figures on the floor. He emerged from the stairwell with Shaw and Beth following behind.

"Nice work," Shaw said as he and Barnes grabbed the rifles from the two men and pulled them roughly to their feet. Barnes attached cable ties to the men's wrists and he and Beth covered them while Shaw guided Kirsty back into the bedroom. "Are you alright?" he asked, looking around the faces.

"Just," Jenny said, joining them.

"I was an idiot to tell you to lock yourself in here. If these people are raiders, this place is probably the highest value target. Get to somebody's house and lock the door. The ones who attacked Stephanie are still on the loose and at the moment there's a convoy heading this way."

"I'm not going anywhere! This is my home," Jenny replied indignantly.

"Jen, it is your home, nobody's disputing that, but just until we figure out what we're dealing with, stop being a stubborn cow and get to safety."

"We'll head to my place," Kirsty said, putting the fire extinguisher down and taking hold of Meg's collar and Jenny's arm.

The two men were still coughing and spluttering in the hallway, and Shaw looked towards them for a moment before turning back to Stephanie. A gunshot sounded and Shaw, Barnes and Beth all looked at each other.

"That was from the campsite," Beth said.

"Shit!" Shaw said, "C'mon. We have to go."

Barnes, Beth and Shaw dragged the prisoners to their feet and marched them into the carpark.

"What do we do with them now?" Beth asked as they pulled them over to the spot where the others lay dead.

Another shot sounded from the campsite and Shaw knew they didn't have much time. "Listen, you tell me what I want to know and your wound will get treated; you don't and you're going to be in all sorts of pain," he said, jabbing the rifle into the man's shoulder.

The man let out a cry as a shudder of sharp pain ran through him. "Don't tell them anything," coughed the other, and Barnes smashed the man in the face with the butt of his rifle. There was a bloody eruption from the man's nose and he fell back, wailing. He desperately tried to move his tied hands up to his face, and as his head banged against the ground he tasted blood in the back of his throat.

"How many are at the campsite? How many of you came in?" Shaw demanded, pressing his rifle against the shoulder wound once more.

The man wailed as he became increasingly light-headed. "I...I..."

Shaw took a step back and fired the rifle. The bullet opened up the man's thigh and he collapsed to the ground, screaming like a child.

Beth and Barnes both looked at each other, shocked that Shaw would shoot a wounded, unarmed man. "I'll ask you again," Shaw said, "Unless you want to go for a matching pair." He grimaced, pointing his rifle to the other thigh.

"No, no please—there are thirteen—thirteen of us. Four caravans. Please, my shoulder...my leg...it hurts."

Shaw kept his rifle aimed. "And how many are in the convoy?"

"Keep your mouth shut!" gargled the other man as blood filled his throat.

Shaw looked at Barnes, who booted the other man in the ribs hard, winding him, and silencing him for the time being. Shaw stood on his prisoner's thigh, sending shards of pain streaking up and down the man's body. He screamed and cried again.

"How many?" Shaw growled.

"There were about sixty of us—about sixty in total."

"And what was the plan?"

"Please, I...don't feel good—" The man suddenly threw up and began to choke; Shaw turned him onto his side and hit him on the back repeatedly to clear his airways.

"Answer me and this will all be over."

"The pub, the meds, the food...then we were out of here—we were going to head down to Kyle—honest! We just wanted the supplies then we were out of here. We didn't come to hurt anyone," he spluttered.

"That why two of your blokes attacked one of our nurses?"

The man coughed. "Those two are bad 'uns. Not all of us are like that. Most of us just want to survive, we don't want to hurt no-one."

Shaw looked down at the pathetic figure lying on his side with vomit residue on his face and large red patches of blood on his shoulder and thigh. "Y'know what, I believe you." Shaw fired point-blank, then turned the rifle towards the coughing figure with the broken nose and fired into the back of his head. He looked towards Beth and Barnes. "That's five down, seven to go across at the campsite. We'll go back to the village hall, see how many of the militia has shown up, then we storm the place."

Shaw marched away, his limp only barely noticeable now. "Shaw," Beth called, "What the hell?"

Shaw turned. He looked down at the men then back towards Barnes and Beth. "We don't take prisoners. Someone strikes against us, it's a death sentence. We'll help, we'll feed, and we'll house strangers, but that doesn't make us weak, that makes us strong, and these people are about to find out how strong."

*

Wren climbed across towards Mike, occasionally glancing down at the monsters below then immediately wishing she hadn't.

"What the hell are you playing at Wren?" Mike shouted to be heard over the growls of the beasts.

"Yeah, nice to see you too. I've come to get you out of here."

"My arm's numb—I can't climb."

"Yeah well that's why I'm here, numbskull," she said looping her arm into the netting for a moment for support and fishing for the end of the rope. "I'm going to help you climb up."

"Wren, I don't know if you've noticed, but the netting doesn't go all the way to the top."

"Duh! You don't say. Yeah, let me worry about that. I've done a bit of rock climbing. It's not that far between the end of the netting and the clifftop; we can make this. First thing I need you to do, Arnie, is put that shotgun away."

Mike looked at the shotgun in his hand then across to the barricade. The only reason he had withdrawn it was to help as a diversion, but it was no longer needed. He extended it towards Wren. "Can you put the safety on for me?"

Wren was not big on guns, but she had watched her grandad tinkering with them in the workshop and had learned the basics. She flicked the safety on and Mike reached round to place the weapon back into his rucksack.

"Okay, now what?"

"Now I need to get a bit closer and tie the end of this rope around your waist," she said, edging across further, placing one hand through the netting near Mike's hip to support herself while she slid the end of the rope around his waist. The side of her face pressed against his chest as she looped it around.

"Wow...this must be like all your dreams have come true at once," Mike said with a smile.

"Oh yeah, I love risking my life for some gung-ho idiot with schoolboy humour." She knotted the rope then pulled hard to make sure it was tight. "Right. That was the easy part."

"What now?"

"Now I need you to face the wall, find a footing, grip onto the netting with your good hand and pull your numb arm out."

"Erm, it's numb. I don't have much control over it at all."

"I'll help you, but first things first."

Mike did as she asked. He secured his feet on thick wire rungs and grasped onto the netting with his left hand, pressing his face against the cold wet stone. He began to withdraw his arm as much as he could, and then he felt Wren's warmth as she helped. After a few seconds, his right arm was dangling by his side.

"Okay, and now?"

"Now we wait a little while for you to get the feeling back."

"You're pretty bright, aren't you?"

"Right now I feel like a genius, but it's a lot to do with the company I'm keeping."

"Thank you, Wren."

"Don't mention it."

*

The radio hissed, "This is Shaw. Over."

Sarah picked up the handset and hit the talk button. "Shaw, this is Sarah, go ahead."

"Where are you?" Shaw asked.

"We're about five minutes away from the barricade point."

"Okay, listen. There are about sixty men. It's nothing like what we've faced before, but it's important we deal with them just like we dealt with Fry's crew."

"Understood," Sarah said.

"Listen, we don't want to release the boulders and logs if we can help it. It took us weeks to clear those the last time. Concentrate on immobilising the first vehicle with all the mangonels, then move on to the others. We're just heading back to the hall now, then to the campsite. Over and out."

"Erm, roger," Sarah said, hitting the talk button once again. "I feel sick."

"Don't worry, poppet," George said as he caught up with another two cars that were travelling in front. "It's not as if we haven't done it before?"

Sarah looked out to the water and saw a motorboat speeding across the waves. "That'll be our navy then," she said drily.

George reached across and placed a hand over hers. "Listen to me, Sarah. These people have no idea what they're getting into. This will all be over very soon."

They carried on for just a few more minutes before the cars in front slowed and turned right, up a steep and bumpy track. Sarah and George swayed and bounced as they hit dips and potholes, but soon their vehicle emerged onto a flat plain where several constructions lay underneath thick sheets of tarpaulin.

George pulled on the handbrake and cut the engine. The pair of them climbed out of the car and walked straight to the first covered object, immediately untying the ropes that held the green waterproof cover down. They peeled the thick sheeting back to reveal a weapon from another time, while the men and women who had come in the other cars did the same.

George could not help smiling proudly as he regarded the medieval siege weapon. Another vehicle approached; he looked up to see Richard and David park their car next to his. He waved and they waved back.

George, Richard and David had been responsible for these creations. The two librarians had brought a wealth of books with them from Skelton including one about weapons of the middle ages. Together with George, they had redesigned and built the giant catapult devices that had helped defend Safe Haven against marauders. They had even fitted one to the deck of a boat, so now, if anyone tried to breach Safe Haven they would come under attack from land and sea. Since the great battle, more of the weapons had been built. Two were positioned at the summit of Dead Man's Pass, one was out on the waves, and the other four were here.

Beside each device lay piles of rocks and boulders, which people now started to load into the deep buckets of the weapons, ready for firing.

When the last of the mangonels was loaded, Sarah headed back to the car and grabbed the handheld radio. She hit the talk button. "Shaw this is Sarah, over."

"Sarah this is Shaw, go ahead. Over."

"We're in position and ready, over."

"Okay Sarah, we're heading to the campsite now. Good luck. Over and out."

The words *good luck* echoed in Sarah's ears and her nerves began to jangle wildly once again. "Erm, yeah, good luck to you too."

9

"My arm's starting to feel better," Mike shouted over the persistent growls.

"Good. Do you think you're ready to climb?"

"Yeah, I think so."

"Okay, we'll head up together. When we reach the top of the netting, I'll carry on and find a path to the top."

He looked up the steep cliff face. "I really hope you know what you're doing, Wren."

"Don't tell me you're scared of heights, Mike," she said, smiling.

"No, I'm scared of people I care about getting hurt."

Wren looked at him and had an overwhelming urge to reach out, to touch him, but she took a breath and started to climb the thick wire netting.

"Come on," she said, "we've got work to do."

The two of them began their ascent, matching each other rung for rung. With each step higher, the volume of the growls diminished a little more, and it was not long before they reached the top of the netting. They both paused for breath and angled their heads upwards, looking at the remainder of the cliff face.

"It's only about another five metres," Wren said.

"Yeah, five metres without any kind of safety equipment over wet rock," Mike said.

"God…you're beginning to sound like my sister," Wren said.

Mike smiled. "What climbing have you done?"

"Enough," Wren said, reaching up to take hold of a fist-sized nub of rock jutting out. "Watch where I'm going; I'll find us a route."

The teenager squeezed her fingers into a crevice and pulled herself higher still before letting go of the first nub and reaching across to another narrow ridge. It was slow going; she could not afford any mistakes. With each nudge upwards, she released a little more rope behind her.

Wren moved her head from side to side, looking for the next ledge or crack, but she could only see flat rock. She looked down to see how much room her feet had to manoeuvre, and that's when she lost her grip.

Her startled scream soared over the sound of the growls and echoed throughout the small canyon as she fell.

*

"Mason, we're pinned down. Where the hell are you?" shouted the voice over the radio.

Tanya picked up the handset and was about to hit the talk button when Mason reached across and grabbed it from her. "What the fuck do you mean you're pinned down?"

"We're under fire, they've got us cornered, there's no sign of Colm and the others. There was shooting earlier. I think they might be down."

Mason had known Colm longer than any of the others. He was the first one he had met and he was the nearest thing he had to a friend. "What do you mean *down*?" he asked, his face suddenly contorting into a grimace of animalistic rage, that made Tanya's skin prickle with goosebumps.

"I…I…" Gunfire sounded in the background.

Mason hit the talk button again. "Your job couldn't have been any fucking simpler and you still managed to fuck everything up. We're on the coast road heading to you now. These are just villagers. What the hell is wrong with you?"

"Hang on there's—wait—" there was the sound of more gunfire and the radio suddenly went dead.

"Jesus!" Mason spat angrily. "This was so fucking straightforward a kid coulda done it! These dimwits couldn't—" Something caught his eye. At first it was just a blur, but as he looked up he realised just exactly how much trouble he was in.

"What is it?" Tanya asked.

Mason did not answer, but jammed on the brakes and steered the motorhome into the rock face to the left. The sound of tearing metal drowned out Tanya's terrified screams as the first of several boulders the size of beach balls ripped through the roof of the motorhome. Another came down on the bonnet like a thunderbolt from the hand of God. It caved in the front end, smashed the windscreen, and halted all forward motion, making Tanya and Mason lurch forward in their seats. Two airbags deployed, and Tanya screamed again as she could feel one of her ribs fracture under the pressure against the seatbelt.

More brakes screeched, and there was another cacophonous ripping sound as the next vehicle ploughed into the back of them, jolting the wrecked husk further along the tarmac. Mason put his hand up to his face and brought it away covered in blood. He looked across towards Tanya, whose face was equally bloody. She was screaming from both pain and fear, and at that moment he felt nothing but revulsion for her as he grabbed his rifle, unhooked his seatbelt and opened the door.

*

The three caravans were already riddled with bullet holes, but the occupants continued to put up a fight. Fifteen of the twenty Safe Haven militia members had assembled in the village hall by the time Shaw, Barnes and Beth returned.

They headed to the campsite to find the residents had fled as the raiders, a number of them now high on the various meds they had stolen from the hospital, tore through the small dwellings like tornadoes. Shaw spotted two young men who matched the description Stephanie had given. They were the first to go, and now they had the remaining five pinned down in and around their vehicles and caravans.

"Please," a red-haired woman shouted as she came rushing out of one of the caravans with her hands raised.

Shaw raised his rifle and shot her without hesitation. Barnes and Beth gave each other concerned looks once again as the militia continued their advance.

"Ceasefire!" came a shout from inside one of the caravans and everyone stopped firing on both sides. "Look we're going to lay down our weapons and come out. You've won. Okay?"

"Okay," Shaw shouted as one of the caravan doors swung open, followed by a second.

A woman stepped out of one, and seeing the eighteen armed men and women pointing weapons at her, raised her hands. Next to step down was a young man who was holding a stomach wound, and finally, two rough-looking middle-aged men.

"You've won—okay," one of the men repeated.

"And now what?" Shaw asked.

The man looked confused. "What do you mean?"

"I mean now what? We lock you up? Let you eat our hard-earned crops, mend your pal's wound?" he said gesturing to the injured man. "Or do we let you go on the promise that you never set foot here again?"

"That," the man said. "The second one. We'll never come back here. We'll head out and you'll never see us again."

"And what about all the damage you did here? What about the girl you attacked? What about all the meds that you stole?"

"The meds, most of them are still in there. The girl? That was those two," he said, pointing to the two dead brothers with their mother lying near them. They were always trouble. We're not like them."

"And the damage?" Shaw asked. The man could not answer, and Shaw smiled. "Y'see the thing is, we've been here before. We've dealt with your kind before. You talk a good game but you're liars and thieves and lowlife scum."

The man's face hardened as Shaw spat the last words out. "That's not true. We're just trying to survive, like everyone else."

"What, by taking what others have? By mistaking people who are trying to do the right thing as people who are weak? As easy targets?"

"We just stay on the road and try to stay out of reach of the biters. Try to keep food in our bellies. We're no different from you. We just want to live."

"Yeah well, that's too bad," Shaw said, raising his rifle and squeezing four rounds in quick succession. The echoes from the first shot were still dancing around the campground when the last body dropped. Shaw slung the rifle back onto his shoulder and turned around. Seventeen stunned faces looked back at him. "We need to head to the barricade. They might need us there."

The militia dispersed, but Barnes and Beth held back.

"What's going on? Since when do we shoot unarmed men and women?" Barnes asked.

"Are you telling me you believed their cock and bull story that they would go in peace and leave us alone?"

"But they'd put down their weapons," Beth replied.

"Both of you, listen to me. People like this, people like Fry, they don't ever change. So they lost today. If we let them go they'd be back again, six, twelve, eighteen months down the line. And in between then and now they'd have tried the same thing with countless others…others who aren't as strong as us."

"But they were unarmed," Beth said again.

"You keep saying that, but it doesn't change the way things are."

"What gives us the right?"

"What gives us the right, Beth? You of all people asking that? The most important thing is Safe Haven's security; we do whatever we have to to protect it. People like this are only ever interested in themselves. They don't know what it is to look after others, to be part of a community. All they do is take."

"But don't you think a decision like…that…should be talked about? We could have locked them up and the council could have decided what to do," Beth said, looking towards the two dead teenagers who had attacked Stephanie.

"It has been talked about," Shaw said, starting to walk away.

"By the committee?" Beth asked.

"By me and Mike."

"What?" You two decided unilaterally?"

"Yep," Shaw replied.

Beth ran after him, taking hold of his shoulder and spinning him back around to face her. "How dare you make that decision for everybody else."

"You've just answered your own question. Because we dare. Look around you, Beth. The world has ended. We're doing something here, we're giving people a chance, we're building a community and a decent society. But for those things to exist you can't let bleeding hearts prevail. If someone attacks us we take them out, and we never have to worry about them trying it again. Now if you don't mind," he said, looking down at her hand still on his shoulder. "We're still under attack."

*

Mike looped the slack rope around his arm as many times as he could before he had to tense his muscle and take the full strain of Wren's deadweight. He growled as the pain from the jolt ran through his shoulder and fencing felt like it was going to cut through his fingers like a cheese wire.

Wren's terrified screams continued as she dangled like a piñata at a child's birthday party, just a few centimetres out of reach of the grabbing fingers of the beasts. The growls consumed her as she swung horizontally, with the rope still tied around her stomach.

The foul-smelling RAMs, with their necrotic grey flesh and piercing, ebony pupils jostled for position below her and for a moment, Wren dared not move, but finally, she heard something beyond their morbid song.

"Are you okay?" Wren's body slowly rotated and she looked up towards the barricade where her four friends stood with looks of terror on their faces as they had all watched the last few seconds unfold, but the voice had not come from any of them. "Wren! Are you okay?" Mike shouted again.

"Yes," Wren replied, but it came out as little more than a whisper. "Yes," she shouted this time.

"I'm going to bring you in to the wall," he said, arcing his arm back around.

Wren still horizontal, gratefully took hold of the narrow, rocky ledge that jutted out from the cliff face. She realised if not for Mike's quick thinking, she could have easily landed on this, which would have cracked her skull open like a hard-boiled egg. She reached up and grabbed the highest rung she could, dragging herself further out of reach of the horde below her. Wren took one step after another. With each one, she felt Mike reeling in more slack to make sure that if she slipped, it would not be down to the bottom.

She finally reached Mike's side and looked into his eyes. He could see she had been crying. "You alright?"

She sniffed and wiped her eyes with the heel of her palm. "Yeah, having a great day. You?"

"You haven't lost your sense of humour. That's too bad," he said. "Wren, what rock climbing have you done before?"

"We'd better get a move on before one of those drones appears again."

"Answer me."

"There was an indoor climbing centre near us that I went to a few times," she replied sheepishly.

"So you've never done rock climbing outside, in the wilds?"

"No."

"What possessed you to take such a risk?"

"You were in trouble, and I know if it had been the other way around you wouldn't have hesitated. If that wasn't worth taking a risk for, I don't know what was."

"Thank you," he said.

"Yeah well, I'm not doing a great job of helping you at the moment, am I?"

"I was looking a little further along. The rock seems to be less smooth there; we might be able to get better grips and footholds. Do you feel up to it?"

"Yeah, I'm fine."

The two of them began to edge horizontally across the fencing, moving further away from the blockade.

"This looks like the best spot," Mike said as he came to a stop on the fencing.

"Okay, we'll do what we did before. I'll—"

"Oh yeah, that worked out so well. We'll take it slow and we'll both climb up together."

"That's not really sensible; if one of us falls—"

"Wren, trust me," he said, and the pair began to ascend, leaving the netting and feeling out their way along the uneven cliff face.

"I suppose at least if we fall we'll be dead before those things get to us," Wren said.

"That's the spirit, Wren," Mike replied.

10

Mason watched in disbelief as fireballs emerged from the bay and headed towards the trapped convoy. "You fucking stupid bitch, Carol," he spat, as he cursed the woman whose one job had been to highlight the settlement's defences.

There was a series of crashes followed by small explosions as the convoy continued to get demolished from both sides. His own, already immobilised, vehicle edged forward even more as the rest of the convoy continued to pile up. Mason ducked down behind a rock as he heard a *whoosh*. Within a second, he felt heat lash above him and there was the familiar boom of a fuel tank igniting followed by the screams of at least a dozen trapped occupants. That was the bus.

More boulders whistled through the air from above, colliding with the vehicles in a metallic dissonance. A shriek of tearing metal split through Mason's head like his very brain had been bisected by piano wire. He dared to edge up from behind the relative safety of his rock to see the back end of the flaming bus rise into the air as the assault from above had knocked the front end over the edge of the cliff face. The burning figures inside renewed their helpless screams as they were thrown by the sudden movement.

He watched as the bus upended completely before disappearing from view. It was just two seconds, but it seemed like a lifetime to Mason as the flagship of his road warrior flotilla exploded on the rocks below. Another flurry of fireballs began to grow in size as they launched from the bay. Mason knew then these people had been severely underestimated. They were not the simple, peaceful village folk he had hoped; they were a well-drilled, relentless and brutal militia.

He wouldn't live beyond this day, but he was going to take some of his enemy with him. He began to climb the rocky incline. For the time being, he was invisible to the small army above. He cast a withering look over his convoy. Flames clung to the surfaces of most of the cars, caravans and motorhomes. Another barrage of rocks and boulders battered two more vehicles from the road, just as the fireballs erupted against the biggest of the motorhomes. Everyone he had spent the last few months with was gone in a matter of minutes.

*

Mike reached the summit, scrambled over the top, and immediately lowered his hand for Wren to take a hold of. He felt the cold flesh of her fingers wrap around his and he pulled at the same time she kicked with her feet. She landed in a sprawl by his side and they both lay there for a moment, looking up at the sky while they untied the rope from around their waists.

"And now we need a plan to get back down," Mike said.

They both got to their feet and cautiously leaned over the edge of the cliff. "This may sound a little odd, but I was in kind of a similar situation a few months back," Wren said, angling her head down at the beasts as they continued to look up towards them.

"Oh yeah? What did you do exactly?"

"I dropped a load of filing cabinets on their heads."

Mike gave her a strange look. "I told you it sounded odd, but it worked," Wren said.

"Filing cabinets?"

"Yeah, obviously, we're not going to use filing cabinets." She turned to look behind her. They were stood on a grassy plateau that gave way to another rocky incline and finally a peak about thirty metres above them. "Rocks," she said, reaching down and picking up to fist-sized stones. They leaned over the edge again to watch as Wren dropped the first. It landed in between two of the RAMs. It may possibly have broken one of their toes or even a foot, but that was not something that would register the blink of an eye with these things. She dropped the second, which possessed a slightly more aerodynamic shape. It pivoted slightly in the air before landing on the forehead of one of the beasts. The creature collapsed, disappearing from view as the others bunched together.

"Great! One down, ninety-nine to go."

"I didn't say it would be quick."

Mike turned and scanned their surrounds. There were hundreds of rocks and stones of all sizes and descriptions. "Oh well, better get to work," he said.

Mike unzipped his jacket, tied the arms together, and placed them around his neck, holding the bottom of the jacket out in front of him like a cradle. He crouched down and began to bundle in any rocks and stones fist-size and above.

"That's not a bad idea," Wren said.

"I'm not as stupid as I look."

"I didn't think you could be."

Mike laughed. "Seriously, what is it with the women in my life. They all think they're comedians."

"Let's face it, you give us plenty of material," Wren replied.

Mike collected twenty rocks in his jacket and walked back to the edge of the cliff with his left hand on one corner and his right hand on another before jerking the whole thing upwards like he was tossing a giant pancake. The stones launched into the air and seemed to hang a brief second before beginning their speedy descent. Mike and Wren looked over the side and six creatures went down at once, either stunned or killed by the various falling missiles.

They carried on; gradually the throng of creatures diminished and the growls decreased in volume.

"Mike!" yelled a voice from the barricade.

Mike looked towards where Hughes was pointing. "Shit!" he said, as three more drones came into view. They hovered there for a moment in mid-air like cyborg birds of prey deciding which quarry to attack. Then, as if responding to a starter's pistol, all three shot towards Mike and Wren.

*

Hughes began firing immediately, then Jules and Emma took aim with their SA80s. Lucy's Glock 17 was not designed for target practice at such a distance, but if just one bullet could hit one of them, then it was worth it. "Take cover, Wren," Mike said, pulling the jacket sling from around his neck and positioning himself in between her and the fast-moving drones. He pulled the shotgun from his rucksack and quickly loaded the remaining shells he had in his pocket.

He heard a loud hollow clunk followed by a high-pitched whir as a bullet hit one of the drones. The machine spun out of control and smashed into the opposite cliff face. The large jar of acid it held in its mechanical claw smashed against the stone, and in a hissing cloud of vapour, the wrecked aircraft plummeted to the ground.

Mike heard and saw bullets dink and clink the remaining two drones, but other than causing them a little mid-flight turbulence, they continued their trajectory. The smaller one held the by now familiar jar of acid in its clenched claw, and partially obscured the larger one.

Mike fired, pumped the forend of the shotgun, and fired again, repeated, and fired again. The small, inbound craft carrying the jar spiralled down like a fly hit by a plume of Raid spray. Now all his attention was on the bigger drone as the volley of shots continued from the barricade. It was closing way too fast for Mike's liking; suddenly, he spotted a device attached to the top of it with duct tape.

"What is it?" Wren asked.

"I told you to take cover," he said, pushing Wren out of the way as hard as he could. Wren went stumbling to the ground and Mike took aim once more. "Stay down!" he shouted over the increasing volume of the approaching flying machine.

"I don't under—"

Mike fired, then fired again, and with his last shell, the sky lit up like a supernova. He felt the heat of the flames even from fifteen metres back, and he watched as shrapnel from the drone spread into the air like a flaming hailstorm. "Fuck!" he said, instinctively taking a few steps back while the remainder of the craft ditched in a fiery dervish. He stood there for a moment looking towards the burning wreckage below.

"Are you okay?" he asked Wren.

Wren stared at him in disbelief. "That was a bomb."

"Yeah, I figured that out already."

"Another few seconds and we'd be dead."

"That's kind of the point of a bomb, Wren."

"Smart arse," she said, climbing to her feet. "I mean. Whoever is doing this, they've got some knowledge and some equipment."

"I know. When we faced Fry, he had some weaponry that he'd raided from barracks, but they never had anything like this. Whoever we're up against, they're playing on a completely different level." Mike looked down towards the RAMs below, "Come on, the sooner we finish this lot off the better."

*

Mason heard a shout of ceasefire from above. He looked again towards his once-formidable convoy and now every vehicle was consumed by flames; there was not a hope of finding a single survivor. The attack had been fast and brutal with no ambiguity in its intention.

He heard the hiss of a radio from above as messages were passed from point to point. If this was the result here, he had little doubt that the same fate had befallen the rest of the group across at the campsite. Mason took a deep breath and scrambled a few more feet upwards before running along a narrow stretch of rock. They had not passed anything resembling a road or a track up to the peak on their journey, so the course to the summit had to be further along.

After a few seconds, the rock gave way to grass and he came out onto a track. He looked down and saw it joined the road, so he doubled back. He would come at them from behind. As he approached, he heard elevated levels of chat as the militia realised they had stopped the marauders. A maniacal grin crept onto Mason's face as he reached the summit.

None of the militia was looking in his direction as he opened fire; figure after figure dropped as his bullets cut through them. Some were women, some were men, some were young, some were old. It meant nothing to him. Everything that had meant anything to Mason was burning now.

"See how you like some of your own medicine you fuckers!" he yelled at the top of his voice as he continued to spray bullets from side to side like Jimmy Cagney in a gangster movie.

Eventually, the rounds ran dry and as he reached into his jacket for another magazine, he heard a gun fire, once, twice. He pressed his hand against his stomach and stared at his fingers as they dripped crimson ooze. Mason raised his head and saw a woman in a grey sweater. She had a pistol raised in his direction. She had tears in her eyes and one hand held against her rib cage as blood trickled through her fingers.

The woman wavered on her feet for a second longer before collapsing to the ground. Mason stood there, the grin had left his face now and everything was getting darker. He tasted copper in his mouth and tried to spit, but the effort was too great. He fell facedown, his nose folding beneath the weight of his head, and his bottom teeth biting deep into his upper lip, stapling his mouth shut. He began to suffocate, and as much as he wanted to turn, his strength had left him. Revenge always came with a price.

*

Mike huffed as he unleashed another jacket full of rocks on the crowd below. There were no more than half a dozen creatures still standing and they were becoming increasingly difficult to hit. He looked towards the barricade and cupped his hands around his mouth. "We're going to the edge…get an idea of the geography of this place, then we'll head back towards you. Take the rest of the RAMs out with the rifles."

Hughes raised two thumbs, and Mike patted the sludgy grime from his jacket. Wren did the same with her jacket and joined him as they began to walk along the clifftop to the north face. "We work pretty well together as a team," she said.

"I suppose we do," Mike replied, "but we've got a long way to go before we start congratulating ourselves, don't you think?"

"Yeah, I was just saying," a slightly disheartened look fell across her face.

"Thank you, Wren, it was really brave what you did. If it hadn't been for you, I don't think I'd have got out of that."

Wren blushed a little and shrugged. "Can't let anything happen to you, you keep me entertained. With all the circuses gone I thought I'd never see a clown again, and yet," she said, gesturing towards him.

"I'm guessing you were beaten up a lot at school."

"No."

"Pity."

"You sound like my sister."

"I like her already. She's obviously had a lot to put up with." Wren went quiet, and Mike looked across at her. The good humour had gone and she was looking down at the ground. Mike placed a gentle hand on Wren's back as they walked. "If she's in there, we'll get her out. We might have to come back with an army, but we'll get her out."

They reached the north face of the cliff and their mouths fell open. The canyon widened into what was an almost perfect oval. It was at least two miles wide and a mile in length. It was surrounded by stone, rising and dipping in height, but there appeared to be just one clear road through the thick forest that carpeted the canyon floor. Their eyes followed the gap in the tree line as far as they could before it turned a bend and vanished into the foliage.

"So what's next?" Wren asked.

Mike stood for a moment longer taking everything in. "Next we follow the road. We'll stay in the trees for cover."

They began to retrace their steps. "Mike, this is just a surveillance mission, right?"

"Kind of."

"So, it's obvious we've been spotted cos of those things."

"I suppose."

"So how come we're not heading back?"

"We need to know what we're up against. We need to suss out exactly what defences they have, and if we can, how many of them there are."

"Isn't that going to be pretty difficult under the circumstances?"

"Well it's not going to be as easy as I'd hoped, that's for sure."

*

Shaw's vehicle was the first to take the bend. He did not smile, but he relaxed a little to see the black plumes of smoke rising from the bombard point. As he got nearer he could see the level of destruction that had been unleashed by the mangonels. The convoy was an inferno; there was little chance anyone could have survived the wreck. He looked into the mirror to see Beth and Barnes in the back seat with contemplative looks on their faces, then saw further back to his own convoy as the rest of the militia followed them.

"Looks like our guys and gals over here did their bit," Shaw said.

He took the turn and began to ascend the track. The moment the vehicle reached the brow of the hill, all levity left him. Bodies littered the ground. He saw crying women and bewildered-looking men desperately trying to come to terms with what had just happened.

Shaw and Barnes jumped out of the car, darting straight towards the fallen stranger, dragging the rifle away from him before checking for a pulse. When they were satisfied he was dead, they both stood and their eyes met. Beth ran towards the next fallen figure. She looked up at Barnes and Shaw with tears in her eyes. "Her pulse is really weak; she's lost a lot of blood."

Barnes ran over to the next body. "It's George!" he shouted. Looks like an in and out, but we need to get him seen to quick."

"Over here," cried Richard, waving from the third mangonel. Shaw went across as fast as his limp would let him, to see David tying a tourniquet around a woman's arm. "He came from out of nowhere. Before we could—"

"How many?" Shaw interrupted.

"Ted Gold and Kim Raines are gone. Sarah and George were hit but—"

"I know about them, Dana, what happened to you?" he asked, looking towards the younger woman who was receiving treatment from David.

"It's just a flesh wound," she replied. "Is Sarah going to be okay?"

"We're going to get her to the hospital now. Come on, you can ride up front with me."

Shaw was about to drive off when Richard banged on the car bonnet. "David and I will take care of clearing the road," he said, pointing back to the bulldozer parked behind the last mangonel. "You just make sure Sarah and George are okay."

Shaw nodded and raised the window. Barnes and Beth were kneeling by the side of the two patients desperately trying to stem the bleeding as Shaw reversed.

"Well, if anyone can help her, it's Lucy," Dana said.

"That's true, but right now Lucy is about a hundred and fifty miles away on a wild goose chase. Unfortunately, the best we've got this second is Raj."

"So you're telling me George and Sarah's lives are in the hands of an animal doctor?"

"Yep."

"Oh shit!"

"Yep!"

11

Mike and Wren navigated their way down the crags and crevices, finally placing their hands gratefully around the rockfall netting. They both let out sighs of relief and continued down with more confidence before dropping the last few feet. They smiled as their feet hit the road once more, then they headed towards the barricade. Hughes, Jules, Lucy and Emma had finished off the remainder of the creatures, and now the coast was clear.

"Okay, throw us the rope up and we'll get you two out of there," Hughes said.

"What are you talking about? We came here to check this place out; we haven't even started yet," Mike replied.

"Mike, I think it's safe to say the element of surprise has gone," Hughes replied.

"Beyond this cliff, it opens out into a huge forest either side of the road. There is no way they could find us in there. We head through, check what's on the other side, see what we're facing."

"We know what we're facing," Emma said. "Flying drones carrying acid, bombs, and god knows what else? It's mental to head back in there."

"Look, if we come back here with an army, we'll get spotted straight away, even if we do go through the trees. If just the six of us head in there, yes there's a risk, but—"

"But nothing. We've been spotted, we've been fucking dive-bombed by kamikaze drones, we've had a bloody army of RAMs unleashed on us. At what point do you think we're outmatched here? When they roll out a division of tanks?"

"Well, yeah, but as for the rest of the stuff, we dealt with it, didn't we?"

"It's a good job you're down there right now, because if you were up here I'd punch your fucking lights out," Emma replied.

"I say we should put this to a vote," Lucy said.

"Ha!" Emma shouted. "A vote? You've got to be kidding me. We did put this to a vote. We voted *no we wouldn't come*, but then my idiot brother, your idiot boyfriend with his Messiah complex, guilted us all into coming along. And now we've just been attacked, multiple times. We've lost an old man who Mike thought it was a good idea to bring along, but anybody with half a brain realised it was a really, really fucking bad idea and now he wants us to have a rematch with these fucking people with more than half our ammo already spent." She turned from Lucy to look at her brother. "What the fuck is wrong with you?" Emma yelled.

"So was that a yes or a no? I kind of tuned out halfway through there," Mike said.

"I'm going to fucking kill him," Emma said, marching across the barricade towards the slide.

Jules, Lucy and finally Hughes grabbed hold of her like rugby players trying to stop a determined prop forward twice their size. Emma's anger carried her another few feet before they managed to slow her down.

"Look! This is doing us no good," Lucy shouted. "Mike, stop being such a wiseass. Emma, calm down. This is a shitty enough situation without us all losing it with each other."

"Lucy's right," Jules said. "I understand both sides of the argument, but Mike's got a point. If that forest is as big as he says, we'd be protected from the road by the trees and from above by the foliage. We've come all this way; it would be mad not to take a look now we're here."

"I don't believe I'm hearing this. You don't think it's mad to carry on after everything that's happened?" Emma replied.

"You have my answer; I say we carry on," Jules said.

"Me too," added Lucy.

Hughes looked towards Emma. "That's four in favour, love."

Emma shook her head. "It's insane, but why am I surprised," she said, continuing to the edge of the barricade and sliding down. The others followed.

Aware that another drone might arrive at any minute, the moment Hughes made his way down the slide, the six of them began to run down the road. Each stride brought them closer to the cover of the forest, and just as the high-pitched sound of whizzing propellers began to sing in their ears once more, they reached the tree line and ducked immediately left into the thick woods. They headed in a few metres then crouched down with their freshly loaded weapons raised in readiness. One of the big drones passed by, and as soon as it did, they headed further into the forest.

*

The car came to a skidding stop in front of the static caravans that constituted the Safe Haven hospital. Shaw banged his hand down hard on the horn. Raj, Talikha, Humphrey, and a host of nurses bolted from various doors to greet them.

Shaw climbed out of the car and it was Raj that he zeroed in on. "It's Sarah and George." Raj's eyes widened. "George's wound is an in and out below the left shoulder. He's unconscious but his pulse is pretty strong. Sarah doesn't have an exit wound and she's losing a lot of blood, her pulse isn't so great."

Raj looked towards Stephanie, who had now rejoined them. "Prep the operating room and get Sarah straight in."

Stephanie and three of the other women immediately ran into one of the wards and reappeared with two stretchers. Barnes and Beth climbed out of the vehicle, gently dragging George towards the boot opening. The end of the first stretcher was placed on the lip of the boot and George's legs were raised onto it before they slid him further down and more of the medical staff could join in to help. When he was securely in the centre of the stretcher, two of the trainee nurses carried George into the ward.

"You want me to clean his wound, see if I can stop the bleeding?" Stephanie asked. "Talikha and Lisa will take care of George for the time being; I would like you to assist me with Sarah."

Stephanie suddenly tensed up. She had been a nurse in an accident and emergency ward dealing with all sorts, but never gunshot wounds. "Erm, are you sure?"

Raj smiled. "Stephanie, you are the most qualified member of medical staff I have. I need you with me."

"Okay," she said, disappearing into one of the static caravans once again.

Barnes and Beth climbed back into the rear of the estate car and one of the other trainee nurses passed them the second stretcher. Together they lifted Sarah onto it with as little disturbance as possible. When she was in position, two of the trainee nurses took the bottom end of the stretcher while Barnes slowly guided out the other end. They paused, resting it on the edge of the boot, then Shaw and Raj took the handle and lifted it onto a gurney. Several of the trainee nurses then wheeled it to the bottom of the stairs of Ward One before manoeuvring it through the door.

Once they were out of sight, Raj looked at Shaw. "You do realise, I have never had to remove a bullet from anything before. I have operated on sheep that have been shredded by barbed wire. I have opened up dogs that have swallowed pairs of socks, but bullet wounds were not really a thing in Candleton."

There was a high-pitched whine and both Raj and Shaw looked down to see Humphrey with an expression that echoed Raj's concern. Shaw crouched down and made a fuss of him, tickling him behind his ears, and slowly his tail began to wag once more.

"I know that, Raj," Shaw said, looking up at the vet. "But I also know you'll do your very best. That's all any of us can do. Now, I'm going to have to head out again—Ted and Kim didn't make it."

"Oh no. Ted had just started seeing Kirsty," Raj said, sadly.

"I know," Shaw replied, giving Humphrey one final stroke and then standing up. "Kim had no one, but that doesn't make it any easier. She was only in her twenties, nice girl. As if she hadn't gone through enough shit to deserve a little happiness, and then bang. It's all gone."

"Would you do me a favour?" Raj asked.

"Of course, name it."

"Will you take Humph over to Jenny's? Talikha and I are going to be tied up for some time, I believe."

"No problem, he can help me break the news to Kirsty."

*

Since they started their journey into the forest, they had heard the drone pass overhead a few times as the camera searched tirelessly for them. The cover of the foliage and the vast area made it an almost impossible task, but the hum of the blades let the group know they were still being hunted, which kept their senses on high alert.

"Right," Hughes said, bringing them to a stop. "This'll be a good place for a five-minute break." He craned his head to view the thick canopy above them, and then pulled his water bottle from his rucksack.

"How far do you think we've come?" Jules asked.

"We were travelling northwest for a while to make sure we got away from the road, but for the last few hundred metres, we've been heading north. I dunno, about a kilometre…ish."

They stood in a close circle as they drank and rested for a few moments, but conversation was scarce. They put their bottles away and were just about to set off again when Lucy stopped them. She spoke in little more than a whisper. "Okay, I don't want to alarm you guys, and don't start looking around, but I think we're being watched."

"What?" Emma said, immediately beginning to look around.

"Erm, remember that whole don't start looking around thing?"

"What makes you say that?" Hughes asked.

"I thought I saw something earlier on, but hell, so much weird crap has happened today I just put it down to my imagination. Then I saw movement in the trees again just now," Lucy said.

"And you think it's a person, for sure? I mean, there might be deer and stuff around here," Hughes replied.

"It's not a deer."

"Okay Luce, whereabouts?" Mike asked.

"About thirty yards to my left."

Mike suddenly began to bound through the trees, leaving the rest of the group in suspended animation. He managed to get several metres in before their pursuer even realised what was happening. He didn't see them at first, he just ran off in the direction Lucy had told him. But as he moved closer, the spy broke from the cover of the tree and started sprinting in the opposite direction. They were nimble, weaving in and out of the trees like a native, but whoever it was did not possess Mike's speed or resolve as he glided through the forest after them.

He kept focussed; each time the figure zigged, he zigged, each time they zagged, he zagged too. They had been running flat out for a minute when the pace of the spy began to slow. Mike's, however, did not. Sensing his chance, he ran faster than ever, finally making his gambit. He launched through the air and tackled the spy to the ground. He immediately scrambled up to his knees and flipped them over, ready to unleash a hammer blow to their face, when he froze.

It was a young woman, whose delicate features had suffered due to malnutrition. She had a depth of fear in her eyes Mike had never witnessed.

An uncontrollable flow of tears began to run down the woman's face and Mike looked towards his fist. He unclenched it and climbed to his feet.

"Who are you?" he demanded. The young woman did not answer; she just sobbed. Mike offered her his hand, but she did not take it. "I'm not going to hurt you," he said.

Mike heard snapping twigs and the rustle of branches behind him as the others caught up. First to join him was Hughes with his rifle half raised, fully expecting Mike to be in the throes of hand to hand combat. When he saw the woman, who was now curled up in a ball, he lowered his weapon.

"What the?" was all Hughes could manage to say.

Wren, Lucy, Emma and Jules joined them and stood around as if they were watching a street artist perform. The woman did not move.

Lucy approached her and crouched down. "Sweetie?" she said, placing a gentle hand on the frail figure's arm. "It's okay…I promise, we're not going to hurt you."

The woman brought her hands down from her eyes. "You *are* a woman," she said almost in disbelief.

"Erm, yeah." Lucy looked a little confused.

The foetal-posed figure wiped her eyes, but the tears kept flowing a little longer. "All I could make out were figures…I thought I heard a woman's voice, but I…I thought it was my mind playing tricks."

"It's not playing tricks. There are four of us," Lucy said, moving a little to the side to reveal Emma, Jules and Wren as well.

The spy regarded them through blurry eyes, then Lucy noticed her tension return when she looked towards Hughes and Mike. "They caught you? You're taking me back?" she said, starting to get upset again.

"No. They're with us and we're not taking you back anywhere. Come on, let's get you to your feet," Lucy said, offering her hand.

The woman took it and stood up cautiously. Her wide, staring eyes looked from face to face, her breathing was heavy from fear and from not having recovered from the run.

"You don't want to take me back to the compound?" she asked.

"No. Look, I'm Lucy. How about you tell me your name?"

"I...I'm Cordelia."

"Cordelia," Lucy said, nodding.

"But...but people call me Coco."

"Coco? I love that. Listen, Coco, we're not here to hurt you. You mentioned the compound, what is that?"

Coco tensed again and her eyes shot from one face to the next, wondering if this was some elaborate, sadistic trick and she would see an evil grin appear on their faces, especially the men. She had seen plenty of evil in the faces of men. But as she looked, she saw only concern. "The compound is where they kept u—me. It's where they kept me."

"They kept you? You were being held?"

Coco's brow furrowed and she nodded. "They—" she could not bring herself to carry on; the mere thought of what she had gone through brought tears to her eyes once more. "I can't go back there."

"Nobody's taking you back there darlin'," Jules said, stepping forward. She handed Coco her bottle of water and the young woman unscrewed the top and glugged the contents thirstily.

She wiped her mouth and handed it back to Jules. "Thank you."

"You look like you could use something to eat," Emma said, reaching into her bag. She pulled out a small, carefully wrapped parcel of bread and tore a chunk off, handing it to Coco.

The young woman held it in her hands, looking down at it like she had just been handed the keys to a palace. She brought it up to her mouth and tore at it with her teeth. She chewed quickly, still not sure if it was some kind of cruel prank and the food would be taken back from her. Coco did not speak; she just ate and watched. When she had finished the bread, Jules handed her the bottle of water again and the startlingly thin woman took another thirsty drink.

"Better?" Lucy asked.

Coco looked at her wide-eyes, "Thank you...where have you come from?"

"We're here to try and find my sister," Wren replied.

Coco looked at her. "Your sister?"

"She might have been taken by Fry's men. We're here to see what—"

Mike glared at Wren and she immediately shut up.

"Coco, what are you doing here in the forest?" Mike asked in the softest voice he could muster.

Coco looked at him with suspicion in her eyes, then towards the women and her anxiety eased a little. "I...I escaped."

"You were a hostage?" Lucy asked.

"Coco!" called a voice.

Everyone looked in the direction of the sound, other than Coco. She took the opportunity to turn and run. It was a second or two before the others realised she'd gone, and Mike began to sprint after her again, with the rest close behind.

Within a few seconds, Mike had caught her and she let out a scream. "Let go of me," she shouted.

Mike did not do as she asked, he kept hold of her sweater as she struggled. "Why are you running from us?"

"Leave me alone," she said, hitting out, but Mike managed to avoid all the swings.

A young woman wearing a black leather jacket and carrying a spear appeared in a clearing in front of them.

"Let go of her!"

12

For a moment, Wren's heart stuttered, but as the young woman stepped out of the shadows, it sank. Maybe it was the clothes, maybe it was the light playing tricks on her eyes, but for a brief moment, Wren thought the woman was her sister.

Mike let go of Coco, who immediately stopped struggling. She looked shocked that the other woman had revealed herself so willingly.

"Who are you?" Mike asked.

The woman did not answer, but walked towards them. She looked less emaciated than Coco, but still painfully thin. Her pale complexion contrasted vividly with her black attire, and despite the spear, she seemed a lot less threatening up close. "I'm Vicky. Welcome to hell. Who are you people?"

"We're looking for someone," Lucy said. "We think they might have been taken."

"You realise once you're in here there's no escape?" Vicky said.

"Says who?" Lucy asked.

"Says me. We've been in here for months. We've lost so many."

"Months?" Mike asked. "And you couldn't escape?"

"How did you get in?" Vicky asked.

"It wasn't easy," Lucy replied.

"You didn't get attacked by drones?"

"We did," Jules said, "A few of them, but we managed to get through all the same."

"And now you're hiding in the forest?"

"We're not hiding," Wren said, "We're just using it for cover."

"Isn't that the same thing as hiding?" Vicky replied.

"Well—"

"You said you'd lost so many. What happened? Who are you?" Lucy asked.

Vicky let out a long breath and looked around at the faces. "Well, if you're here, you're stuck up shit creek just like us. You might have got in, but you're never getting out. Come with me, I'll introduce you to everyone."

She began to walk off and Coco walked beside her. The rest of them glanced at each other before following.

*

Shaw and Humphrey arrived at the pub to find Jenny sweeping away broken glass.

"Jen, am I glad to see you?" Shaw said.

Jenny looked down towards Humphrey, then her eyes moved back to Shaw. "Are Raj and Talikha okay?"

"Raj and Talikha are fine."

"Something's wrong."

"Yeah Jen, something is wrong."

"Is Kirsty here?"

"She's nipped home; she should be back in a few minutes."

"Listen, I need to head across to the hall and sound the stand-down siren. Can you look after Humph until I get back?"

"Of course I can, but you're really worrying me. What's wrong?"

"Make us a couple of drinks, stiff ones, and I'll see you soon."

Shaw disappeared and Jenny just stood at the door watching him. Her heart was pounding fast as she went back inside and poured two double measures of Jura whisky. The unnerving howl of the siren rose into the air and Jenny closed her eyes. She took a drink of her whisky and wiped her mouth as the siren began to diminish again.

It was only then that she heard the synchronised barking of Humphrey and Meg. "Settle down you two," she said, taking another drink from her glass before refilling it to its original level.

Two minutes later, Shaw appeared by her side. "Is this mine?" he asked, a little out of breath.

"Yes. Now, what's wrong?" Shaw knocked back the double measure in one go and banged the glass back down. Jenny drained hers as well and poured them both two more.

"It's bad, Jen," he said, taking just a sip this time. "Kim and Ted didn't make it."

Jenny's eyes opened wide. "Oh my god. Things were just starting to get serious between Kirsty and Ted."

"I know, and that's not all."

"Tell me."

"Sarah and George were shot too."

Jenny just looked at Shaw. It was sad about Kim and Ted, but Sarah and George were family to Jenny. "And?"

"The bullet that hit George went straight through. He's unconscious, but his pulse is strong and it's looking positive for him."

"And Sarah? What about Sarah?"

"She's…" Shaw took another drink from his glass. "She's in a bad way, Jenny. The bullet's still inside her. Raj is going to do the very best he can, but by his own admission, he's never dealt with anything like this before."

Jen started to cry and the mascara ran down her face. "If anything happens to Sarah it will kill Emma."

"I know," Shaw replied.

"And...the...did we stop them?"

"They're all dead. Every last one of them. The drills, the planning, it all worked, but it doesn't change the fact we lost people today."

They both took another drink from their glasses. The entrance door swung open and Kirsty walked in. "Got the good stuff out have we?" she said, walking up to the bar and picking up the bottle of Jura whisky. Shaw and Jenny just looked at her. "Don't mind if I take a jolt, do you?" It was only as she arrived at the other side of the bar and poured herself a drink that she noticed the smeared lines of mascara on Jenny's face. "What's wrong?" she asked, holding the half-full glass in her hand.

Jenny's eyes filled with tears once again, and that's when Shaw knew it was down to him. He took another drink of whisky. "Kirsty, Ted didn't make it."

Kirsty fixed Shaw with a stare as her mind struggled to comprehend his words. "Didn't...make it?"

"He got shot. Ted and Kim were dead by the time we got there."

Kirsty looked at the glass in her hand and downed the double measure in one go. Tears pooled in her eyes, and this woman who was so strong, who had put thousands of rowdy and randy pub goers twice her size in their place over the years, flopped limply onto the nearest stool.

Her whole body began to shake and Jenny rushed to the other side of the bar. "I'm so sorry my love," she said. "I'm so sorry."

"I can't tell you how sorry I am, Kirsty. Ted was a really nice guy, and what he did saved a lot of other people from getting hurt," Shaw said.

Kirsty remained on the stool with her legs dangling like a small child, but now she had the face of an old woman. The usual joy that radiated from her smile and her eyes was buried beneath hopelessness. "So…Kim got killed too?" Kirsty said eventually.

"Yes, and George and Sarah are both shot, they're at the hospital now," Shaw said. "But what they did made sure the rest of Safe Haven was safe."

"It's not right," Kirsty said. "It's not right. The others went off like they did on that fool's errand. If they'd have stayed here I bet there wouldn't have been any casualties. Instead, Ted and Kim are gone and who knows what's going to happen to Sarah and George."

"We don't know that, love. The ones to blame are the people who did this. Nobody else, just them."

*

The group followed Vicky and Coco for a quarter of a mile until they reached a cave at the edge of the forest. The entrance was concealed by bushes and branches.

"It's me," Vicky shouted before moving a few of the branches out of the way. "Come out here, we've got guests."

The group stood, watching the gap for a moment before the first head emerged. In total there were seven women. One had a wooden splint strapped to her leg, another had some severe facial and skin disfiguration, and yet another wore a hood, completely hiding her face. All of them looked badly underfed.

"This is all of you?" Lucy asked.

"This is all of us," Vicky replied.

"How long have you been here?"

Vicky looked at the women and they all shrugged. "A few months," Vicky replied eventually.

"Were you held at the compound?" Emma asked.

All the other women looked down to the ground almost as if they were ashamed. "They called it 'the whore pit.' You can imagine what went on there. It was a never-ending nightmare. Some women got taken by the men, they became their property, but most were held prisoner in the community hall. Armed guards kept watch day and night.

We were used for whatever they wanted." One of the women began to cry and another placed her arm around her.

Something approaching a snarl appeared on Mike's face. "This is Fry you're talking about? Fry's men?"

All the women's faces looked towards Mike. "You know him?" Vicky asked.

"I killed him. We destroyed his army."

"You didn't destroy all of it," Vicky replied

"How many are left?" Hughes asked.

Vicky sat down on a rock and pulled a mint leaf out of her pocket. She tore a small strip from it and placed it in her mouth. "When the army didn't come back it became like *Lord of the Flies*, little boys fighting for position. I couldn't tell you exact numbers, but going by what we've heard from the girls from outside, it couldn't have been more than a hundred. As time went on, it looked surer and surer that Fry wasn't coming back and a guy called Webb took charge. Now he wasn't like Fry, he was something very...different."

"How do you mean?" Jules asked.

"Well, whereas Fry was a bludgeon, Webb was...is more of a scalpel. Calculating. Very, very clever. He's the one responsible for the drones as well as all the other little tricks," Vicky said.

"What other tricks?" Hughes asked.

"You'll see soon enough. Anyway, there were about a hundred or so of us in the community hall, and we realised the numbers had evened up. The big problem was, we took too long to act. We had become so subservient, so resigned to the fact that this was going to be our lives from now on, that we just kept waiting, procrastinating, and by the time we made our move, by the time we escaped, we were too late. The barricade had been put up, the drones were operating. Webb had planned everything out in finite detail."

"So how did a hundred become seven?" Emma asked.

"Webb was paranoid. All the women, even the ones the men had claimed, had to return to the hall on a night. He was convinced we'd try to make a break for it at some point. We left about fifty girls there. They were afraid we'd get caught; they thought the men might do something even worse to us, but nothing could be worse than what we went through there. We came up with a plan, all whispers and secret messages. They kept us tethered to the beds, but a few of us had managed to find a way to slip in and out of the manacles without them realising. It wasn't that hard, truth be told. Some of us had grown so thin they couldn't get them tight enough around us and there was a lot of slack in the end. Finally, we waited for the next full moon and made a break for it. There were four guards at the hall. We overpowered them, grabbed the bolt cutters and freed all the women who wanted to come with us. There were four sentries at the gate, and that's where we lost our first two, but we kept on. We made our escape, stayed on the road, heading south, heading to freedom. Until we came to the landslide."

"Huh! Landslide," one of the other women said.

"Well, trying to get over that thing in the daytime would have been hard enough. Trying to do it by moonlight was impossible, and that's when we heard the first of the drones. It was playing some classical music and we thought we were hearing things, to start off with, but then we heard the growls and we knew what was coming.

"That night, we only saw a dozen approaching from the shadows of darkness. We took as many of them out as we could with the guns we'd stolen, but still, a handful got through and attacked us. Anyone who could run, ran, but you know what those things are like. No sooner do they strike you down then they're onto the next, then the next. It was a massacre. twenty-five of us managed to break free and run back down to the forest. We hid high up in the trees that night, and we've spent many a night up there since, too.

You really don't know what you've let yourself into coming here. Just wait until you meet the metalheads."

"Metalheads? What the hell are they?" Lucy asked.

"You'll see soon enough," Vicky said spitting out the small piece of leaf and biting off another. "Anyway, the next morning we heard the drone come back, playing its music once again."

"It was playing 'Ride of the Valkyries,'" one of the other women said.

"I think that's what's called black humour," Lucy replied grimly.

"I don't get it," Jules said.

"'Ride of the Valkyries' is what was playing when the choppers attacked in *Apocalypse Now*," Lucy replied.

"Ah. Yeah, funny."

Vicky continued, "So the next morning it rounded all the RAMs back up, like a flying Pied Piper."

"Rounded them up?" Mike said.

"We didn't know it at the time; it was dark when we made our escape, but we found out soon after that part of the construction at the gate consisted of two cargo containers. They keep RAMs trapped inside and bring them out on special occasions—but I'm sure you already know that. How many of you were there?"

"There was another one," Mike said sadly. "An older guy, we'd only just met him. His niece was brought here. Deb, he said her name was." Mike looked around at the faces, and the women all looked down to the ground.

"There was a girl called Deb. She was one of the first to go when we made our escape," Vicky replied. "Oh well, I suppose he's with her now. But tell me, how did you only lose one?"

"We got up high and dropped stuff on them, then finished off any stragglers with the guns," Mike said.

Vicky looked at the others in her group then back towards Mike. "They usually release a full container. Are you telling me you killed a hundred of those things?"

"Yeah, that sounds about right," Mike replied.

"And the drones? You shot them down?"

"Yeah. One of the drones was what took Will out. It was carrying acid or something," Mike said.

"They got me with acid," said the girl with the disfigurement. "It was a pain I didn't know was possible."

Mike looked at her sympathetically for a moment, then turned his head back towards Vicky. "Then one of the last drones they sent had bloody explosives attached."

Vicky smiled. "Oh man, you must have really pissed him off. He doesn't just break out the dynamite for anyone."

"So you said twenty-five of you escaped the RAMs; where are the rest?"

"Those first few weeks, they sent out search parties. They let the RAMs roam free, they tried everything. They whittled down another five of us. Then, when they were sure we'd run out of bullets for the guns, they released the metalheads. They took out another twelve."

"And the other one?" Lucy asked.

"Fever. We buried her the day before yesterday."

"I'm sorry. What have you been surviving on?"

"Roots, mushrooms, we catch the odd bird, rabbit, rat. It's not exactly haute cuisine," Vicky replied.

"My sister," Wren said, stepping forward. "Her name's Robyn. She's a tiny little bit taller than me? She dyed her hair black, but that would have grown out now. Have you seen her?"

"What's your name?" Vicky asked.

"Wren."

"It doesn't ring any bells, Wren, but that's not to say she wasn't there. We were stuck in the confines of cramped, partitioned cells. Fry was a murderous sadist, but he knew women kept his men happy, so we were a precious commodity. The last few days we were there, some of the girls started leaving *the pit* and not coming back. At the time, we thought it was weird, but figured maybe Webb had relaxed his rule again about the soldiers taking a woman, or that maybe they were doing some of the duties. I mean, they had just lost a couple of thousand men; there was all the shifting and carrying and looking after vehicles and so on. Anyway, more time passed and more girls disappeared…"

"And you never found out what was happening?" Wren said.

"Oh we did, then we wished we hadn't. We overheard two of the guards talking one night. Turns out, the girls weren't being put to work and they weren't being taken by the men," she said, looking towards Mike, Lucy, Jules, Hughes, Emma and finally Wren.

The look in Vicky's eyes sent a chill through them. "So what was happening to them?"

"Webb was using them for experiments."

13

Shaw entered the campsite and saw many of the residents were already busy patching up holes from stray bullets and generally trying to return things to a state of normality as quickly as possible. Barnes and Beth were in the process of hitching the caravans that had belonged to the spies for the raiding party. He waved, and they both waved back. They stopped what they were doing and headed across to Shaw.

"How's everything going?" Shaw asked.

"People seem on edge still," Beth replied.

"That's only to be expected after what happened. I'm going to head there now, see how it's going."

"We'll come with you," Beth replied.

The three of them walked in silence across the campsite. The physical damage was minimal, but what had happened would leave mental scars for a long time to come. As the three of them arrived at the hospital, Talikha appeared from one of the static caravans, carrying two handfuls of gauze. She smiled politely, but was clearly preoccupied and began heading straight towards one of the other entrances.

"Talikha!" Shaw said, flagging her down.

"I apologise, but I am really very busy," she replied.

"Have we heard anything?" Shaw asked.

"Raj is in theatre. We have hooked George up to an IV and stopped the majority of his bleeding. I am sorry, I must get back," she said, continuing towards the door.

"Oh no!" Beth said.

"What is it?" Shaw asked.

"Sarah's kids from the school."

"Oh shit," Shaw replied. "I didn't even think about that. If anything happens to Sarah it will be a nightmare for them. She's the only one who speaks fluent sign language."

"What about Ruth?" Barnes asked.

"She knows a bit more than me," Beth said, but we're both still learning."

"Let's not think the worst. Sarah is strong. She can pull through this, she's a fighter." They all nodded as Shaw spoke, but each of them suddenly felt sick to their stomach.

*

"Experiments?" Lucy said, horrified.

"That's where the metalheads came from," Vicky said looking towards the woman in the hoodie who was sat with her head down and her hands in her pockets. "Prisha. Show them," demanded Vicky.

All heads turned towards the figure in the hood who withdrew her brown hands from her pockets and slowly peeled her hood back. Wren let out an involuntary gasp and Prisha's eyes immediately weighed a little heavier with shame. "Oh my god," Lucy said, walking across and kneeling down in front of the girl. She gently pushed the hair back from Prisha's face, revealing the full extent of the girl's wounds. "What did they do to you?"

"Go on," Vicky said, "Tell them."

"They made me watch," Prisha began, only her words were garbled, they sounded like: *"they mae me woh"*.

The rest of Lucy's group crowded around so they could hear Prisha speak. Whenever she said something they could not understand, they looked towards Vicky for a translation. The difficulty in comprehension was nothing to do with a language barrier; the young woman had a vocabulary that oozed of a good education. The difficulty to understand her came from the horrific injuries she had suffered.

"Tell them everything," Vicky said.

"They strapped me to the bed. Webb wanted me to see what he was doing." Prisha paused and wiped away excess saliva from her mouth. "The girl in the bed next to mine had been put to sleep. Webb sliced her cheeks open," Prisha said, pointing to the horrific scars on her own face and suddenly looked down as the memory brought a quake to her voice and tears to her eyes.

Lucy reached out and took hold of the girl's hands. "It's all right Prisha. Go on."

Prisha raised her head once more. "Then he…clamped her mouth open wide. He pulled out four of her teeth with pliers and took a cast. I could not see, but I heard and smelt burning, then a sizzle as if something hot went into water." Prisha paused and wiped more saliva from her mouth. "Webb came back to the table with a metal plate that he had taken from the cast. He had attached tiny brackets to the four extra lengths where the gaps were from the teeth he had removed. He wedged the plate to the roof of her mouth, then screwed it into place through the teeth." Prisha began to sob.

"What the fuck?" Mike spat angrily. "Why would the sick fuck do something like that?"

"Wait," Vicky said, "You haven't heard the worst of it yet."

Prisha brought her tears under control as one of the others comforted her, and then she continued. "He stitched her cheeks back up and then fitted this metal helmet over her head. It covered from the base of the skull to the top lip." Prisha paused and illustrated with her hands where the helmet started and where it stopped. "There were metal gauze and Perspex covering the eyes. When he made the final adjustments and tightened the mask securely, he stood back and smiled. Then he turned to me. The last thing I remember was him standing over me as the anaesthetic kicked in." Prisha burst out crying, and Lucy stood while two other women embraced the poor girl.

"I still don't think I understand fully. So what, he's just a whack job sadist?" Jules asked.

"The metalheads are all infected. He keeps them in the second container, lowers his new creations in through a small porthole in the top, then watches as the already infected ones attack," Vicky replied.

"How do you know this?" Mike asked.

"You hear the men talking. There were more than a few who were horrified by what was going on, but there was no way they were going to step out of line. Anyway, the helmets are really tough, but with bullets you stand a slim chance, if you hit them around the eyes. The plate in the roof of their mouths means you can't thrust the spears up through their brains. Because of the design and rigidity, they can't angle their heads up so well. If you're high up, chances are they'll miss you."

"This man sounds like a monster," Emma said.

"I'm not exaggerating, he is the Devil."

"So how did Prisha escape?" Lucy asked, looking back down at the girl, who was still in tears.

"She was being escorted out to the containers when we made our break. That's when I missed my opportunity to kill Webb, but it all happened so quickly. There was a firefight, and Prisha and another girl were just left, standing in the middle of the road while bullets were flying around them. The other girl got hit, but Prisha was still standing when we took out the sentries. The rest of the men were beginning to rouse from the barracks by now and Webb had vanished amid all the confusion, so we opened the gate and just ran as fast as we could. The next time we stopped was at the barricade, and you know the story from there," Vicky said, taking another bite of mint leaf.

"And...how did you get that thing off..." Lucy trailed off looking down at Prisha.

"I don't suppose any of you have any fags?" Vicky said, needing something more than the mint to calm her nerves as she relived the story.

"Here you go," Hughes said, pulling out a packet of cigarettes from his pocket, taking one for himself then offering one to Vicky, who gratefully accepted. Hughes offered the packet to the other women too, but there were no more takers. He gave Vicky a light, and she inhaled deeply, as something close to a smile appeared on her face.

She brought the cigarette away from her lips and looked at it. "I never thought I'd ever get to smoke one of these again," she said before taking another long drag and letting out a blue plume of smoke that drifted up towards the forest canopy. Vicky looked towards Lucy. "I was a nurse in the life before. I saw lots of awful stuff, car accidents, industrial accidents, stabbings, shootings, but I never had to deal with anything so horrific as what happened to that poor girl. Getting the helmet off her was painful. It involved us loosening the bolts and smashing the small hinges until it broke. Getting the plate out of her mouth...I don't want to relive it, if it's all the same to you, but Prisha no longer has any upper teeth barring two molars at the back. After we removed the plate, I cauterized both cheeks; still, it was an absolute miracle her wounds didn't get infected." A grimace appeared on Vicky's face and she looked back towards Prisha; she remembered the screams and howls of agony that had issued from the poor girl.

Silence befell everyone. Mike and Lucy looked at each other, struggling to comprehend what kind of person could do something like that.

"Dear Jesus," Jules whispered, and Hughes gently stroked her arm to comfort her.

Emma turned towards Wren, but now Wren had gone to sit on a large log a few metres away with her back to everyone. Emma went across and sat down beside her. The teenager was sobbing hopelessly and Emma put a motherly arm around her.

"What if...what if they've turned Bobbi into one of those things," she said between cries.

Emma leaned in and kissed her on the head. "Don't think like that Wren. There's no reason to think it. We don't even know if she's here."

"I know...but what if she is."

Emma let out a sigh. "Come here." She held Wren for several minutes until the cries finally subsided and they went to rejoin the others.

"In all this time you never tried scaling the cliffs rather than staying trapped here?" Jules asked.

"Are you kidding me? We tried everything. Climbing was how Sandy broke her leg. After that we realised that we were just stuck here, hoping that one day something might happen," Vicky said.

"You didn't try going back to the barricade to see if you could get over?" Hughes asked.

"The drone does a circuit at least once a day. Always different times. Once a week, one flies over with a bag of supplies. I'm pretty certain they've got a spotter on the other side."

Hughes looked at Mike. "Yeah, I think Wren spotted him," Emma said, still with a comforting arm around the young teen.

"So now all we need to figure out is how we're all going to get out of here," Jules said.

Mike was about to speak when Lucy interrupted. "We're not going anywhere."

Jules looked at her. "What do you mean?"

"She means, this ends today," Emma replied.

All the women suddenly looked up. Mike had a proud smile on his face as he looked from Lucy to Emma. "If we'd have known where this camp was back when we got rid of Fry, we'd have come down here then," Mike said. "This has gone on long enough." He turned towards Wren. "We're going to find out if Bobbi's here." And then he looked towards the women. "We're going to free your friends, and then these fuckers are going to pay for everything they've done."

14

Richard and David both gave Ruth a hug as she climbed down from the steps of the bus. When the *all-clear* had sounded, she had started the journey back to Safe Haven, blissfully unaware of the tragedy that had unfolded. Despite having a radio, she kept the volume down to a bare minimum so the children would not be disturbed by the messages.

"Your two faces are a sight for sore eyes," Ruth said.

Their smiles were weak; it was Richard who finally spoke. "Let's get the children in, and then we can tell you what's happened."

The joy drained away from Ruth's face. "Oh no. I don't like the sound of that."

Richard climbed onto the bus, "Okay, let's get you all inside. I think there is some soup on the pot, and afternoon lessons will be cancelled today."

The children filed off the bus and followed Ruth and David into the village hall. Sammy, Jake, Ann and John were the last to leave. Sammy walked up to Richard. "What's happened?" she asked with a maturity way beyond her years.

Richard crouched down to look her directly in the eyes. "You know I'll never lie to you, don't you?" he said, taking hold of her by the hand. "What I need you to do right now is go in with the others, get a bowl of soup, and then I'll tell you everything, deal?"

The young girl looked at the librarian long and hard, but finally nodded. "Deal."

They all left the bus and walked into the village hall as the aroma of vegetable soup warmed the air. Some of the distraught-looking campsite inhabitants were huddled around tables, sharing their woes with each other, and the pupils had been taken to a long table towards the front where there was little danger of overhearing any of the adult conversations. Ruth put a fifteen-year-old called Natalie in charge, while she, Richard and David went into the back office with their bowls.

The two men took it in turns to tell different parts of the story, and Ruth had not taken two mouthfuls of her soup before she pushed her bowl away, unable to stomach any more. She became glazed as she stared at her two friends, but eventually broke her silence. "Sarah's one of the sweetest people I've ever met. What she did with those kids…"

"It's not over yet," David said. "Raj is a very clever guy. He's not somebody who'll give up."

"Yes," Richard added, "and George's bleeding has stopped, so don't lose heart."

"But…Kim…and Ted…Kirsty must be distraught."

Richard let go of her hand and looked down at the floor. "Jenny's looking after her. They got a sedative from the hospital and she's in bed. Jenny's a good friend. She'll keep a close eye on her."

They all sat there for a moment, contemplating the morning's events when a light tapping came at the door, which was already ajar. Sammy was stood there. Her eyes were wide in a valiant effort to stave off tears. "Sammy, sweetheart, are you okay?" Ruth asked.

Sammy stood there for a second trying to compose herself. She looked at Richard and then towards Ruth. "I went to one of the other tables. I found out about Sarah. I'd like to go to the hospital please."

"Sammy, Sarah's in theatre; she could be in there for a long time. As soon as she's out, we'll all head across, okay?" Ruth replied.

Sammy stepped into the room. The young girl was still fighting hard to keep the tears back. "Emma, Mike and Lucy aren't here. Jake and I are her only family. Her family should be there with her." A single tear ran down her cheek and Ruth realised if she did not give in to the young girl's wishes, all the steadfastness and pride Sammy was hoping to maintain would be lost in a flood.

"You know what, Sammy? You're right," Ruth said, standing up from behind the desk. She walked around, crouched down, dabbed the tear from Sammy's face with a clean handkerchief and gave her a hug. "You and Jake should be there. Do you mind if I keep you company?"

Sammy swallowed hard. "I'd like that."

*

"Don't get me wrong, I like your pep, but how do you propose to take the entire compound with so few people?" Vicky asked. As soon as the words had come out of her mouth, the sound of a drone could be heard. "Come on, quick," she said, and despite the cover of the trees ensuring they could not be seen, she ushered everybody into the cave. They heard the blades travel closer before gradually becoming inaudible again.

"I don't understand why they haven't sent more RAMs out," Coco said, looking at Vicky.

Mike thought for a little while, then finally answered. "Well, if what Vicky said is right, and one container held RAMs while the other held metalheads, we've already taken out all of his RAMs. So he's got a couple of options. He can wait for our next move, or he can send in some of his Metalhead thingies or more troops. The fact he hasn't already, tells me he doesn't want to risk it while he knows we've got ammo."

"Webb never struck me as the waiting kind," Vicky replied.

"Perfect," Mike replied.

"Why perfect?" Hughes asked.

"Well he's not going to be sending them in here unarmed, is he? If they're coming in, they're not leaving, and we get their guns and their ammo," Mike replied.

"Okay, there's one tiny little thing that I think we need to clear up here," Jules said. "What makes you so sure they're going to be the ones not leaving this forest?"

"Because, Jules, they might be good at raiding villages and towns, but we're really, really good when it comes to guerrilla warfare now. And we've got people on our side who know the terrain."

"And what if he doesn't send ten or fifteen, but he sends fifty of his men out looking for us?" Jules asked.

Mike smiled. "Then we'll have a proper fight on our hands."

"He hasn't sent men out in months. I'm pretty certain he suspects we're all dead and the drone just comes out as an insurance measure. But if he does send a group out, they might find us. We used to move around all the time. Never stayed in one place for more than a night, but then, after a few weeks, he stopped sending out the RAMs and the metalheads and we kind of settled here. It's not much, but it gives us shelter," Vicky said.

Mike looked around the dark interior of the cave. "One way or another, after today, you won't need this place again."

"Oh, bravo! Way to rouse confidence there, Mike," Jules said.

"If we win this, you're all welcome to come back with us. We have food, shelter, and a community. You, and your friends in there, you could all join us," Mike said.

"For real?" Coco asked.

"For real," Lucy replied. "We've got a hospital, and we're crying out for nurses," she said smiling towards Vicky.

"We're next to the ocean," Jules said. "We fish, we grow, we forage our own food. We have a huge campground where people can live while we sort something more permanent out. Nobody goes hungry; we have a communal breakfast lunch and dinner in the village hall."

"And we've got a school and a library," Wren said. "It's not exactly how life was before, but it's good. It's something...something worth fighting for."

"And you'd take us with you?" Prisha asked.

"Every last one of you," Emma replied.

The women all looked around at each other and for the first time in a long time, they felt something beyond despair.

"How? How do you intend to do this?" Vicky asked.

"Yeah," Hughes replied, "I'm curious myself."

"You say his army is about a hundred strong?" Mike said.

"About that, and then there's the drones and the metalheads," Vicky replied.

"There are only thirteen of us, but you say there are another fifty women in the hall. If we can make it to them and give them weapons, all of a sudden we've got a proper army," Mike said.

"Arm them with what, though?" Jules asked.

Mike looked at her and then walked out of the cave. "This guy's pretty intense...and more than a little crazy," Vicky said as he disappeared.

Jules looked at her watch, "He's getting better, though. It took you much longer to notice than it did the rest of us."

They all looked towards the entrance as Mike reappeared with a long straight branch. He pulled the rucksack from his back and placed it on the ground then drew his hatchet from it. He hacked off some of the smaller twigs, then began to chop at the end. The brown bark gave way to the cream coloured wood beneath, and within two minutes, the bough had been transformed into a primitive spear. "Granted, it's not perfect, but it's a weapon," he said.

So we're going to fight a hundred heavily armed men with pointy sticks?" Vicky said with the beginning of a smile on her face.

Mike laughed. "Exactly."

"And there was I worrying," she replied.

*

There had been a short tussle for power after Fry and his army had left Loch Uig, never to return. But there was never a doubt in Webb's mind that he was the one who would take charge. The other men were terrified of him, despite him not having anything like the physical presence of the big Glaswegian.

Fry was tall; Webb was average height. Fry had fiery, untamed, red hair and whiskers, while Webb had a neat, below collar length cut and was cleanly shaven. Fry's voice was booming and he swore incessantly. Webb never swore and spoke deliberately and quietly.

Webb was impeccably clean; his fingernails always carefully manicured, his clothes always tidy and pressed. To look at him, he was the last person anyone would expect to be the leader of an army of marauders. But beneath the exterior, there was something very different. Someone far more menacing than Fry ever had the potential to be. Fry was a vicious madman, but Webb's insanity was far more sinister.

In his life before, he'd been a clerk, a pen pusher with grand designs who told his colleagues that he was going to *be someone*, that he was going to go places.

He escaped the claustrophobic prison that was his mother's cottage, the place where he had spent nearly every day of his wretched life, to go on survival weekends. There he was a different man. He was even given a nickname, the Professor. Unlike every other nickname he had been given up to this point in his life, it was not to hurt or mock him, but because he possessed an almost encyclopedic knowledge of survival skills. He had read about them for years; in his head, he had performed them a thousand times, or maybe more. Out in the wilds, as his weekend survivalist brethren struggled to tie a knot or set a trap, he would help them, and for the first time in his miserable existence, he became liked and respected. Like him, a number of the weekend survivalists went on a few longer courses and whenever they had to pair up, there was a rush of willing partners to join the Professor.

On Monday mornings, he was back to the job he hated, the people he hated, the boss he hated, the place he hated—the life he hated. Conversations stopped when he walked into a room. Women giggled behind their hands. He knew they called him the forty-one-year-old virgin. How clever they were to adapt the title of a film to make fun of him. But the last laugh was his. Where were all of them now?

He knew where one of them was, just one, but that one was all he needed. That one was the breakthrough. That one had made him the man he was today. When everything had gone to hell, when anarchy and chaos had erupted on the streets, he knew that his time had come.

Now, as he stood over the operating table and looked down at his next experiment, he felt a sense of pride. He had come so far. The girl in front of him was unconscious; she'd need to be for what he was about to do to her with his scalpel, but the girl whom he had strapped down on the table opposite was most definitely awake. A captive audience, her terrified, tear-filled eyes watched his every movement, knowing soon it would be her turn.

"I like you, Melissa. I always have," he said to her, but she could not respond through the thick duct tape he had placed over her mouth. "I was just reminiscing, remembering how things used to be," he said as he began to slice the unconscious girl's cheek. Melissa began to cry even more and turned her head away.

"Y'know, the first day when all this happened, I packed a rucksack and left the house. I knew this was the start of something for me, not the end. I remember looking back at my mother's white cottage and seeing her in the window. She was sobbing like a baby; I could see the betrayal in her eyes. She didn't understand. She had never understood. I walked down the street, hearing screams and sirens and gunfire, and I felt more alive than I'd ever done, because while everybody else was confused and scared, panicked wondering what they were going to do, I knew exactly. I arrived at a small block of flats and headed straight to the third floor. I reached Flat B and knocked on the door. Then I saw the speck of light through the peephole darken for a second before the safety chain went across and the door opened a crack."

Melissa's head turned back, her morbid curiosity getting the better of her.

"'Damien,' she said. 'What are you doing here? How do you know where I live?'" A wide grin bled onto Webb's face. He looked across towards Melissa then stopped speaking for a moment while he sliced through his experiment's left cheek, causing Melissa to howl beneath the duct tape once again.

"Anyway, I smiled at her for a moment, and then booted the door with everything I had. The safety chain shattered, and the force knocked Hazel from her feet. I walked in and closed the door behind me while she scrambled on the ground, desperately trying to get up." He put the scalpel down and walked across towards Melissa. She froze as he stood over her, and the bloody latex glove covering his left hand went up to her face. His thumb gently wiped away her tears, leaving red streaks in their place.

"You have to understand, Melissa, since I'd known this woman, there had always been a look of derision, of scorn on her face towards me, but now, as I stood over her, there was only abject terror. That was nothing compared to the fear I saw in her eyes over the next few hours. She started by feigning defiance, then she tried to bargain, then finally she pleaded," he said, letting out a small laugh. He looked down towards Louise and ran his gloved hand from her face and down her body. He took a deep breath. "I could smell her fear. All the times she and her friends had mocked me and laughed at me, and now it was me laughing at her. I left that flat a different man. I knew then that no one would ever make fun of me again."

Webb looked down at Melissa. He saw the same terrified look in her eyes that he'd seen in the eyes of Hazel White. Her turn would come soon enough. He walked back to the other table with a calm smile adorning his face. Now he was a leader, the most powerful man in Loch Uig…perhaps in all of Scotland. He had the entire top floor of the hotel to himself where he could carry out his experiments, where he could entertain himself, and even if someone thought him strange, they would never dare say it.

He heard the stairwell door squeak open from further down the corridor, and he immediately removed his gloves. "Dammit, this is inconvenient timing. Keep an eye on Louise here, will you, dear?" Webb said before removing his smock and heading to the door.

A man in his thirties walked towards him. He was over six feet tall and took up a good portion width of the hallway. Webb walked to meet him; they entered another room which was where he held most of his meetings with his second in command, Barker. "I want a search party to head out there," said Webb.

"Okay boss, how many?" Barker asked.

Webb looked towards the laptop on the desk. There was a freeze-frame of the group who had traversed the barricade and killed all the RAMs. "There are six of them. Send eighteen. I sent a drone out earlier, but didn't see anything. They'll be hiding in the forest somewhere."

"You don't want to send the helmets out there?"

Webb smiled. "Not yet, Barker. While they've got bullets there's a risk they can damage my girls. When it's hand to hand, they won't stand a chance. If the men can flush them back out into the open, I've got a few drones ready. Then we'll put these intruders down once and for all."

"Yes, boss," Barker said, turning to leave.

"Tell me when the men are ready and I'll coordinate operations from here."

"Sure thing, boss."

Webb picked up the laptop, walked to the door, and looked down the corridor as his subordinate disappeared through the stairwell exit. Webb walked along the hallway, and as he passed one of the rooms he could still hear Melissa's muffled crying. He would get back to the two women later. Right now, there were more pressing matters at hand.

He opened the door to the honeymoon suite at the end of the corridor. What had once been the venue of so many happy beginnings was now a control room. He plugged the laptop in, flicked a power switch, and monitors gradually began to flicker on. Over on one side of the once luxurious suite were tables full of electronics, soldering equipment, tools, drones and various projects he had been working on.

Webb looked again at the monitor and to the six intruders. "Well, you won the first round, but this game has only just begun."

15

Mike, Lucy and the rest of the group along with Vicky, stood in a circle. The other women had already started to fashion spears using the homemade knives they had crafted soon after entering the forest.

"Pretty nifty," Mike said, nodding towards the knife tucked into Vicky's belt. For a second she did not know what he was talking about, then she looked down to where his eyes were levelled.

"What can I tell you? We all watched Rambo a few too many times. The first thing we did was make weapons. We thought we'd need them for fighting, but in the end, we used them for everything but," Vicky replied.

"Well, they're being put to good use now," Mike said, looking across to the women busily working away at the mouth of the cave.

"Okay, what's the plan?" Vicky asked.

"That depends," Mike said, turning to Hughes. "What do you think? Do we go looking for them or wait for them to come to us?"

"Depends what we want to achieve. They might never find this place—it's a really big forest. If we want their guns, we bring the fight to them. If we want time to prepare, we stay here; if they find us, we put up a fight."

"What's your gut telling you?" Mike asked.

"I say we go after them. As far as weapons and ammo goes, at the moment, we're struggling. Our hardest job is going to be getting through the gate. To be honest, right now, I don't have a clue how to do that, but however we do it, having more ammo wouldn't harm."

"So we're going looking for trouble, is what you're saying? We're looking for a fight with these people?" Jules said.

"We're already in a fight with these people, Jules. It's all about tipping the balance in our favour now."

"I would think they'd get a search party out pretty quickly. The day's dragging on and they won't want to send people out here at night, so whatever they're going to do, it will be soon," Hughes said.

Lucy zipped her jacket, checked her Glock and placed it in the back of her jeans once again. "Okay, enough talking. Let's start moving."

*

Beth sat at the table with Jenny. For the first time in a long time, she had not opened the pub. Instead, she had spent the day sat by Kirsty's bed watching her sleep. But now, with the arrival of her friend, she relished the opportunity for a few minutes of conversation.

"...Everything was just falling into place for her, and now this. She's devastated," Jenny said.

"And how are you?" Beth asked.

"I'm fine, love. You and I have been in plenty of tough scrapes before. I've got the window boarded up, had myself a stiff drink, and now I'm as right as rain. It takes more than a bunch of thugs to rattle this old bird…but I'm worried sick about Sarah and George."

"I think George is going to be okay, from what Shaw said, but Sarah's the one I'm really worried about. They're still in the operating room," Beth replied.

"Raj is quite capable," Jenny said.

"I know. But it doesn't help when your friend's in trouble."

"Sarah's a strong girl, a fighter. She'll fight this."

They sat in silence for a moment, and Beth took a drink of her tea. "I should really get back; I just popped by to find out if you needed anything. They've got all the vehicles shifted off the road up at the blockade, but there's still more work to do up there," Beth said.

"I can imagine."

"I…"

"What is it?"

"Today…it's just, Shaw shot those men in cold blood, the ones in the carpark. Then we went to the campsite and he did the same thing over there. I was horrified, but he was right…he was right to do it. I've been struggling with that all morning. I was brought up in a Christian family. I mean, not devoutly Christian, but we went to church at Easter and Christmas and we always did what we could to help others…and…"

"You're worried about what your parents would think of all this?" Jenny asked.

"No! Yes…I suppose. I'm just confused. I couldn't believe it when Shaw gunned them down, but as soon as I heard about our own people, then I was glad he'd done it. Does that make me a bad person?"

Jenny smiled. "Well my love, I never really did the whole church thing. I take people as I find them. There are good people and bad people, builders and destroyers. We're builders; look at what we've done here. If people come to us with no food and no clothes, we feed them, we clothe them, we give them shelter. It's the right thing to do and it's the decent thing to do. There are so few people left in this world now; we should look after each other. Those people who tried to steal from us, who hurt our friends…we fed them like we would feed any strangers. We gave them a safe place to stay and they took advantage. They tried to destroy what we had built." Jenny took a sip of her tea, "And let me tell you, if we hadn't stopped them, they would have gone on to do it to someone who couldn't defend themselves."

"That's what Shaw said."

"Shaw was right. Being good doesn't make us weak, and being good people doesn't mean that sometimes we don't have to get our hands dirty to protect our way of life. Never get confused. They came here. They started all this trouble. We stopped it."

*

The group had been walking for fifteen minutes when a rumbling sound began to vibrate through the air. "That's not a drone," Emma said.

They all stopped to get a fix on where it was coming from. "Whatever it is, it's getting closer," Lucy said.

"Hang on, I know that sound," Hughes said, "It's quad bikes. A lot of quad bikes."

"They never had quad bikes before," Vicky said.

"Obviously they've been adding to their arsenal since you've been gone. I wonder what other surprises they're going to have in store for us," replied Emma.

"They're coming up on us, fast. We'd better find some cover," Hughes said.

Vicky immediately scrambled up the nearest tree like a lizard. The rest spread out, using the width of trunks to shield them. "I can see one," she called down.

"Whereabouts?" Mike asked.

"About a hundred and fifty metres straight ahead. It's coming in this direction. There's another to the left about thirty metres away."

Mike looked at Hughes and smiled. "Don't even think about it Mi—," Hughes said, but before he could even get the words out, Mike was sprinting back the way they had come, weaving in and out of the trees, making himself as visible as possible. "Shiiit!" Hughes said. "What the fuck is wrong with your boyfriend?"

"Don't ask me, I'm not a shrink," Lucy said, taking the Glock from the back of her jeans.

The engines got louder, and over the top of them, the crackle of radio messages could just be heard. The group all looked at each other. Right now there were two, but they knew any moment, the whole hunting party would be heading their way.

The sound roared to a climax as the first quad bike sped past the copse of trees the group were hiding behind. Hughes trained his rifle on the rider, but before he could fire a shot, he saw a small object blur through the air, and the rider fell forward over the handlebars, his unfastened helmet tumbling onto the ground. The quad bike slowed to a complete stop, and the man slumped off the bike onto the forest floor.

Hughes spun to his right to see Wren with her pistol crossbow raised, cocking the handle and carefully positioning another bolt. The sound of the second engine made him swing around, and this time he was the first to fire. The bullet entered the rider's abdomen from the side, making him and the quad bike tip. The sound of other engines began to draw closer, and the group looked up towards Vicky. "Can't see anything yet," she shouted, as she climbed higher up the tree.

Mike approached the struggling figure, who was desperately trying to reach around to his back to remove whatever object was stuck in there. He grimaced and grunted as he continued to slide across the forest floor towards the cover of the brush.

Mike looked towards the others, who were all preoccupied with the sound of the advancing engines—all but Wren, anyway. Unbeknownst to Mike, she was still watching his every move.

Mike stepped onto the arm of the wounded rider and the man let out a gasp of pain. He shifted the weight of his body to look up at the owner of the boot pinning him down. "Please!" he said, flicking off his sunglasses to take a proper look at his captor.

"How many are coming?" Mike growled.

"I don't know...I don't—"

Without hesitation, Mike pulled one of the machetes from his rucksack and whipped it down, slicing through the rider's left hand below the knuckles. "How many?" he shouted.

It took a few seconds for the pain and the horror to register with the fallen rider. His widened eyes almost seemed to pop out of their sockets as he looked down at his hand, now just a fingerless stump with a thumb. He let out a high-pitched scream and Mike unleashed a powerful kick to his ribs, winding him, almost silencing him, but not quite. "Please," he whispered.

"Answer me or I'll make the design symmetrical, then I'll move on to your other body parts," Mike said with no hint of a smile.

"Eighteen!" he cried. "There are eighteen of us."

Mike noticed the rider was wearing almost the same attire as he was, dark t-shirt and jeans. "How many men are in the compound?" Mike demanded.

"Wh...what?" the man asked feebly.

"How many of you are there?" Mike demanded, bringing up the machete one more time.

"No, please, I'll tell you. There are eighty-four of us. A lot of us don't want to be there, please, we just—"

Mike brought the machete down with lightning speed, slicing through the man's skull as if he was a RAM. The split second of terror that glistened through the tears in the man's eyes gave way to nothingness as all thoughts ended in a loud crack. Mike jerked the blade back out of the rider's head and blood gushed spontaneously from the wound. Mike stood and looked across to see Wren's eyes were fixed in his direction. The look on her face was unreadable. They stared at each other for a moment before Vicky shouted, "They're coming!"

For a few seconds Mike thought about taking the helmet and the glasses, climbing on the quad bike and posing as the fallen rider, but then he realised that would be a great way to get hit by friendly fire. He pulled the strapped rifle from the rider's back and checked the man's body for ammunition. There was one extra magazine, which Mike put in his rucksack.

"Feel better now?" Hughes asked as Mike took his position behind the tree.

"There are another sixteen," Mike said, leaning the newly acquired rifle against the trunk. "Eighty-four in total."

"How do you know he was telling the truth?" Jules asked.

Mike looked at her. "I just know."

"I can see three spread about fifty metres apart—they're almost in a line," Vicky shouted down.

"On my count," Hughes called, as the engines got closer and closer. "Three! Two! One!" All of them broke from the cover of the trees at the same time, immediately training their weapons towards the incoming vehicles. The first two riders were down before they had time to react, but the third had started to pull his rifle from around his back when a bullet ripped through his chest, knocking him from the quad bike.

"Talk to us Vicky!" shouted Lucy, her Glock still panning around the tree line, searching for any movement.

"I can see movement. Get back—there are a few of them. They've ditched the quads, they're on foot," Vicky said.

The whole group ran back behind the trees. "Can you see how many, Vicky?" Mike asked.

"No. A few though."

"What should we do?" Mike asked.

"Wait. We'll wait to see if they head this way," Hughes replied.

"Hang on. Something's happening. *What the fuck?*" Vicky said.

Suddenly they all heard a *whooshing* sound and shouts. "What the hell's happening?" Lucy said.

"They've launched flares," Vicky replied.

"Flares? What's the point of—Oh shit. The drones. The flares are a marker for the drones. Run!" Lucy shouted.

Vicky shimmied down the tree as fast as she could, and a volley of bullets flew towards her. Mike and Hughes kept low and hurried across while the rest of the group began to run back towards the cave. Hughes knelt down, and although not able to get a clear shot, he fired in the direction the bullets were coming from, while Mike caught Vicky as she jumped the last few feet out of the tree.

"Thanks," she said, and Mike handed her the rifle. "That's the first time I've actually been shot at."

"Don't worry," Hughes said, "now that you've met us, you'll find it happening more and more."

"Good to know," she said as the rumble of more motors could be heard elsewhere in the forest.

"Come on, let's get out of here," Mike said, taking Vicky by the arm and beginning to run back in the direction of the cave. Hughes took one final glance back around the tree and then followed them. The others were already so far ahead, they were out of sight, and Mike, Vicky and Hughes sped up even more as they heard the quad bikes start up again. They'd not travelled more than fifty metres when the sound of a drone made them look up.

They saw a small object fall from the claw beneath it. Within a second there was a bright explosion, and Hughes, Mike and Vicky all dove to the ground. Soil and small fragments of forest floor detritus rained onto their heads. "Jesus!" Vicky said.

"Come on," Hughes said, climbing to his feet again as the engines got louder behind them. "That was something homemade, not like what they used before. Hopefully, they've run out of the big stuff."

Another drone appeared above them. "Take cover," Mike shouted, and they each ducked behind wide and ancient trees. They stayed there for a few seconds, but no explosion came. Hughes peeked his head around the corner and saw a small device sitting harmlessly in the middle of an opening.

"It's a dud!" he shouted as a quad bike emerged from between two trees twenty metres in front of them. Hughes brought his SA80 up and fired four shots, centre mass. The rider flew back from his seat and the bike rolled into a tree. Hughes remained there with his rifle raised, ready to fire again, but nothing else appeared.

Mike pulled his shotgun from his rucksack and aimed towards the same spot. The sound of another drone came from above them. He could see it manoeuvring into the small gap in the canopy as it prepared to drop another homemade IED. He raised his shotgun and fired. There was an almost immediate explosion and the three of them dove for cover on the other side of the trees. When the sound of the eruption and the falling debris had settled, Hughes was the first to get to his feet to see if any more quad bikes had appeared, but now the engines were in the distance, ensuring the riders did not get in the way of the bombs.

Hughes helped Vicky to her feet as he looked towards Mike. "Without a shadow of a doubt, you are the maddest bastard I've ever met in my life. What the bloody 'ell were you thinking?"

"One less drone. He can't have an endless supply, can he? The more of their men we take out, the more of their machines we take out, the more of their ammo we use, the weaker they become."

"I get your point but, shooting at a bloody bomb when it's directly over your head isn't the best way to go about it."

"We're all still here aren't we?" Mike asked.

Hughes shook his head. "You're bloody certifiable, you really are."

Mike smiled. "Do you think they've headed back to base?"

Another drone sounded above. "Yeah, I'm guessing they're hoping the air force will take us out. Come on, let's get out of here."

"I'll catch up," Mike said, raising his shotgun to the skies once again. Hughes and Vicky began to sprint just as the drone came into view above the small clearing. Mike pumped the fore-end, aimed and fired, immediately ducking back behind the tree as another explosion singed the upper foliage. There was a loud *clunk* as the charred wreckage of another drone smashed on the ground. He stayed there for a full minute, waiting to see if anything else emerged, but nothing did. When he felt sure this wave of the attack was over, he headed towards the rider Hughes had taken out.

Mike took the rifle from him and slung it over his own back before climbing onto the quad bike. The engine was still running. For a moment, he looked towards the direction his friends had run off in and thought about following them, but instead, he headed back towards the other bikes and riders that they had brought down. He meticulously collected the weapons and ammo up from each of them before climbing back onto the bike. He was about to set off again when he heard laughter and spun around.

It was Fry leaning up against a tree with his arms folded. *"The way you got information out of your prisoner, boy...that was just a thing of beauty. No hesitation, just lop,"* he said, clapping slowly.

"Stay the fuck away from me," Mike hissed.

Fry breathed deeply and smiled. *"I started out just like you. It's an amazing sense of power, isn't it? I mean, watching someone beg for their life and you having full control over whether they live or die. I mean, it's like playing God. But let me tell you, boy, the way you handled it was something else. I'd have given him two or three chances, but no, not you. Cold as a witch's tit, you, boy...the look on his face as he stared at his stump. Oh, that was beautiful."*

"We needed that information. My friends and family are more important to me than some low life piece of shit. He chose his life, I chose mine."

"Oh that you did...you did, just like I chose mine. We all forge our own paths in life, Mikey boy. Another few years and you'll be a scarier, sicker bastard than I could ever hoped of being," Fry said, grinning.

"I will never be anything like you."

"We'll see. We'll see."

Suddenly, Mike heard shots. They came from the direction of the cave. He looked back to where Fry had been stood; there was nothing there but a tree.

"I will never be anything like you," he said again as the quad bike accelerated towards the sound of the shots.

16

Talikha had been busying herself in Ward Four, looking out of the window every few minutes, desperate to see her husband emerge with a victorious smile on his face. But as she saw him now, walking down the steps from Ward One, she saw a worried and haggard expression, the likes of which she had only witnessed before in the most testing times they had suffered.

She ran out to greet him, and for the first time in a long time, not even her appearance could put a smile on his face. "I am frightened to ask," she said as she wrapped her arms around him tightly.

"I have done absolutely everything I can do," Raj replied.

"That is all that anyone can expect," she said, pulling back and looking into his soulful eyes.

"She has lost a great amount of blood; we have managed to transfuse some. I have removed the bullet, but I don't know if it will be enough."

Talikha placed her hands on each of his cheeks. "Sarah is strong, she will fight, and you have given her the best chance. You will see. I have faith."

Raj took one of Talikha's hands and kissed it. "I hope you are right my love. I hope you are right. How is George?"

Talikha's face lit up. "Why don't you ask him yourself?"

"He is awake?"

"Yes," she said, taking hold of Raj's other hand and leading him into Ward Four. As Raj approached the bed, he could see George's colour was much better than it had been when he was first admitted.

"Ah, speak of the devil and he shall appear," George said with a tired smile on his face.

Raj sat down on a visitor's chair. "How are you feeling, my friend?"

"Like I've been shot."

"Good answer."

"These ladies have been giving me top-notch care, though. I think I might move in here. I could get used to this."

"Don't get comfortable. We'll have you back home in no time," Raj replied.

"Oh, that's too bad. How's Sarah? Talikha told me that we both arrived in here together," he asked, his tone taking a serious turn.

"She is hanging on, George, I managed to remove the bullet...but...I am not a surgeon."

"Sarah's a tough girl, and you don't give yourself nearly enough credit."

"I hope you're right, George; I hope you're right."

*

Mike arrived back at the cave to find no sign of anyone. He cut the engine to the quad bike and climbed off, pulling the shotgun from his rucksack and walking towards the cave entrance. He stepped inside to find it empty. He walked back out into the afternoon light. "Hello!" he called, placing his finger gently over the trigger. He heard shuffling to his right and swung around with the shotgun raised.

Coco was standing there with a frightened look on her face. "We heard the bikes coming this way and we scattered."

"Where are my people?" Mike asked.

"It all happened so quickly," she said.

"What happened? Where is everyone, Coco?"

"Mike!" came a shout. He turned his head to see Wren running towards him. She did not stop, but threw her arms around him and pressed her face into his chest.

He pulled back, immediately spotting the tears streaming down her cheeks. "Wren, what's happening?"

"They've taken them, and I think Hughes is dead."

"Wren, what the hell are you talking about?"

"Hughes! I don't think he's breathing."

"What? I was just with him a few minutes ago."

"Come...come with me," she said as she ran back into the forest. Mike looked towards Coco, and then Prisha and Sandy as they both emerged from the shadows. "Come on Mike!" Wren shouted and eventually he snapped out of his bewildered daze and followed her. They both ran flat out for the best part of a minute, eventually coming to a stop at a large grey boulder.

Mike saw Hughes lying there. A metal dart was protruding from his leg and there was a palm-sized bloodstain to the lower left-hand side of his stomach. Mike felt for a pulse. "He's still alive," he said and let out a relieved breath. He rolled up Hughes's shirt revealing a deep cut, roughly the size of a thumb. The surrounding skin had a green residue on it. "It looks like he might have got caught on a branch or something. He moved down to the small arrow and pulled it out. "This is a tranquilizer dart. Tell me what happened, Wren."

"We were all running back to the cave, then we heard two bikes. Somehow they'd managed to get in front of us. We scattered; I hid until I heard the bikes move off then I came back this way and Hughes was the only one I could find."

"Give me a hand," Mike said to Wren as they pulled Hughes from the ground. Wren propped him up while Mike hoisted him onto his shoulder. "Jesus Christ! Fat bastard, Bruiser," he said taking the full weight of his friend as they began to head back.

"What are you thinking?" Wren asked.

"I'm hoping the rest of them are back at the cave."

"And if they're not?" Mike didn't respond, he just gave Wren a look. They walked in silence the rest of the way back and paused at the edge of the tree line to observe the cave for a moment. Mike carefully placed Hughes down and pulled the shotgun from his rucksack. He and Wren stepped into the clearing.

"Hello?" Mike said, looking towards the covered cave entrance. The branches moved and Lucy came running out. She flung her arms around him and the pair embraced.

"Oh Mikey," she said, taking his face in her hands and kissing it roughly.

"Hughes is injured—I think he's been drugged."

"They're tranquilizer darts. They got Em, Jules and Vicky. I saw them take some of the others too.

"They *took* them?" he said, and the words hung between them like the smell of death itself. Lucy caught a flash of something beyond rage in Mike's eyes.

"We'll figure out a way to get them back," Lucy said, but Mike did not hear her; he became deaf to everything as the thought of his sister being held by a maniac overwhelmed him.

"He's over here," Wren said, guiding Lucy over to where Hughes lay.

Mike walked to a rock and sat down. He glanced back to see Prisha, Sandy, Coco, and Amy, the woman with the terrible burns, heading back into the cave. He stared at each of them without realising how self-conscious he was making them. There was no malice intended in his gaze, but his mind was beginning to spin out of control. The man who had Emma, Jules and the rest of the women was capable of monstrous things, and now, as Mike's eyes fixed on the scarring on Prisha's face, he knew he could not let that happen to his sister.

The conversation between Wren and Lucy was white noise to him as his mind wandered deeper and darker, but then something dragged him from his thoughts. It was barely perceptible, but…it was music. "Oh shit," he said, jumping to his feet. He ran across to Lucy and Wren, who looked at him like he had gone mad. "Music!" he shouted.

Their confused looks remained for a few seconds more until they could hear it too. It was very gradually getting louder as the drone moved slowly towards them above the canopy of the trees.

"Oh shit!" Lucy said. "Give me a hand," she demanded, and she and Mike took one of Hughes's arms each, lifting him from the ground and into the cave. They placed him flat, behind the wide rock that blocked a good portion of the entrance. Lucy removed his rifle and all the ammo from his backpack then covered him with leafy branches. "Huh. He brought his night vision goggles. Talk about wishful thinking; we'll be lucky if we get through the next half hour, never mind see nightfall."

"What do we do?" Wren asked.

"There is nothing to do except hide," Sandy said, "but if those are what I think they are, heading this way, then this is where I bow out. I can't climb into a tree with this leg."

Mike grabbed the rope from his rucksack and handed it to Wren. "Get them safe," he said.

Wren did not hesitate, she walked over to one of the tall trees near the cave entrance and handed one end of the rope to Coco, who tied it around her body and scurried up the trunk as if she had done it a thousand times before.

"These will be those metalhead things they talked about," Lucy said. "That drone is sure moving slow."

"He'll be trying to keep them together. When the drone was guiding them along the road, it was all pretty straightforward, but through a forest, it will be a lot harder to keep them all together. He'll have to take it slow."

"We wouldn't want a straggler to miss out on the feast, now would we?" Lucy said bitterly.

"Hang on—I've got an idea that might buy us some time." He reached into his rucksack and gave Lucy the remainder of the shotgun shells then headed over to Wren. "I need you to stay here."

"I don't know if you've noticed, Mike, but I don't really take orders."

"This isn't an order, it's a favour. If any of those things get through I need someone I can trust. My best friend is lying on the ground in there."

Wren nodded. "Okay. What are you going to do?" she asked as Lucy came over to join them.

"I'm more a 'make it up as I go along' type of guy," he said with half a smile. He walked across to the quad bike and started it up then looked towards Lucy. "You're riding shotgun—literally."

She climbed onto the seat with Hughes's rifle still strapped to her back, the Glock in the back of her jeans, and now a pump-action shotgun in her hand. They began to accelerate away from the cave, leaving Wren watching them, a little bewildered.

"So what exactly is the plan?" Lucy shouted in Mike's ear as the roar of the motor sliced through the forest air.

"We take down the drone and get the RAMs to follow us."

"That's it? That's the plan?"

"That'll buy us more time than we have now," he replied.

"But, I mean, what's the bigger plan? How are we going to get Em, Jules and those girls back?"

"Still working on that one," Mike said as he slowed the quad bike to a stop so he could get a fix on the sound of the drone. They set off again, and hadn't been travelling for more than a minute before they saw the first of the creatures, just as Prisha had described. Mike slowed the quad bike down to a stop once again as another, then a third, metalhead came out of the trees.

Lucy looked up towards the sky; the music could be heard clearly as the drone hovered into view. "Come on you son of a bitch," Lucy said, waiting to get a clear shot as the flying machine emerged.

Mike saw more of the beasts appearing. "You might want to hurry this up, Luce," he said as even more came into view. His body tensed as the deafening boom of the shotgun exploded behind him. He looked up towards the drone, watching as it plummeted from above the trees like a giant mechanical bird shot through the heart. The instant he confirmed the kill, he turned the handlebars and they sped away to the north. All the creatures began to follow the sound of the bike as Mike negotiated his way through the forest. When they had travelled a hundred metres, he stopped. He and Lucy looked back as the horde of metalheads sprinted after them.

"How many do you reckon there are?" Lucy asked.

"Hard to say...thirty...maybe?"

"We've taken a lot more than that out before," Lucy replied.

"Yeah, they weren't wearing helmets though. Plus..."

"Plus what?"

"Never mind, let's just get out of here," he said. He steered in a wide arc to face west, pointing the beasts back the way they had come.

"I know you too well, Mike. There's something going on in your head."

"I've got an idea...but you're not going to like it."

17

Emma was already awake when Jules finally roused. "Where the fuck are we?" Jules asked.

"That was my first thought, but in all honesty, I don't think I want to know," she said as she desperately tried to free herself from the restraints.

"Oh shite! This is the place Prisha was talking about. This is the fucking mad scientist's lair," Jules said, as she turned her head to the right. "Vicky! Vicky!" she called as she saw the woman lying unconscious next to her. "How did we get here?" she swivelled her head to the right to face Emma again.

"I'm pretty certain we were drugged. I remember seeing a dart heading towards me, and Hughes got in the way. The next second, he dropped like a stone."

"Well Vicky's not waking up," she said, turning her head back towards Emma. "And I can't see properly, but I think some of the other girls are here too...are any of you awake?" There was no response.

"Those girls are really malnourished. I'm guessing the effect will last longer on them than it will on us."

"Are you calling me fat?"

"I'm glad you've still got a sense of humour, Jules, 'cos we're going to need it if we can't get out of this place."

"If I could just wiggle my fingers free…"

"It won't make any difference," Emma said. "As well as those belts strapped across us, our wrist restraints are cable-tied to the table, too."

"Fuck."

"Yep."

"There's got to be something we can do. I had a small knife in my pocket, if I could just…"

"I'm pretty sure they'll have gone through our pockets. I can see our backpacks over there; they'll have gone through everything."

"We've got to do something, Em. We can't end up like those other women."

"Yeah, but do what, Jules? Tell me, what? I mean, we're strapped down, we're unarmed, we're in the middle of a compound full of heavily armed men."

"So what then? We just lie here?"

"You're making it sound like we have a choice."

"Right now, I'm just hoping they didn't get Mike and the rest of them. They're our only hope."

"Don't get me wrong. I love that mad fucking bastard to bits, but even he's not going to be able to rescue us in here. We're going to have to hope an opportunity arises and take advantage of it."

"Yeah…good luck with that, Jules."

"Nooo!" came the cry from another table. "Nooo!" Jules turned her head.

"Vicky! It's alright, calm down," Jules said as she saw the younger woman desperately straining against the strapping that held her to the examination table.

"Nooo!" she screamed again. "This can't be happening. This can't be happening."

"Calm down," Jules said again.

"Calm down?" she screeched. "I swore I would kill myself rather than end up here. This is all your fault! You and your fucking friends! They had no idea we were out there. They thought we were all dead. If you hadn't shown up, they'd still think that. This is all on you, and now...now we're going to become those monsters! And before we do, we're going to undergo pain you can't even imagine. Have you any fucking idea what Prisha went through? Every day I look at that girl and ask myself how she had the strength to carry on, because if that was me, I'd have killed myself," she said as tears streamed from her eyes.

"Oh no! Oh no! Oh no!" came another voice from one of the other tables as they woke up from the effects of the tranquilizer.

"Look we'll figure something out," Jules said, desperately trying to calm both women.

"You don't know what this place is like. This is a living hell. We didn't think things could be any worse. Do you honestly have any clue what we went through? And then...then we found out about these things, the metalheads, and we saw and heard what Prisha had suffered and we realised, yeah, things could be worse. What's about to happen to us will make Hell look like a day spa."

*

Jenny did not usually allow dogs, other than Meg, on the seating in the pub, but Humphrey was an exception...especially today. He sprawled across the woven material and rested his head on Raj's lap. Raj never drank alcohol; there was a strong cup of tea on the table in front of him, but he looked longingly towards the bottles behind the bar and wondered if he should break the tradition. He gently stroked Humphrey's head and felt the dog's warm breath on his leg through his trousers. Jenny and Talikha were sat with Raj. They had all just been up to check on Kirsty, who was still fast asleep.

"Do you think she'll be okay?" Jenny asked.

The vet did not answer, and Talikha gently prodded him to coax him out of his glazed state. He looked up. "Hmm? Sorry? What did you say, Jenny?"

"I said, do you think she'll be okay?"

"It is good that she is sleeping. That will be the effects of the sedative...and the spirits you gave her...not a very wise combination, I must add. But loss is a very difficult thing to cope with. The initial reaction will be shock."

"I've never seen you so preoccupied, Raj," Jenny said.

"I need to get back to the hospital," he said, taking a drink of his tea. "I just wanted to take a little break."

"I'm glad you came here," Jenny replied.

"I am too," he said, smiling.

"You and Talikha should come round one night; I'll make us a meal."

"That would be very nice," Talikha said. Raj had drifted into his thoughts once again. "Wouldn't it, Raj?"

"I'm sorry. Sorry, yes...that would be lovely."

The forced conversation came to an abrupt halt as the radio handset hissed to life.

"Raj! Raj! This is Stephanie. Over."

Raj jumped from his seat, startling Humphrey, who let out a small bark. The vet barged into the table and tea slopped over the sides of each of the cups. He ran across to the bar and picked up the handset. "Stephanie! Go ahead."

"Raj, Sarah's having convulsions. Get here quick!"

Raj did not even look towards Talikha or Jenny. He sprinted across the pub and out the rear door. There was a part of him that had been looking forward to hearing Stephanie's voice, and another part that was dreading it. He had hoped that good news would have prevailed, that Sarah would wake up. But the realist inside him knew that was a long shot. As he ran through the small wooded area behind the pub and to the hospital, fear filled his heart. He had never felt so out of his depth.

*

Mike let the engine idle for a moment as they waited for the metalheads to catch up. The road was dead ahead and beyond it lay another part of the forest...the part he intended to lose the predators in. He felt Lucy's arms tighten around him as the creatures got closer. They both craned their necks and watched. Whoever did this to these women was sick, evil, and to think that Emma, Jules, and the other girls were all in the clutches of this mad man now sent chills running through them. Neither of them said anything, but both of them felt it. It was real fear. A dark, relentless fear born from the most primal nightmare.

When the nearest beast was just twenty feet away, Mike set off once again. They left the tree line and headed across the tarmac of the road. Both of them immediately looked to the left and saw the downward inclination leading to the roadblock and the gate to Loch Uig. Mike had deliberately come out so close so that he could take a proper look. Cliffs with the same rockfall netting lined either side of the road, just like the ones he had clung onto for dear life earlier that day. The entire geography of the place was like a colossal hourglass in reverse; a narrow channel either end with a big something smack in the middle. As they looked down towards the barricade, the guards on duty were taken by surprise and they watched in bemusement as the quad bike chugged across the road ahead of them. It was only when the bike had made it two-thirds of the way that they thought to bring up their rifles and start to fire, by which time, Mike and Lucy had disappeared into the trees on the other side.

The few seconds they had were enough to take in everything they needed to. To the left-hand side were two cargo containers, both open, both empty. On top of those were the four guards. The gate looked like a huge metal quilt, stitched together with whatever scrap they could find. Vicky had told them that, when they had made their escape, they had discovered the gate was essentially a wooden construction with a metal front. It had been several months since their escape, but there was no reason to believe it had been changed.

Lucy looked back as the gunfire came to an abrupt stop. Behind them, the procession of metalheads continued their pursuit. "Are they all following?" Mike shouted.

"Seem to be."

"We'll keep going for a few hundred metres, then we'll pull a really big U-turn and head back as fast as we can."

*

Wren remained crouched down in the cave with both of her pistol crossbows drawn. It had been some time since Mike and Lucy had left, and she had not seen a single RAM emerge from the woods, but she had made a promise to keep Hughes safe, and she did not intend to break it.

"What the…" Hughes said groggily as he started shifting the leafy branches that had been piled on top of him.

Wren removed the last branch covering his face and gave him an enthusiastic hug. "I was so worried about you," she said.

"What the hell happened?"

"You were hit by a knock-out dart. You should probably just stay flat for a couple of minutes."

"Like for a wild animal?" he said as he reached towards the gash on his stomach.

"Yeah, but we think you got impaled on a branch or something there. The dart was near your bicep. Well, as near as I could judge your bicep to be…you're pretty flabby around there," she said, smiling.

"Thanks, kid. The longer I spend with you the more I understand why you were alone for so many months. Where is everyone?" The smile washed away from Wren's face. "Spill it."

"They got Emma, Jules, Vicky and three of the other girls. They released those things…the metalhead things that Prisha told us about and Lucy and Mike are luring them away from us right now."

"Oh shit!"

"Yeah, I've been sat here trying to think of every possible way we can get them back and I am drawing a blank every time."

Hughes sat up slowly and touched the puncture on his arm. "Tranquilizers?"

"I thought you were dead. I was so scared."

"Don't celebrate yet, Wren. Before the day's out who knows what could happen."

*

Emma tried to clear her head, desperate to come up with a seed of an idea at the very least. It was hard; the four women who had spent the last few months in the forest were crying and screaming. It was clear they all felt the same as Vicky, that they would rather be dead than trapped in this room.

"I don't mind telling you, this whole thing is really starting to give me the shits," Jules said, angling her head around towards Emma. Emma's eyes were looking directly towards the ceiling. "What are you thinking?"

"I'm thinking I wish I was back at home with Sarah and we'd never come here."

"Yeah, I don't blame you. As much as my brothers drive me insane, I'd give anything to see any one of their ugly mugs right now."

The door creaked open and all the women instantly stretched their necks as far as they could. Webb was stood in the doorway with a smile on his face that made Hannibal Lecter's seem inviting. "Hello ladies," he said, cordially.

Vicky and the others immediately began to scream at the top of their voices. The sounds echoed around the large room, and Webb's smile broadened as he stepped in and closed the door behind him.

"Help! Help! Help!" one of the women screamed repeatedly.

"Let us go, you sick bastard," Vicky yelled.

Webb walked along the arrangement of tables and Jules and Emma lost sight of him as he went down to the far end. The woman who was screaming for help stopped and began to sob. "I don't know who you think is going to help you. We have the whole floor to ourselves and at the moment, my boys are busy keeping a lookout for the rest of your gang."

The radio clipped to Webb's belt crackled. "Boss, it's Barker," came the garbled message.

Webb unclipped the handset from his belt and walked quickly to the other end of the room, past Emma and Jules's tables. He looked irritated. "What is it?" he demanded, releasing the talk button.

"We've just seen them."

"What do you mean you've just seen them?"

"One of the lads from the barricade has just reported to me that two of them crossed over the road on a quad with the Helmets close behind."

Webb brought the handset up to his mouth, then brought it down again. He turned and looked towards Emma and Jules, and the creepy, lecherous smile he'd worn when he'd first walked in reappeared.

"No matter. It will be getting dark in a couple of hours. We'll leave the girls out to do a little night hunting, and then I'll round them all up tomorrow morning. By that time—"

"Help!!!" one of the women screamed again.

Webb released the talk button. "Silence!" he demanded, and for a few seconds, all the women fell still.

"Is everything okay, boss?" Barker asked.

"Everything is fine. I'll be working late, so I don't want disturbing unless it's absolutely necessary. Do you understand?"

"Yes, boss. Over and out."

The radio went dead and the sounds of the women sobbing began again. "There now. My apologies, ladies, I don't like interruptions. I'm glad you've joined me. I am so happy to see you, I've actually put two of my other projects on hold. It's the very least I can do for such special guests," he said, placing his hand over the straps across Emma's stomach and stroking her like a pet.

Emma glared at him, and the smile left his face temporarily. Her expression reminded him of the looks he used to get from the women at work. The disdainful glances and stares that made him feel like he was being made a laughing stock the moment he left the room. He brought his hands back up and walked across to a bench at the side of the room.

Webb picked something up and placed it in his pocket, before beginning to stroll up and down the row of assembled examination tables. "Help!" one of the women shouted hopelessly again, as if the word still had meaning.

Webb laughed to himself. He loved the sense of power he had over the men, but to have the power of life and death over six captive women, was intoxicating; it felt like a drug-induced high. "You see, ladies, I went for a walk this afternoon. Some of you never got to leave the Fun House, so you won't have seen what else we have going on here, but we have thriving vegetable plots and gardens," he said, walking to the side of Vicky's table and placing his hand over the strapping where her breast was, for no other reason than to demonstrate he could do anything he wanted. He brought his hand away and began parading up and down once more. "So, there I was, paying my royal visit, and I had a revelation. Tools! Tools were designed to cut down on man's labour...to make his life easier. I watched as a woman in one of the polytunnels knelt down to prune a fruit bush, and I looked at the small shears in her hand. That's when it came to me."

"Please. Please let us go. We're sorry. We'll go back to the Fun House," one of the women said, crying.

Webb looked in her direction, temporarily irritated at being interrupted, but then that awful smile returned. It turned the women's blood to ice.

"As I was saying...I want you to do something for me. Take your tongues and push them against the walls of your cheeks on both sides. Push as hard as you can. You see, those walls are thick aren't they? All this time I've been using surgical equipment. Do you have any idea how hard it is to slice through the cheek wall with a scalpel? I'm guessing not. But today, thanks to my botanical visit, I realised how much easier my life could become if I started thinking a little bit further outside the box." Webb continued walking up and down for a moment, and then paused for effect. He pulled an item out of his pocket and held it high in the air so all the women could see it with a minimal craning of their necks. "I give you...secateurs."

Two of the women screamed, one more started crying, and the defiance and hatred that had bubbled up inside Vicky finally left her. "Please...please don't do this," she said softly.

He ignored her comments and went to stand by Jules's table. He grabbed her cheeks between his thumb and the rest of his fingers and brought the shears up in front of her face. Webb moved in closer until he could feel his own breath on the back of his hand. "Can you imagine how much easier this is going to make my life? Can you? There'll be no more laboured slicing and pulling and wrenching." He squeezed the handles of the shears and the sharp, shining blades crossed over with a metallic grind. He mashed Jules's face even harder and now, tears of fear appeared in her eyes, too. "It will be as easy as cutting through bacon rind with a pair of kitchen scissors," he said, releasing his grip and standing up. "So now, there is just one piece of the puzzle left for me to fathom: who is going to be first?"

18

Jake had quietly been reading a book in one corner of the static caravan. His sister had insisted on helping the nurse. She had brought fresh jugs of water for the only two patients in ward one, then she had helped prepare the meals for them, the nurses, herself and Jake.

"You're quite a little worker aren't you?" said Sophie, a former doctor's receptionist, but now a trainee nurse. They just put the finishing touches to the basic but nutritious plates of food.

"My nana always said that when you're worried or upset, it's always best to keep busy, keep your mind occupied. That way you don't dwell."

Sophie let out a small laugh. "Your nana sounds like a remarkable woman, I'm guessing you're going to be a chip off the old block. Wisdom must run in the family."

"She wasn't my nana by blood. She was my brother's gran, but there's more to family than blood."

"Did she tell you that too?"

"No...Mike taught me that."

"Well that's very true as well," Sophie said.

Sammy picked up two of the plates and took them out to the patients. She had already placed knives and forks on their over bed tables and made sure that water had been poured into their glasses. She returned to the compact kitchen and picked up two more plates for her and Jake. "Are you coming to eat with us?" she asked.

Sophie smiled again. "That would be nice! I'd love to eat with you and Jake."

The pair of them walked across to the counter that George had built from old Formica kitchen surfaces, which acted as the Nurses' station. They smiled at the two elderly patients as they headed through. Sophie and Sammy reached the station; Sophie stayed at the front, and Sammy beckoned Jake to join her on a stool behind the counter. The meal was a simple salad with carrots, cucumber, lettuce and tuna.

"We grew the cucumber," Sammy said, proudly.

Sophie smiled as she placed a slice in her mouth. "I'm going to have to come up and pay your famous polytunnel a visit someday," she said.

"You should," Sammy replied. "Sarah and I spend a lot of time in there." She took a mouthful of tuna. "Did you know there are sea cucumbers too?"

"Do you pick those when you go foraging?"

Sammy giggled. "No. Sea cucumbers are actually animals. They live on the sea bed. Sarah told me that. She knows lots of stuff about nature."

"She's a very clever lady," Sophie said, placing a fork full of food in her mouth.

"I wish Emma was here," Sammy said. "She'd want to be here." She looked over the top of the nurse's station and down through the hall to the room that Raj had rushed back into about half an hour ago.

Sophie followed her eyes, and then looked back towards Sammy. "Your sister will be happy to know that you're here. You were right, it's important that Sarah had family here. You're her family just as much as Emma." Sammy dragged her eyes back away from the door and down to her plate. She had only had a few mouthfuls, but now she placed her fork down.

"I'm sorry," she said. "I don't really feel like eating anymore," and a single tear trickled down her cheek.

*

Lucy gripped onto Mike hard as the quad bike accelerated back across the road. They were much higher up now and could barely make out the top of the manned barricade as they sped across. They had lost the horde of metalheads a few hundred metres back.

Mike brought the quad to a standstill at the side of one of the other vehicles whose riders had been killed. "Follow me back on that?" Mike said, turning to Lucy.

"Are you going to tell me what the hell is going on in that head of yours?"

"I Love you, Luce. I love you so much. Remember that; whatever else happens today, remember that."

"What do you mean?" she asked looking him straight in the eyes.

"I mean, I am who I am. I'll never change. Sometimes I have to do bad stuff for the people I love, but it's still me underneath."

"Mikey," she said, pulling back from him with a concerned look on her face. "Where is all this coming from? What's going on?"

"Sometimes I...sometimes I worry that doing some of the things I do will make you think less of me."

Lucy shook her head and moved her lips to his. It was one of those magical kisses that he had only ever experienced with her; the kind that made the rest of the world stop around them. "There is nothing you have done and nothing you could ever do that would make me feel anything but love for you. You're my Mike, and I know you. I know that everything about you is for us, for the group, for the good guys. So whatever crazy doubts you've got going on in your head, get rid of them now. We're about to go to war with these people. They've got your family, our family, in there, and they're going to get what's coming to them."

"I..."

"This isn't the nineteenth century, Mike. There is no honour in war, no respect between enemies. These fuckers kidnapped Em and Jules. They deserve everything they've got coming to them."

"Luce...there's something I need to tell you..."

"What is it? You can tell me anything."

"I've been seeing—"

"Fry."

Mike's eyes widened. "I don't understand. How do you know?"

"That night...a couple of weeks back when we'd been for that beach walk." They both smiled knowingly. "You know the one I mean. I woke up at about three in the morning and went to put my arm over you, but you weren't there. I got out of bed and headed downstairs, and I heard you talking. At first, I thought something really bad had happened. Who the hell would you be talking to at three in the morning? Then I got to the bottom of the stairs and I heard it was just you talking. You never said his name, but from what you were saying, I knew you were talking to Fry. I thought it was some kind of parasomnia but—"

"What's parasomnia?"

"Weird sleep behaviour. But then it happened again one afternoon, a few days later."

"Why didn't you say anything?"

"I knew you'd tell me when you wanted to. I hoped it would be at a time when we could sit down and talk about it, but beggars can't be choosers," she said, gesturing around.

"So, your boyfriend's crazy as a loon. You must be so proud," Mike said with a heartbroken look on his face.

"Now you've told me, I can help you. That was the first step," she said taking hold of his hand.

"Doesn't it scare you? Aren't you worried?"

"We've all got stuff that we need to work through. No offence, Mikey, but I knew what I was getting into, you weren't a poster boy for good mental health before this. But you've been through more than anybody. It's a form of PTSD. I think it all goes back to those school kids."

"School kids?"

"The ones in Inverness that had turned. You had so many nightmares the days and weeks following that. Whatever it is, whatever is happening, we'll deal with it together. Nothing you can do will change the way I feel about you, but I need you to focus now. Forget everything else, we need to get Em and the rest of them back to us."

"You're right...you're always right."

"Yeah, it's a cross I have to bear."

"Thank you, Luce...for everything."

"Hey, for better or worse right?" she said, smiling.

Mike looked at her long and hard. He combed his fingers through the hair on the back of her head and pulled her face towards him. They kissed again. "Maggie Tyson was a registrar. She's able to marry people and stuff. She's done hundreds."

Lucy's brow furrowed. "And?"

"Maybe we should make it official."

"Did you just ask me to marry you?"

"Erm...yeah."

"Let me get this straight. We're in the middle of a forest being chased down by RAMs and cyborgs. Your sister and our friends have been taken by a band of ruthless bandits, you've just admitted to me that you're having conversations with a man you killed last year, and you want to know if I'll marry you?"

"Well, when you put it like that, I suppose—"

"Yes!"

"Yes, what?"

"Yes, I'll marry you! Of course, that's on the assumption that we don't die in the next few hours."

"Well duh!"

They climbed onto the quad bikes, started them up, and within a few minutes were back at the cave. They entered the clearing to find no one there, but as soon as they pulled up the bikes everyone emerged from the entrance. Hughes had his shirt open and Wren had taped gauze to his wound.

"The wanderers return," Hughes said.

"I'm sure it won't be too long before they're all heading back this way, but we're safe for the moment," Lucy said.

"So what's next?" Wren asked.

"Well...I've got a plan," Mike replied, "but you're not going to like it."

"I've never liked any of your plans, but just for old time's sake, let's hear it," Hughes said.

"Okay, Mike replied, it goes like this…"

19

Webb went over to the workbench and picked up a syringe, placing it in his pocket. "Now this will be the hardest part. Decisions, decisions."

"Please don't do this," Vicky begged. The four women who had previously been guests of his were crying uncontrollably now. Jules and Emma did their best to remain stoic, but their resolve was weakening with each moment that passed.

"You beg me now? You destroy my drones, you kill my men, and you want forgiveness?"

"It wasn't us," Vicky cried. "It was them. We never did anything, it was all them."

Emma's mouth fell open in surprise, and Webb walked across to the space in between their two tables. "Is that so? It was all you two, was it?"

"Yes," shouted another of the women. "It was them and the other ones they arrived here with."

Webb smiled as he saw looks of disbelief form on Emma and Jules's faces as the women all blamed them.

"I know that expression," he said while the others continued to shout out. "Disbelief; betrayal. How can people offer you up so readily to save their own hides? You two still have faith in your fellow man...and woman. I think that's admirable, or at least quaint," he said with a small huff of a laugh. "Alas, you have been outed. You are guilty; you shall suffer the most." He walked across to Emma's table and dragged it away from Jules's.

"No!" Jules shouted. "No!" Leave her alone you sick fuck!"

The table slid across the carpet, and Emma remained silent, staring Webb straight in the eyes as he continued to smile.

"You're heavier than you look," he said, finally bringing the table to rest and pressing his left palm down on her stomach. "Wherever you come from they must be feeding you well." He moved his hand lower to assert ownership, to see if he could get any kind of reaction from his victim, but she just stared at him. His smile wavered for a moment before he removed his hand and walked over to one of the tables at the far end. Emma and Jules could not see what was happening from their position, but they could hear another of the tables being dragged across the carpet. More than that, though, they could hear another of the women screaming hysterically, then the others joined her in a banshee chorus as it dawned on them one by one what was happening.

Webb carefully guided the table he was dragging into the gap between Jules and Emma. The woman who was now stuck between them was no more than twenty. Once, she would have been beautiful, but her emaciated figure made her cheekbones and chin too prominent now, not to mention the marks of this new horror that had befallen her. She was ageing before their very eyes.

"I remember you pretty," Webb said, standing over the terrified young woman. "We had lots of fun together back in the day, didn't we," he said with a leery grin. The girl did not answer; she just cried and howled.

Despite being betrayed by these women, Emma could not bear to stomach such cruelty. "I'm guessing the only fun for her was laughing at the shrivelled up little cocktail sausage that was hanging between your legs."

Webb's face contorted into a hateful glare as he stared at Emma, but the second he saw the defiance in her eyes, he smiled. It was a natural response. It was how people dealt with fear...false bravado. He disappeared out of her line of sight again. They looked towards the table between them, to the poor young woman who was bound there awaiting her fate. Webb came back into view, wheeling a small trolley. He put the brakes on and grabbed a syringe full of clear liquid.

"Now, let's find a vein, shall we?" he said, examining the gaps of skin that could be seen beneath the straps.

"What made you like this? Let me guess, mummy didn't like the idea of her little boy going out with girls, so he had to stay at home and wash her hair. That's it, isn't it? Little mummy's boy," Emma spat.

Webb slammed the syringe back down on the trolley and marched over to the bench. He pulled a roll of duct tape from the countertop, and tore off a large strip, almost running back towards Emma. She wrenched her head from side to side as he tried to put the tape over her mouth. He managed to adhere one corner, but then she clamped his thumb and a mouthful of tape between her right molars. It was Webb now who let out a pained howl as he desperately pulled to try and get his thumb out of Emma's mouth. The more he tugged the greater the pain became, and his fleeting and impulsive notion to keep yanking finally gave way to a greater panic. Like an injured animal, he began to lash and strike at her, but Emma bit down all the harder.

Webb stumbled and the trolley toppled. He continued to scream and his eyes filled with tears of pain and frustration, but Emma showed no sign of relinquishing. Then came the taunts and jibes. It was just Jules at first.

"Go on Emma! Go on girl. Tear the bloody thing off!"

"Kill him! Kill him!" Vicky shouted, happily switching loyalties once more, seeing that it was Webb on the back foot now.

"Go on Emma! Make the little shite scream for his ma!" Jules called.

The rage and pain; the fear and hate and shame all hit Webb at once like a wall of sewage, drenching him in the foulest smelling humiliation a man could suffer.

He raised his left fist high like Thor's hammer, and was about to bring it down to smash Emma's skull when she jerked her head violently. Webb stopped screaming immediately. For a split second, he thought he had dragged free from her bite, but then as he brought his hand up to his face and saw the squirting red stump that used to be his thumb, he screamed louder and higher than any of the women could. Emma turned her head back around to face him. The duct tape hung from her face by one corner, and blood painted her lips, she peeled them back in an ice-cold grin to reveal the pulsating thumb.

Despite being covered in Webb's blood, her nose twitched as she smelt something out of place. She looked down to see her captor had lost control of his bladder and a football-sized wet patch had appeared on his beige chinos. She spat the thumb towards him with all the force she could muster and it hit him square in the forehead, stamping him with a fleshy red seal.

He continued to scream, but Emma's campaign was not over yet. "He's pissed himself. Look! What a big man."

Jules began laughing mockingly. She found none of it funny, not for a second, but she understood what Emma was trying to do. "Oh, that's beautiful. Hey big man, you better run and get your ma to change your nappy."

Webb just looked on in horror, focussing on the stub, then looking at Emma, then looking back to the stub. He could not comprehend the words that were coming out of her mouth, he could not comprehend anything right that second. All he could see was the blood fountain spurting from his hand. All he could hear was the blood rushing around his head. When he finally gained control of his senses once more and heard the mocking laughs, the words assaulted him: *pissed himself...pissed himself.*

He looked down and real horror swept over him. He was nine years old again. They were at the herpetarium on a school visit. Webb had always had a morbid fear of snakes, but his teacher had assured him all of these were behind thick glass and there was no reason to be scared. Then a huge python had locked Webb in its gaze. Despite the glass, despite all the safety features of the enclosure, fear took hold of him as he stared into that creature's eyes, and he lost control of his bladder as he had done now. Mocking laughs and hoots had come from his deriding classmates and now rose from his prisoners, and his tears flowed now as they had then.

"Let me out of these restraints you little shit, I'll give you something to cry about," Emma shouted.

Webb looked at his hand one more time, looked back towards Emma and ran out of the room. The laughter came to an almost immediate halt. "I'm guessing he's not going to be in the same playful mood when he comes back in," Jules said.

"Do any of you have any give at all with the straps or the cable ties?" Emma shouted, but all the responses that came back were negative. She angled her head around the best she could, looking for anything that might give her inspiration. She knew there were an array of tools and sharp objects scattered over the floor, but she had no hope of getting to them. This was it. She had played her one ace and Webb held all the rest. She turned back towards Jules, ignoring the young woman between them who now lay there with her eyes tightly shut, desperately hoping that she would soon wake up from this nightmare. "Listen, I know we're both probably going to die in here, but if by some miracle you get out. Tell Sarah that I love her. Tell her she's the only person who made me truly happy."

"Don't be daft. If one of us gets out, both of us'll get out, and if neither of us get out then it doesn't really matter, does it?"

"Promise me."

Jules looked up to the ceiling. These were the empty promises of dying women, designed to bring nothing more than a last moment's comfort. "Okay love. I promise."

*

The light was fading fast. Mike had the night vision goggles on his head, raised, but ready for when he needed them. As he scaled the rock face, feeling out every bump and crevice, he kept looking down to make sure Wren was okay. They were bound by rope at the waist and the whole of the plan Mike had devised depended on the two of them succeeding.

"Hang on a second," Wren called.

Mike paused. "Do you want to rest for a while?"

"No," she replied, "I'm just struggling to get a firm grip."

Mike looked down to see Lucy and Hughes forty feet below, the features on their faces becoming less discernible with each passing second. "Let me know when you're ready," he said, clinging to the cliff face.

"Okay. I think I'm okay," she said and they began to climb once again.

"I really don't like this," Lucy said as she, Hughes, Prisha, Sandy and Coco watched them.

"Which part? Them climbing the rock face in the dark with no safety equipment? Or us raiding a compound full of heavily armed scumbags with just a few guns between us?" Hughes asked.

"Yeah," she replied.

"I'm the first to criticise Mike's schemes, but under the circumstances, I don't honestly see any other option. Us leaving while Em, Jules and those other girls are trapped in there is a definite no, and we don't have the numbers or equipment for a full assault. I'd prefer it if it was me up there with Mike, but one, I'm injured, and two, I can't climb for shit anyway, so if we were bound together, we'd both be heaped in a pile of broken bones in front of you."

"Well, there is that I suppose."

"Listen, this plan is better than nothing," he said, unclipping the radio from his belt. "We're using a different band, so they're not going to hear our comms, and Wren is pretty capable. She got Mike out of that jam in Inverness and she's a smart cookie. And Mike is...well, y'know...."

"Don't remind me."

A broad smile suddenly swept across Hughes's face. "Remember when we thought it was all over, back in Morecambe? The RAMs had forced the door and it was just a matter of time before they got to us." Lucy looked at Hughes and burst out laughing. The other women didn't understand why as they looked at the pair of them. "We were stuck in a small cupboard in a hospital ward waiting for the end and the next thing we know there's all this white stuff floating in the air. It looked like a snowstorm."

"What was it?" Coco asked.

"It was that mad bastard. He'd only gone and got himself a fire extinguisher. He sprayed foam everywhere, blinding them, making them slip on the floor as they tried to rush him, then he just started taking them out one by one," Hughes said, smiling and shaking his head.

"I don't think a fire extinguisher is going to help here," Coco replied.

"That's not really the point of the story," Hughes said as the fond reminisce faded.

"So what is?"

"Mike doesn't give up. He was outnumbered; it was a real cat in hell's chance that he'd make it out of there, but he did it anyway. He won't stop until he's got your friends and ours to safety."

"Or he's dead," Coco replied.

*

Shaw, Barnes and Beth all walked through the back entrance of the pub. Jenny and Kirsty were sat at the bar. There was half a bottle of Jura whisky sitting between them and both had been crying. Humphrey and Meg lay in front of the fire, snoring.

"Have you heard anything?" Jenny asked, gathering three more glasses and pouring each of her guests a measure.

"No," Shaw replied. "We're just about to head over there. We were up at the barricade. All the vehicles have been cleared. The mangonels have been covered up and more rocks have been piled in case we get attacked again," he said, taking a drink.

"Perish the thought," Jenny replied.

"We just wanted to check in here," Beth said, looking towards Kirsty.

"Don't worry about me," Kirsty replied, raising her glass, "I've got my best pal looking after me." She drained the glass and stood up, staggering a little at first. "And on that note, I think I'm going to call it a night," she said.

"Are you sure, love? It's only early," Jenny said.

Kirsty put her hand on Jenny's shoulder, leant down and kissed her on the cheek. She picked up one of the lanterns from the bar and staggered a few paces before turning back. "I just want to put today behind me," she said. "Goodnight."

"I'm guessing she's not doing too well," Shaw said as they heard Kirsty climb the stairs.

"Would you be?" Jenny asked, taking another drink.

"No, I guess I wouldn't." Shaw drained his glass. "Right, we'd better be heading across to the hospital.

"You won't stay for another?" Jenny said disappointedly.

"When we know what's going on, we'll head back this way. Keep that bottle out; hopefully, we'll be toasting good news," Shaw replied.

"And if we're not?"

"Well, you'd better have another one ready, too."

20

Mike scrambled over the edge of the cliff face and dug his fingers into cold, damp, grass-covered earth. He turned over onto his back and took the weight of the rope in his hands. "I'm going to pull you the rest of the way up," he called, beginning to tug at the tow rope.

"Waaarrrgghh!" was all Wren could say as she was hoisted like a girder on a building site. Her arms and legs flapped in the air for a few seconds before she too felt the cool earth against her skin.

"You okay?" Mike asked as she climbed to her feet.

"I was. A little more warning might have been nice," she said, brushing herself down. They untied the rope from their waists and Mike placed it back in his rucksack. Darkness had now fallen, but the glow of the spotlights from the gate gave them enough light to make their way along the top of the cliff face.

"You'd better take these," he said, handing Wren the night vision goggles.

"Erm...okay," she said, stopping and looking at them. "I've never used these things before." Mike stopped too and helped her put them on. She felt his warm hands on her cold chin as he adjusted the strap. He moved closer and felt his way around the back of her head as he fastened them into position. He took hold of her hand and moved it to the "on" button. He pressed her finger against it and the goggles activated. "Wow," she said. "these things are really cool. I can see everything."

"Okay, to turn them off, it's this button," he said, moving her finger to a different position.

As quickly as everything had been cast in a green hue, it all vanished again. "Roger," Wren said.

"Now, whatever happens, don't turn them on until they've taken out the spotlights, otherwise you'll be blinded and no good to anyone."

"I can see how Lucy fell for you. You really know how to make a girl feel special."

"Yeah, it's a gift."

They carried on walking slowly along the edge of the cliff. Wren caught Mike's shoulder, "Hey!" she said.

"What's wrong?"

"Seriously. I'm not an idiot, Mike. I know the chances of us pulling this thing off are like a million to one. I just want to say thank you. Nobody but my sister has ever stepped up for me the way you did."

"It's like I said, you're one of us, Wren, so no thanks necessary. Plus, I don't want to live in a world where this stuff goes on. One day I might tell you about my childhood, but for now, let's just say bullies and men who abuse women and think of them as property…" Mike's fist clenched and a familiar hatred began to come over him. "They have no place sharing the same air as the rest of us."

Wren went cold as Mike spoke. "You mean your dad? I heard a little bit about what happened to you."

"Really?"

"I wasn't prying—it just came up. I…I'm sorry. My dad was about the best a girl could wish for. I can't imagine what it must have been like for you and your sister."

"There's not much further for us to go," Mike said, changing the subject and continuing along the clifftop.

"I didn't mean to upset you."

"You didn't."

"I just meant, I think it's pretty amazing the way both of you turned out. I mean, you could have been so different."

"Different how?" Mike asked, stopping once again.

"Different like them. Like these men."

"I've done stuff in my life that I'm not proud of, but I would never become one of them."

"That's what I mean," Wren said.

"Just because I'm not like one of them, Wren, it doesn't make me a good man. I've got a lot of skeletons in my closet and a lot of them are going to surface tonight. When we take the barricade, stay with the others; you don't want to be anywhere near me when this kicks off."

Wren did not need to see Mike's face; she could hear the intensity and foreboding in his words. He carried on walking again, eventually drawing parallel to where the powerful spotlight beams were shining from below. He pulled the rope back out and started to tie it around his waist, but then noticed the sprawling shadow cast by a rock to the right of him. He walked over to it and tugged. It was not a separate boulder, but part of the cliff itself. He looped the rope around, tying it firmly.

"This is perfect," he said. "We can abseil down as far as the rope will let us, then we can just climb down the rest of the netting. That's going to save us time."

"Goody!" was all Wren could manage.

Mike took the radio from his rucksack. He looked at Wren briefly, then hit the talk button. "We're in position," he said. "Standby!"

*

Jake had curled up on one of the beds and gone to sleep shortly after dinner, but sleep was the last thing on Sammy's mind. When the door to the operating room opened, she stopped in mid-step. She was heading towards the kitchen with Sophie to make a cup of tea so the two patients could take their nighttime medication. Sophie stopped too, and the pair of them stood there, frozen like statues waiting for someone...anyone to emerge from the doorway. Raj appeared in his blue scrubs. The mask had been pulled down from his mouth and as he walked out into the corridor, he pulled the surgical cap from his head. The generator had been running all day and the lights were still burning brightly in the hallway for Sammy and Sophie to see the look on his face.

At first, he did not even notice them, he was too wrapped up in his own thoughts. But then, as he lifted his face towards the nurse, and finally to Sammy, they could both see the tears that had welled in his eyes. For more than a heartbeat, Sammy willed herself to believe that they were tears of happiness, but as Raj's breaking voice said, "I'm sorry," she knew her worst fears had been realised.

She ran down the hallway past him and despite his protestations, she burst into the room to see another of the young nurses, along with Stephanie, carefully placing the surgical instruments into a tray ready for sterilisation. Sammy ran up to the operating table; she was crying long before she reached it. Raj had already sewn the wound up and the bloody covers had been replaced by clean ones. Sammy looked at Sarah; she looked peaceful, almost as if she was sleeping. Her skin was always pale, but now it was nearly snow-white, the fine colouration made Sammy cry even more.

The little girl put her hand on Sarah's head and recoiled immediately; her temperature had already started to drop. She had hugged and kissed and cuddled and held hands with Sarah a thousand times, but as she felt the cold flesh beneath her own, she realised Sarah would never hold her again.

Sammy felt a presence in the doorway and turned to look. It was Sophie. She looked at the distraught little girl and was flabbergasted for a moment to see the other women were not rushing to comfort her, but then she looked closer and saw that even while they were busy clearing away the instruments and cleaning down the surfaces, their shoulders shook with weeping.

Sophie walked to the side of the table and took Sammy's hand. "We were going to go into the woods this afternoon. We were going to pick mushrooms. It was our day together. Why would somebody take her away from me? Haven't I lost enough? I lost my mum, I lost my dad, I lost my gran. isn't that enough? Did they have to take Sarah too?" she said, breaking down.

Sophie knelt down and pulled the grieving child towards her, holding her tight. "I'm so sorry, Sammy. I'm sorry, sweetheart."

*

Raj stepped out of the static caravan, his breath tremored as he exhaled. He brought his hands up to his eyes and wiped away the salty streaks. He walked in a dark, blurry haze towards the lantern-lit figure of Talikha, who was in one of the other wards, carefully tucking in the bedding of an elderly patient. He paused outside the window just watching her. He had failed, and right this second, he did not want her words of comfort, he wanted to suffer. He deserved to suffer.

Approaching voices drifted through the air. He recognised those of Barnes and Beth, but right this minute, he did not want to see anyone. He did not want to face anyone. Raj ran for cover to the side of one of the wards. He saw their silhouettes head across towards ward number one, then made a break for it through the clump of woodland at the back of the hospital to the Haven Arms.

He entered the pub through the back door and headed straight to the bar.

"That was quick; did you forget something?" Jenny said. "Oh, Raj, it's you. Is everything okay?" He emerged from the shadows and into the white glow cast by the rechargeable lanterns. She could see sadness painted on his face. "Oh no," she said.

"I think...I think I'd like a drink," Raj said.

Jenny pulled the stool beside her out from the bar and patted the seat for Raj to join her. He walked across and sat down. She poured him half a glass of the thick amber liquid. "I don't know if I've got any tears left in me today," Jenny said.

Raj lifted the glass and drank the whisky down in one go. "Then I will cry for both of us."

*

"He's been gone a long time," Jules said, arching her head up to look towards the door.

"He'll be back and I don't think he'll be in the mood to play anymore," Emma replied.

On cue, the lock disengaged and the door opened, revealing Webb. He stood there in black jeans and a black roll-neck sweater. His thumb and hand were heavily bandaged and as he walked into the room his eye twitched.

"Good thinking. If you piss yourself again, it will be harder to spot in black jeans," Jules scoffed.

Webb said nothing, he walked up to her and without warning unleashed a powerful blow on her breast bone. Jules shrieked with pain. "You little fucker. Untie me and see if you want to try that again."

"Oh, I'm going to untie you. I'm going to untie all of you," he said, noticing his thumb on the floor and bending down to pick it up. His face twitched a second time as he looked towards Emma. "Up until a few months back, we had a surgeon here who might have been able to reattach this, but now, I fear, I am going to spend the rest of my life with just one thumb."

"Yeah, and you know where you can stick it," Jules said, for which she received another powerful hammer blow in the same place. She coughed and wheezed and in between the defiance and bravado there was writhing pain, too, but she did her best not to show it.

Webb was far more introspective now, almost as if he was thinking out loud as he spoke. "As I was saying before I was…interrupted, I'm going to untie you. I've managed to stem the bleeding from my hand, but I am not really in the mood to carry on here this evening."

"What are you planning to do with us?" Emma asked.

Webb's head turned towards her slowly and menacingly. "Nothing. Tonight, I am going to do nothing to you," he said as the door to the stairwell further down the hall squeaked open and clattered shut. A few seconds later, Barker walked into the room followed by five armed guards. Webb's second in command walked straight towards Emma, unfurled a length of duct tape and placed it firmly over her bloodstained lips, then did the same with Jules. The other men continued down the line with the duct tape and before long, all the women were breathing heavily through their noses and frantically trying to make themselves heard through the gags. "However, as a kind of celebration of your arrival, I've decided to give the rest of the girls in the Fun House the night off. You six are going to be the sole attractions for the men tonight," he said with a sickening grin on his face. "I dare say you'll be worn out by tomorrow morning when I come for you, but as you've spoiled our original plans for this evening, it's only right that the boys get to show you a good time." He looked towards Barker. "Take them away," he said, heading back out.

The four women who had been residents at the Fun House before began screaming and pleading beneath the gags as the men untied them. Emma and Jules cast knowing looks towards one another. They had no intention of being any man's slave. Whether they lived or died, they would not enter that hall.

*

When Shaw, Barnes and Beth reached the doorway to the operating room, Sammy was draped across Sarah. Her tears had soaked through the light blue cover and she did not hear them as they walked in. Sophie had stroked Sammy's head for a long while, thinking the young girl had drifted off to sleep, but she had not. Her eyes were open and a thousand thoughts were flickering through her head.

"Sammy?" Beth said.

The little girl slowly brought her head up and her red eyes looked straight towards Beth. She had known Beth longer than nearly everyone else in Safe Haven, and she ran to her now. Beth knelt down and the pair held each other tightly. "She's cold. Her skin's cold already," was all Sammy could say.

"I'm sorry, Sammy. I'm so sorry," she said squeezing the little girl even tighter.

"I haven't told Jake yet," Sammy said.

"Don't worry about that just now. Jake was asleep when we came in."

"I wish Emma was here."

"I know you do, Sammy, sweetheart. We all do. But you know what, she'd be proud of you. You were here for Sarah. She was never alone, she had family here, and that's going to make Emma feel better when she finds out."

"Will you stay with me for a while?" Sammy asked.

Beth looked back to Barnes and Shaw at the door, who both nodded and made their exits, then Sophie and the other nurses left as well. Beth took hold of Sammy's hand and they both went to stand by the bed. "Do you think we can bury her next to Nana Fletcher?"

"That will really be up to Emma, Sammy. She needs to decide what to do now, but whatever happens, I know she'll be looked after."

Sammy's hand tightened around Beth's. "She looks like she's asleep."

"Well Sammy, she's at rest now. She won't feel pain, or fear, or loss ever again. She'll never have to worry, she'll never have to fight, she'll never have to suffer."

"I know you're trying to make me feel better, and I know what you say is true, but…"

"But what Sammy?"

"But she'll also never feel happy, she'll never laugh.

She'll never see Emma again. Nothing's ever going to be the same."

21

Wren and Mike crouched down as they approached the edge of the cliff. She handed four bolts to Mike and loaded a further two onto her pistol crossbows.

"Explain to me again why you're here if I'm the one doing all the shooting," she whispered.

"Moral support...and to reload your crossbows," Mike replied.

"So you're a bit like a caddy," she said with a smile.

"Yes Wren, I'm like your caddy...you cheeky little gobshite. Okay, I'm going to radio through to Bruiser. Are you ready?"

Wren reached out her hand and placed it on Mike's arm. "Just give me a minute."

"Are you okay?"

"I'll be fine, I just.... It's a long time since I've taken somebody's life. It doesn't exactly come easily to me."

"Are you going to be able to do this, Wren? Cos if you're not we need a Plan B."

"I'll be fine, just give me a minute," she said, trying to get her breathing under control. "It seems to come pretty easy to you." She regretted the words as soon as they had left her lips. "I didn't mean it like that."

"Don't worry yourself," he said.

"I'm sorry. I shouldn't have said something like that. I'm sorry."

Mike reached through the dark and found Wren's hand. "You're a really sweet girl Wren. You're a good, decent, honourable person with a conscience, and that's something you should be proud of."

"You are too."

"No Wren, no I'm not. You're right about me. Whereas you're agonising over taking the lives of these men, I can't wait to get the job done. They're scum. They're bottom feeders, living off the hard work of others, preying on the weak, using people, hurting people. Whereas you're wondering whether you should be doing this at all, there isn't a doubt in my mind that this world would be a better place without them. That's what I thought before; now they've got my sister and Jules in there...well now it's become something completely different. Now you're going to see what I'm really like, because the second someone hurts my family or my friends, well then, it's a new game and all bets are off."

Wren slid her hand away from Mike's. "You're scaring me talking like that."

"I'm just warning you. You haven't seen me at my worst. Don't put me on a pedestal."

"Duly noted."

"Okay, are you ready?"

"Oh yeah, that was a great pep talk; I feel much better now, thanks."

Mike brought the radio up to his mouth and hit the talk button. "We're ready. Repeat...we are ready. Over!"

*

The radio hissed and Hughes sprang into action. He reached into his rucksack and grabbed the suppressor, fixing it to the end of the SA80.

"Okay, does everybody know what they're doing?" he asked, moving nearer to the road.

Each of the women answered yes, and as he crept through the darkness, he could feel Lucy's presence behind him. "Good luck," she said.

"It's not me who needs the luck, it's Wren and Soft Lad. I've got the easy part. Taking out four spotlights is a doddle; it's not as if they're moving targets. Are you sure the others won't let us down?"

"They don't really have that much to do, but they're good. I think the slimmest of chances of escape gives them more hope than they've had in a long time, so they're going to do everything they can."

"Coco can barely lift that bloody rifle," Hughes said.

"I know, but if it sounds like there are more of us who can shoot than there actually are, that might work in our favour. It's all about perception," Lucy replied.

"True enough. Okay, here goes nothing," Hughes said, crouching down and sweeping the barrel of his rifle around the corner. The barricade was a hundred metres down the road and although the spotlight cast a powerful beam, Hughes was still in the shadows as he took aim. The sound of breaking glass masked the muted shot of the suppressed rifle, and all four men standing on top of the barricade looked towards the extinguished spotlight in confusion at first, as if maybe a bulb had blown. By the time the second spotlight went out, the four men had been reduced to three, but the three had no idea of that at the time. One of them ran for the radio, and as they watched him fall, the other two reached for their rifles. The remaining spotlights blew out, and suddenly the men were fumbling in the dark.

*

Wren brought the night vision goggles down over her eyes as Mike passed her a reloaded pistol crossbow. Before the third man had even had the chance to raise his rifle towards whoever was further on up the road firing at them, a bolt entered his chest. He let out a pained gasp and fell heavily on top of the metal shipping container with a clatter, leaving one last man standing.

He looked around in the dark, his eyes still not fully adjusted to the night. He held the rifle to his chest like a small boy holding a teddy bear.

"Please," he begged, "Please!"

Wren paused. "Do it, Wren!" Mike demanded.

"He's surrendering," she replied.

"Do it now!"

"I...can't."

Mike grabbed the night vision goggles from Wren's head and now it was her whose eyes were struggling to adjust. He placed them on his head, grabbed hold of the rope and began to abseil down the rock, leaving Wren alone and night-blind. "Drop your fucking weapon now!" Mike demanded, turning his head to look at the man while he continued to descend.

The man immediately dropped the rifle and threw his hands up. He was alone, he was blind, and he was facing an unknown force. Mike came to the end of the rope and grabbed hold of the rockfall netting, climbing down the rest of the cliff face and finally landing on the ground. Without pause he climbed the steps onto the top of the cargo containers and saw the man standing there with his hands still in the air, searching out the darkness for the source of the sound.

"Please," he said as he heard feet hit the metal surface. "I won't put up any resistance. Please."

"If you want to live you'll do as I ask, and if you don't think I'm serious, ask your three dead friends."

"Anything. Tell me what you want."

Mike had intended for all four guards to be put down, so this was a wrinkle in the plan, but he realised it could work in his favour. "How often do you call in?"

"Used to be every hour, but it's been every half hour since the breach."

"When are you next due to call?"

"I...soon."

"When?"

"I don't have a watch. Smitty had the watch."

Mike looked at his own. "It's half-past."

"Now...we're meant to call now."

Mike looked towards the first figure who had fallen. The radio was on a plastic chair, just out of his reach. Mike picked it up and shoved it into the other man's chest. "Make the call."

"I..."

"Make the fucking call!"

The man felt around the radio like he was reading braille and eventually brought it up to his mouth, hitting the talk button. "Gate one—all clear," he said.

"Is that you, Preston?" came the voice from the other end.

"Y-yeah."

"It's me, Lammy. Treat in store for you tonight boy. We got fresh meat in the pit, and an old favourite, too. Vicky's back." Preston remained silent. "Did you hear me?"

"Er yeah, fresh meat."

"You're not turning queer on us, are you? You're usually first in line."

Preston stood there with the radio in his hand wishing a hole would appear to swallow him up.

"I'll be there. Smitty's just cut his hand open on a fucking tin, useless bastard. I'll have to go."

"Alright, my crew's taking over at ten-thirty. See you then."

"Yeah, see you."

The radio crackled and Mike took it away from Preston. "That was nice, that whole Smitty cutting his hand open bit, great improvisation."

"Listen, that guy's an arsehole, he doesn't know what he's talking about."

Mike bent down and picked up a lantern. He pulled the infrared goggles off and put them in his rucksack, then switched the light on, placing it on the plastic chair next to the radio, revealing himself to the tall, well-built guard for the first time.

*

"What the fuck?" Hughes said, looking down the scope of his rifle towards the top of the containers.

"What's happening?" Lucy asked.

"I don't know. This wasn't part of the plan. I was meant to take the lights out, Wren was meant to take the guards out, and then Mike was meant to open the gate and radio through the all-clear to us."

"What's he doing?"

"There's Mike and one of the guards stood on top of a container."

"Where's Wren?"

Hughes panned the rifle around. "I can just about make her out. She hasn't climbed down yet."

"What the hell is he up to?"

"Oh shit!"

*

"So, you're always the first one in line, are you?" Mike said, slipping his rucksack from his shoulders.

"No. He's always the first one in line. I…I've always treated the girls with respect. I…" Preston began to back away.

"You've got my sister in there."

"It's not us. It's Webb. He's…he…"

"He's what?"

"He's sick! He's sick, man…he doesn't speak for the rest of us!"

"And yet you follow him. What does that make you?"

"You don't understand, he's ruthless!"

"You have no idea what that word means, but you're about to find out."

Preston threw a punch, completely taking Mike off guard. "Fuck you!" he shouted, reaching for his rifle, but

Mike rugby tackled him. Preston landed heavily on the metal roof of the shipping container.

"See I knew you wouldn't be able to keep the frightened rabbit thing up for long," Mike said, grabbing hold of Preston's left wrist and pinning it down.

"I haven't got time for this shit," Preston said, unleashing a powerful blow with his right fist against the side of Mike's head. Mike went toppling, temporarily dazed and Preston jumped to his feet. "Didn't you hear? I've got your sister waiting for me." He lunged for his rifle again, but Mike swept his right foot around hard, knocking Preston's legs from under him. "Arggghhh!" he cried, landing heavily on his ribs. As he turned over Mike was on top of him, and this time, he pinned both of Preston's wrists down.

"Y'see, my friend up there, she's a sweet girl. When you said please and put your hands up, it appealed to the part of her that says there's good in everyone. But you and I know better don't we? We know that some people are bad all the way through."

Preston continued to writhe, desperate to wriggle at least one of his wrists free. "You don't stand a chance. You're outnumbered ten to one at least and we've got more bullets than there are leaves in the forest. If you go now, I'll give you a five-minute head start before I call it in. I'm fair like that," Preston said with a snarl on his face.

"You know what you need to do, don't you?" Mike looked to his left; there was Fry crouching down beside him with that mad glint in his eyes. The same mad glint Mike could feel in his own.

"Yes," Mike replied.

"What?" Preston asked, suddenly confused.

"Well? What are you waiting for?" Fry asked.

Mike unleashed a headbutt on Preston, the sound from his cracking nose ushered in a second's silence before a pained scream gurgled into the air as blood ran down Preston's throat. Mike let go of his captive's right wrist and smashed his fist down on his skull like a sledgehammer.

"You—" *punch* "will—" *crack* "never—" *smash* "lay—" *crack* "a—" *crack* "finger—" *splat* "on—" *splat* "my—" *squelch* "sister!" Mike stopped. His breathing was erratic, his fist was coated in blood and he had even more splattered over his face, neck and arms. The figure beneath him was still conscious, but only just. His features had been pummelled to an unrecognisable gory Halloween mask and he desperately gargled for breath as his airways filled with blood. Distorted words and pleas issued from him and the one eye that was not just a swollen slit, spouted tears that glistened in the lantern light.

"You hear him?" Fry said, putting his fingers up to his ear. "You hear him pleading? Oh, he was so sure, so full of himself just a few minutes ago…now look at him. Crying and spluttering like a little girl."

"I hear him," Mike said under his breath.

"I don't think you do," Fry said, standing up and stepping across towards Preston's head. He raised his boot.

"Nooo!" Mike growled.

"Going soft on me, are you boy?"

"No!" Mike said standing. "He's mine." Mike walked opposite to where Fry was standing, raised his boot and brought it down once, twice, three times. He felt give with the fourth strike and knew then that Preston's skull had caved. He looked across towards Fry, but Fry had disappeared. He looked up towards Wren, who he could just make out. She peered over the side of the cliff on all fours. Her mouth was open in horror. Mike went across to one of the other guards, who had a similar build to his own, and peeled off the man's jacket, putting it on himself before reaching down and pulling the rucksack back onto his shoulders. He removed the sidearms from the four dead men, along with the spare magazines, and put them all in his rucksack. He then clambered down from the shipping container and opened the gate. Mike unclipped the radio from his belt. "Gate's open. We've got about twenty-five minutes before they're next due to report. I'm going in." He placed the radio down on the ground and ran into the darkness.

22

"What the hell are you talking about?" Hughes demanded. "Mike! Mike! That's not the plan. What are you talking about? Mike!" Hughes clipped the radio back onto his belt and stood up. "I swear to god, if we make it through this, I'm going to kill that little bastard."

"You're going to have to get in line," Lucy replied.

"I suppose the only thing we can do is carry on with the rest of the plan," Hughes said, heading back towards the others. Lucy looked down the road towards the blockade. The soft light of the lantern still glowed, but beyond it, there was a night darker than any she remembered. She let out a long sigh and followed Hughes.

"Okay, we're ready. Any questions?" Hughes asked, he flicked on a small torch and clipped it to his shirt pocket.

"You'll definitely close the gate as soon as we're through?" Coco asked.

"You don't have to worry about any of that. Now remember, follow Lucy's lead. When she heads back out, make sure you're behind her. Is everybody ready?" Hughes looked around at the faces. Coco, Prisha and Sandy all looked terrified. They had undergone horrors that Hughes could not even imagine, but they had not faced anything like this before. "Right then, let's go." Prisha and Hughes each picked up a bale of the homemade spears that had been bundled together with twine. Hughes placed his on his back, choosing to carry his rifle rather than sling it. "I guess this is it then," he said to Lucy.

"I guess so," she replied, putting her arms around him. "Be careful," she said, squeezing him tight.

"You too. I…"

"What?"

"I don't understand why he does this stuff. I don't know what the hell's wrong with him."

"His sister's in there. This was never going to be a walk in the park."

"But we had a plan," Hughes said.

"Something changed it."

"Yeah, no kidding."

"We'll stick to our part—it's all we can do."

"And if Mike changes the plan again, then we do what we need to."

"One of these days he's going to get us killed. You do realise that don't you?"

"Let's just hope it's not today."

*

The road continued downwards for a while and eventually curved around a bend and into more forest. Mike pulled the night vision goggles back out of his bag and placed them on his head. He continued for another minute and then realised he could hear music. This was not like the tinny tone he had heard coming from the small speakers on the drones earlier in the day; it almost sounded like a rave.

Mike ran faster, and as specks of light began to prick the black blanket ahead of him, he removed the night vision goggles, stuffing them into his rucksack. The music got louder and the lights became brighter and soon he was on the edge of the town. It was like stepping back in time.

The street lights had been replaced by lanterns that hung from wire, but the strobing, multicoloured lights that danced through the windows of the large pub halfway up the street emitted a radiant normality. Mike ducked into the trees that bordered the edge of the town centre and main road. A memory dragged him back to this place. He had been here once when he was younger. On his way up to see his gran, Alex had stopped off here. They had bought a Chinese takeaway which they all agreed had been the worst thing they had ever tasted, but if nothing else, it had filled their bellies.

"Think, Mike, think!"

Mike crossed over to the other side of the road and practically hugged the buildings as he continued towards the bar. At the top end of the street he could hear, if not see, a group of drunks playing the fool, but now he was in the thick of it, he realised he needed more information before making his next move. He carried on to the alehouse and looked beyond the frosted glass of the doors to the multitude of figures inside. It was crowded and still relatively early. He remembered back to earlier in the day. If there were eighty-ish men in Loch Uig in total, well over half must be in this pub right now. As the night went on, the crowd would dissipate. Some would go home, some would be on sentry duty, some would go across to the Fun House, but right now, they were in the pub, enjoying themselves and not suspecting a thing. A barricaded door and a well-placed Molotov cocktail could significantly reduce their numbers, and he could wait in the shadows, picking them off as they tried to escape. It was tempting...very tempting.

*

The lights on the quad bikes bobbed up and down as they bounced over the uneven terrain of the forest floor. The motors rumbled, but to make sure the metalheads really knew they were there, Lucy pressed the heel of her palm against the horn. They had been driving around for several minutes before the first figure emerged from the shadows, quickly followed by a second. Lucy immediately turned and signalled for Coco to turn too. Sandy was sat behind Coco for no other reason than, if she had followed Hughes and Prisha down to the barricade, her bad leg would have got them all killed, or at least her, if they needed to make a run for it.

Lucy brought the radio up to her mouth and pressed the talk button. "That's it, we've found them. We're heading back. Make sure you're ready," she shouted over the noise of the engine.

"We're ready here," Hughes replied. "Just be careful."

Lucy put the radio back down and looked behind her as more figures began to chase them through the shadows. She slowed the pace a little; not only did she not want to lose the metalheads, if Coco and Sandy ran into any trouble, they would not be able to look after themselves.

They continued for a few seconds more and Lucy began to relax as they were back on a track she recognised. She gave a fleeting look back to see Coco was keeping up, then turned to face the front once more. That's when she saw more metalheads approaching from multiple directions. They were surrounded.

*

"Don't worry ladies," Webb said as the women were dragged from the examination tables to their feet. "I'm an early riser, so I'll make sure you're collected at the crack of dawn tomorrow." A smile reappeared on his face. Now the women were gagged, he felt some of his bravado returning.

Jules struggled free from the man who was holding her and kicked out hard, but Webb jumped back, and the momentum from the kick knocked her off balance. She fell to the floor, landing heavily on her cable-tied hands. She let out a stifled grunt of pain and Webb and the other men laughed.

Barker dragged Jules to her feet and was about to strike her, but Webb caught his arm. "No," he said. "Such a nice face...she'll be popular with the men at the Fun House. Don't worry, she'll pay tomorrow. Perhaps I'll give her the procedure without anaesthetic." Webb smiled, but he was the only one. The men knew what he did, but they also knew he kept food on the table, beer in the pub, lights on the streets, bullets in the armoury. And he kept them safe, just like Fry had done.

They were both maniacs, but maniacs were what this new world demanded.

*

Two men stumbled out of the pub door and Mike clung to the wall. They did not notice him as they made their way up the road. They crossed to the other side and turned left down an adjacent street. Mike checked to make sure the coast was clear, gave one last look towards the pub, and then sprinted after them. As he reached the turn, he saw them crossing the road and entering the carpark to a substantial, single-storey building. Lights were on inside, and as Mike watched, he heard the pub doors open again further down the street, behind him. He glanced back to see a larger group of men exiting the establishment this time. He ran down the hill towards the single-storey building. The street was dimly lit by the lanterns, but it was bright enough for him to see the sign for Loch Uig Community Hall crossed out in black spray paint, and FUN HOUSE printed untidily underneath. A shiver ran down Mike's spine, and as the noise of the group who had just left the bar got louder and another group appeared at the bottom of the street, he realised he could not wait any longer. He needed to act.

*

Lucy drew the Glock from the back of her jeans and began to fire, but instantly found that the terrain was too uneven to get any kind of decent aim. She brought the quad bike to a juddering halt, raised the pistol again and was about to take a shot when she heard a high-pitched scream from behind her. She turned to see the other quad heading straight towards her. There were a number of silhouettes in pursuit, but Lucy's eyes were drawn to the one that had just grabbed Sandy in its claw-like hands. Sandy, whose arms were clasped around Coco's waist, held on, but the RAM was too powerful and they were both dragged from the bike. Lucy pivoted to take aim as the figures disappeared into the darkness and the screams got louder. In that instant, she knew it was too late. The quad bike veered off, slowed and stopped, and she could see the silhouettes converging on where the two women had disappeared.

Lucy's heart was racing as she turned back to her direction of travel. The pause had allowed the creatures that were heading in her direction to gain ground. She fired, one, two, three shots towards the creatures' knees and legs, causing black explosions in the quad bike's headlights. Two of the creatures stumbled, causing the one behind them to fall, too. She did not wait to see them rise to their feet. Instead, she adjusted her angle of travel and sped full throttle through the gap she had created. She caught movement out of the corner of her eye as she passed where the beasts had fallen, but now there was a clearing ahead and nothing in front of her but forest. She carried on for a while into the small, tree-lined arena then looped around. The headlights cut through the forest's blackness; she could just make out the remainder of the throng, their shining metal heads dipping and rising as they stole the last vestiges of life from Coco and Sandy. Lucy banged her palm down hard on the horn and the sound echoed through the woods, dragging every last one of the creatures from their frenzied attack. She could not see their eyes through the gauze, but she could feel their malevolent gazes upon her as they began to charge.

Lucy steered the bike three hundred and sixty degrees, pounded the horn one more time, and moved off, keeping a steady course and speed, making sure the creatures could keep her in sight. She kept looking back, but could only see a shifting, black mass behind her getting closer. She increased the throttle to gain a little more distance, and that's when the motor began to splutter.

*

One of the guards pushed Vicky hard through the entrance of the hotel. The door flew open and jammed, while Vicky, bound and gagged, toppled and skidded across the pavement, ripping her already ragged clothing. Five of the guards laughed, while Barker barked: "Stop pissing about and get her to her feet."

The young guard who had used her as a human battering ram roughly dragged the skinny young woman up and pointed her in their direction of travel. Now they were outside, the guards kept firm hands grasped around the women's arms. There was no doubt they would try to run, given half an opportunity.

They walked through the carpark and Emma looked back to the hotel. It was an ugly, modern-looking building, out of place with the quaintness of the rest of Loch Uig, but her eyes were not looking at the architecture, they were drawn to the top floor—the only floor of the hotel that was lit in its entirety.

She turned back around and caught Jules's gaze. They both nodded and in perfect synchronicity, kicked their right foot back with everything they had. Emma made contact with Barker, but the big man saw it coming and managed to brace himself, keeping a tight hold of her arm. Jules's guard was less alert. He let out a cry of pain as her boot heel dug hard into his shin. His fingers sprang open and Jules began to run, but Barker reached his long arm out and grabbed her by the scruff of the neck, pulling her back. Both women struggled, but the big man held them there until the other guard gathered himself.

"Soz, chief," the guard said.

"Watch what you're fucking doing. You've got one job. Is that too much for you? You want me to call in reinforcements?" The other men laughed as the two women continued to struggle.

"No. Won't happen again, chief," he said, rubbing his shin.

"Make sure it doesn't. And you," Barker said, pulling Emma's hair so hard that she was forced to turn around and face him. "Another stunt like that, and you'll be working the Funhouse solo until Webb comes for you tomorrow morning."

Emma wanted to spit in Barker's face. She wanted to bite and scratch and maul him like an animal. It was a primal urge; she wanted to tear him apart for what they had done to these women, for what was happening to her, Jules and the others. But all she could do was flex against the restraints and bundle up her hatred into her stare. A smile appeared on Barker's face. "Oh, you're a feisty one. You're going to be fun," he said menacingly.

Emma glanced towards Jules, who was now back in the grip of the other guard. Her head was bowed, and she could not see the tears that were running down Jules's face, but she could see the jerking movement of her head as she tried desperately to hold them back, to be strong. Emma would not give them the satisfaction. They wanted her weak, they wanted to humiliate her, and once they would have managed, but not now. They carried on walking along the road, and as they left the carpark and the group spread out into a line almost side by side, she could hear the sounds of the other women sobbing behind their gags.

They turned onto a more brightly lit street. At the top of it mulled a group of drunks, jostling each other as they laughed and joked. A third of the way up the street was a single-storey, brightly lit building.

"Here we go, girls," Barker said, laughing, "Welcome to the Fun House." The other men laughed too, and the women who had been here before, began to strain, and struggle, as memories came flooding back to them.

"Come on now, Vicky," said one of the men, "I always thought you liked it here." The guards laughed again.

Emma's resolve dipped a little. How could people revel in the misery of others so much? This new world had brought out the very best of the best and the very worst of the worst. She gulped as they moved nearer, and she felt Barker's fingers tighten even more around her arm. He anticipated that she would try making another move, but Emma now realised it was futile. No matter what she did, she would not escape; they would not kill her, they only wanted her to suffer. But she would cast her mind elsewhere. She would be back at home with her Sarah, walking hand in hand on the beach. Whatever they did, whatever gross, sick acts, they could never take what was inside her head away from her.

That's when a tear did run down her face, because it was then that she realised she would never see Sarah again. She would die in this place and never get the chance to make things right with her, tell her one last time that she loved her. She felt the stinging tear roll down her cheek, over the duct tape and onto her chin. She would give anything to see her one last time.

"Hey, word must have got round. There's a queue forming," said one of the guards as they all looked at the solitary man stood in front of the community hall noticeboard.

"Who is that?" Barker demanded as they continued to walk.

"Looks a bit like Smitty," one of them said.

"No, Smitty's at the gate," said another.

"If that little shit's skipped his duties again, I am going to cut his balls off and stick them down his throat," Barker said.

Emma looked towards the figure stood in front of the noticeboard, as he in turn looked towards them, and then back up the street towards the approaching group of drunks. She stopped in her tracks and screamed a muffled scream through the duct tape. Jules looked towards her, then followed her eyes back towards the man.

"Too late to run now, darlin'" said a guard.

Emma could feel her skin turn raw as she used all the strength her jaw muscles could muster to break the seal of the duct tape around her mouth. She manoeuvred, and chewed, and stretched to find the smallest gap in those split seconds as she knew what was about to happen.

When she could feel the smallest whistle of cold air tickle the back of her throat she screamed, "Get down!"

The women all looked towards her. She did not dive or jump or lurch, she just dropped as if all muscles, all ligaments, all will had been abracadabra'd out of her.

Jules did the same, then the other women. Three of the guards attempted to drag them back to their feet while the other three just looked, baffled by such a feeble protest that would do nothing but delay their fate by a few seconds.

The youngest of the men, an eighteen-year-old who had spent his life in correctional institutes until joining this nirvana for lowlifes, looked towards Barker for orders. "Get—" Barker's head exploded like a watermelon being hit by a high-speed train. The young guard's mouth dropped open, not hearing the boom of the shotgun until it was too late. Barker's almost headless body collapsed to the side, and that's when the second boom sounded. The young man felt something warm and sticky on the back of his head. He turned to see his best friend, now minus any distinguishing facial features flying backwards through the air.

A third, fourth and fifth shot sounded in quick succession, and the boy looked around him in terror as the rest of the guards reeled and fell in gory horror. He fumbled to bring his rifle up as he turned to look towards the direction of the sound. The man from the noticeboard was now just a few feet away, pointing a shotgun towards him. As shouting started from the group at the top of the street, who were sobering up at alarming speed, the boy threw the rifle down in front to him and put his hands up.

Mike placed the barrel against the younger man's head and did not even let the plea escape his mouth before pulling the trigger. Blood, bone and brain matter showered Vicky and another woman who had scuttled across the tarmac.

He turned back around to see the men at the top of the street running. They would be heading back towards the pub to get help. Shadows were moving in the Fun House, and Mike knew it would not be long before the street was swarming with armed men. Whether it went to plan or not, they were in it now. The night would not be over until their enemies were dead, or they were dead.

23

Hughes and Wren looked at each other. They had anticipated hearing the odd shot from Lucy's gun to alert the metalheads, to get them following the quad bikes, but they had hoped whatever move Mike made would be in silence, at least until they got there.

"Do you think that was him?" Wren asked.

"I know it was him," Hughes replied. "That was his shotgun; these guys use army-issue rifles. Mad fucking bast—" He stopped and looked at Wren, "sorry, love."

"I do swear y'know, I'm not like…six. And under the circumstances, I think you're spot on with your analysis," Prisha just looked at them both, not sure how to respond, so she stayed silent.

Hughes looked back up the road into the darkness. "Come on Lucy…where the hell are you?"

"What's that?" Wren asked, pointing to a mere slip of dancing light as it emerged from the trees.

Hughes squinted into the darkness. "Well it's not a bloody quad bike," he said as the light grew closer.

"Ungh!" screamed the voice from the distant shadows.

"It's Lucy," Hughes said. "What the hell's she saying?"

"Ruuun!!!"

*

Mike pulled one of the machetes out of his backpack and cut Emma's restraints, then Jules's. He handed Jules the machete, and she began to free the other women. Emma picked up one of the rifles and Mike handed her a Glock from his bag as she ripped the remaining duct tape from her face. "Let's get their weapons and head back around the corner," she shouted. The women took the guns and followed Emma with Mike at the rear, looking back towards the village hall as the door swung open.

He took the corner before anyone laid eyes on him and ran straight into Emma's waiting arms. "I was so scared I wouldn't see you again!"

Mike broke from her embrace. "You don't get rid of me that easily. The others are on the way too." For the first time in hours, relief warmed Emma's insides.

"In my life, I have never been so happy to see you," Jules said, grabbing his face and giving him a rough kiss on the cheek. "I thought that was it."

"We're not out of the woods yet," he said as shouting in the street began to get louder.

"What's the plan?" Emma asked.

"There's a plan?" Mike asked.

"Funny."

"They're heading here with the spears and the RAMs."

Jules dragged him around to face her, "That's the plan? You're going to overrun the town with RAMs?"

"It's not as mad as it sounds," Mike replied.

"I'm happy to hear that, cos it sounds pretty fucking mad to me."

"Look, right now we need to get into that hall," Mike said. "I've got more weapons in the bag. The more of us who are armed, the better."

He peeked his head around the corner to see ten men, in various states of dress, looking up and down the street to see if they could fathom where the attack had come from. Only four of the men were armed, holding their weapons out in front of them as if they were some kind of miracle shield.

"Not all of them are armed," he said, ducking back around.

"Usually it's just guards who stay armed in the compound. Too many drunken gunfights over card games and shit. It was like the Wild West around here some nights. If they're not on duty or about to go on duty, they won't have a gun," Vicky said.

"How many guards for the hall?" Mike asked.

"Four."

He looked towards Emma and Jules. "There are four of them with weapons out on the street. This will be our best chance." He turned to look at the other women. "Do any of you know how to shoot?"

"I do," replied Amy. "I was on the road a while before they got me. I can shoot a rifle," she said, placing the butt of the SA80 she was holding against her shoulder.

"Okay," Mike said. "Four against four. We don't stop shooting until they're all on the ground, capisce?"

"Hark at Don Corleone," Jules replied, checking the safety and placing her finger on the trigger.

"Give me a gun!" Vicky said.

Mike reached into the rucksack and pulled out a Glock. "Just point and shoot and keep shooting," he said. "Anyone else?"

One of the women raised the machete she had taken from Jules and the other put out her hand. "I'll take one."

"Okay," Mike said as he finished loading the pump-action shotgun. "Don't waste rounds, but same thing—point and shoot until they stop moving. Shock and awe. I doubt if they're used to being shot at...Go!"

Mike ran around the corner before the others even realised they were under starter's orders. A boom shook them into action and all six women followed, emerging into the street to watch the first of the men in front of the Fun House fall to the ground. Mike fired again, then dived onto the ground as a storm of bullets rained above him. He watched as the figures toppled and fell. Two of the men managed to get shots off and he was about to fire another round, but in that short furious volley, it was already over.

All ten men were down. Mike looked behind him and saw the woman next to Vicky, the last one to take a gun from him, had her hand pressed over her stomach. She looked towards Mike, and then fell forwards, the gun skidded over the tarmac as her skull cracked against the ground.

"Lauren!" Vicky cried as she ran to her fallen friend. Vicky turned the woman's body over, but even in the dingy light, she could see she was already dead. Hate filled Vicky's face as she looked towards the men lying on the ground. She marched over to the fallen bodies.

"Hey, Vicky!" Jules called, but there was no stopping her. She emptied the remaining rounds into their corpses, finally flinching from her violent trance as Jules arrived at her side and put a gentle guiding hand around her shoulders. "Come on darlin', we've got a long way to go before the night's over and we're going to need every bullet we can muster.

"Okay," Mike said, "Let's head in. Be careful; there could be more of them." He ran across the road and heard feet following behind him, all the time he was doing sums in his head. He had estimated there were forty or fifty in the pub. They had taken out six men earlier in the day, four at the barricade, six who were guarding the women and now another ten. There would be four up at the other gate...that didn't leave many unaccounted for.

A scream rose into the air and the women who had been residents of the Fun House suddenly felt chilled to the bone. It was the scream of a man, but higher pitched than any note they thought a man could reach.

"It's started," Mike said turning towards them. "Let's get in there," he said, bursting through the front doors of the community hall with his shotgun raised. His breath left him as he was hit in the face by the image that confronted him. He had once applied for a job at one of the largest office supply companies in Yorkshire. He had been given a tour of the facility, including the sales floor. He remembered all the partitioned cubicles that the telephone reps worked from. He remembered what a horrible and oppressive environment it was; there was no privacy, always under scrutiny, always being watched. Now as he looked into the community hall, he saw a similar arrangement of partitions. Each with a thin curtain across the front. Attached to the narrow aluminium strip at the edge of each of the cubicles was a photo of one of the girls inside.

"They never had curtains when we were here," Vicky said, coming to stand by Mike.

"*Fuck!*" was all he could say as he heard sobbing from one of the nearest compartments. He walked up to it and flung back the curtain to reveal a young woman sat on the bed. She stretched the quilt over her naked body and at first, she thought Mike was just another of Webb's men, but then she looked beyond him to Vicky and the others.

The young woman wore a bewildered stare.

"Aggie?" Vicky said.

"Vick?" the woman replied.

It was then that Mike looked down to the woman's foot which was tethered to the bed. The bed itself was a metal-framed construction that looked like it belonged in a prison, which, of course, this was. It was bolted to the ground; escape was impossible without the means to cut the chain or the manacle around the woman's ankle.

Another curtain opened and an Asian woman appeared in the entrance to the cubicle. "Vick, it's really you," she said.

Vicky ran to the woman and threw her arms around her, while Mike continued to gawp. He turned to his right and saw Fry standing there, looking back at him. "You were responsible for this," Mike whispered. "I am nothing like you, and I never will be." Fry spoke, but no sound left his lips.

"What did you say?" Jules asked, placing a hand on Mike's left shoulder.

Mike's head swivelled to the left and looked Jules in the face. "What?"

"I said, what did you say?"

Mike turned his head back towards Fry, but now there was nothing there but an empty space. "Nothing," he said, "it's just...fucking sick."

"Yeah well. You want to meet the guy who runs this place, then you'll see sick, right Em?" There was no response and Vicky turned around to look for Emma. "Where is she?"

Mike spun around too. "Where's Em?" he asked one of the other women.

"I thought she was following me."

"Shite. I bet she's gone back to the hotel," Jules said.

*

Wren, Prisha, Hughes and Lucy continued to sprint as fast as they could, even after the first resident of Loch Uig was attacked.

Lucy shot a glance backwards; there was a forty-metre gap between them and the surging throng of beasts. They had emerged from the darkness on the edge of town into the sparse, seedy light that illuminated it. There was a growing and rowdy crowd up ahead of them still emerging from what she could only assume was a pub. As they entered the town, music had been playing and bright, colourful lights had been flashing from the windows. The music had come to an abrupt stop, the lights were still dancing, but as they got closer, those stopped too.

There was a small group of men holding audience, shouting and pointing towards the entrance to another street. Lucy could not hear the exact words of the exchange, but it was frantic and fevered.

Prisha had kept them close to the building on the left-hand side of the street and for the time being, the crowd was looking at the shouting men and in the opposite direction. The young Indian woman looked back and signalled for them to duck down a small passageway between what was once a hiking shop and a newsagent. They turned and headed down the hill, fully expecting to hear the pounding feet of the metalheads behind them. There were no lights in this ginnel, but Lucy could just make out the bobbing shadows in front of her as the rest of the group blazed a trail down the alley. She shot a glance back to the road; nothing had appeared from around the corner, but it was just a matter of time.

The sound of feet in front of her slowed and she brought her eyes back around. "What is it?" she asked, pulling the small torch out of her pocket and shining it into Prisha's face.

"I think I have brought us down the wrong alley."

"What?" Lucy said. "You're telling me this is a dead-end?"

"No. This leads to the hotel, which is Webb's headquarters. I don't know what to expect there; we will have to travel through the grounds before we can get to the hall."

Hughes looked beyond Lucy towards the dingy light at the top of the ginnel and saw blurred movement. "Kill the torch," he hissed.

Lucy caught the look of alarm on Hughes's face and turned the torch off straight away. She spun around, and now all four of them held their breath, expecting to see the terrifying creatures heading towards them, but instead, the mob ran past the entrance to the narrow passageway. Lucy, Hughes, Wren and Prisha were now forgotten as the beasts sprinted along the street towards the large crowd outside the pub.

A few seconds later, a scream shredded the night air, cutting through the sounds of running feet, cutting through the shouting of the men outside the pub, cutting through the darkness itself. Each of them in the alley felt the same thing. Their skin prickled and even though they knew, for that moment, they were safe, that they had managed to escape the initial phase of the creatures' attack, their hearts raced.

One scream became two, then three, then a chorus of howls filled the main street accompanied by the familiar sounds of panic, running feet, and the odd gunshot.

"Come on love," Hughes said, "if we've got to head through this place let's not dilly-dally. I don't really want to be out here for longer than I need to."

Prisha could not see the faces of the others, but she could feel their fear like it was her own. It was her own. She turned, and the others followed the sound of her footsteps into the blackness.

24

Greg Lambert, or *Lammy,* as everyone knew him, was a career criminal. He had been inside for a good portion of his life for everything from armed robbery to sexual battery. He was a lowlife who had found his own personal heaven in Loch Uig. It was a place where debauchery reigned, and he had made out better than ever, first under The Don, Then Fry, and finally Webb.

His senses had been muddied by the whiskey, and it took him a while to rouse from the drunken conversation he was having with his compatriots, but finally, he saw the group of men who had left the pub just a few moments earlier reappear in the doorway with panicked looks on their faces. Since his conversation with Preston at the barricade a few minutes earlier, he had managed to swap duties. He had been on the cusp of drunkenness at the time of the call, but since getting a substitution, he was now wallowing in the freeing lightheadedness.

It wasn't until the blaring music stopped suddenly that he woke to the realisation that something was very wrong.

"Barker and the others have been shot! The women are making a break for it!" one of the men shouted.

There was a rush for the door. Tables and chairs were knocked over as the men, including the bar staff, piled onto the street, leaving the pub empty. The frigid air, along with the news that their second in command was down, sobered a lot of the men up immediately. They looked towards the small group that had given them the news and who were now pointing and shouting towards the street where it had unfolded. There were multiple mentions of Webb and the armoury key. It was only then that Lammy remembered he had his sidearm, but his rifle was still leaning against the wall back in the pub. He had jostled his way to the middle of the crowd, but making this realisation, he started barging his way back.

Some of the pub's patrons stepped aside, some were too drunk to understand anything of what was doing on, they just followed the herd. Movement beyond the crowd blurred in the corner of Lammy's eye and he looked right. At first, he did not understand what he was seeing…small, flying metal bowls headed straight towards the crowd. He stopped. He knew he was tipsy, but he was nowhere near drunk enough to hallucinate an invasion of miniature spacecraft flying down the main street towards him.

His jaw dropped. He had heard stories of Webb's creations, but up until this moment he had not seen one for himself. Now though, as the crowd slowly began to shift away from the alehouse, he knew what he was seeing. He was glued to the spot. He knew he should run, or at least warn the others, but fear clasped icy fingers around his shins, rooting him to the spot. He had not felt terror in a long time; he did not think he was scared of death, but as he saw these monstrous creations just a few metres away from him, he realised there were many things worse than death.

A banshee's wail filled the air like a siren as Lammy watched the first creature pounce, digging talons into its victim and opening its mouth unnaturally wide to clamp its teeth around its target's neck. The young man had been sat at the same table as Lammy; his shriek of pain made the entire crowd turn. They all registered the same confusion, but soon came to grips with what was happening.

Some froze, some yelled. Some ran, but as the first creature brought its head back with half of the young man's neck between its teeth, many of the other beasts were already in mid-air. The attack was swift and brutal. Blood fountains sprayed, painting faces, clothes, and the very ground red with death. All the time Lammy just stood there watching, knowing he had walked out of the pub and straight into hell.

Finally, he came to his senses and turned to run as more and more of his comrades fell. He pulled the sidearm from his holster and sprayed bullets behind him, turning to see the helmeted beasts rise from the feast and continue their pursuit of the others. They were now joined in their game of devil's tag by the very men they had attacked Their victims climbed to their feet, initially in a bewildered stupor, then, as if a lightning bolt had struck them, they became electrified with purpose and charged after the fleeing men. Lammy and another armed man stopped and fired, taking down two RAMs, then they each targeted one of the metalheads only to hear their bullets merely ricochet off the top or side of the creatures' helmets.

"Fuuuck all of yous!!!" Lammy shouted, firing another two shots that vanished into the night. He turned to run again but felt a force strike him from the side. He went toppling to the ground, rolled over then felt the thing that had hit him roll over him in turn. His body hit the tarmac hard, and for a second, he was dazed. He started to clamber to his feet but was knocked back to the ground as a helmeted head hovered over him for what seemed like an eternity, but was less than a single breath.

The blackest blood the light afforded dripped from its mouth and as Lammy's scream joined the screams of his compatriots as they too fell to these creatures, he swore he saw the hellish abomination smile as it unhinged its jaws to feed like a giant snake. The stitching holding its cheeks together ripped free, and Lammy's agonised scream was muted as the demon's mouth locked over his cheeks. Its teeth sliced through his flesh like rusty razors, clamping around his nose and tearing the cartilage as it pulled its head back.

With no respite for Lammy to fend off the attack, the beast lunged again, towards the neck this time. Lammy felt its jaws close around his larynx and as the blood from where his nose had once been seeped into his eyes and down his throat, everything turned red, then black, then...

*

"Hotel? What hotel?" Mike demanded.

More gunshots were sounding from up the street now as the attacks continued. "The hotel where that bastard had us held," Jules said.

"Fuck!" Mike spat. "Where is it? Where is this place?" he demanded as he took Jules by the arm and guided her towards the door.

"You can't go," she said.

"That's my sister!"

"Mike, it's a war zone out there. She'll be at the bloody hotel by now and she can look after herself. We need all hands on deck here. I mean, look around for fuck's sake," Jules said gesturing towards the cubicles.

Mike balled his fists. "Fuck!" he yelled and Vicky and the others looked startled. He glanced around the room. It was an ugly building from the seventies; high, frosted windows and skylights allowed enough light into it during the day while still shielding whatever was happening in the hall from the outside world. Many a town meeting, a pantomime, a council vote, had taken place in the time before, but now the purpose of this place had become a far more sinister one. "The entrance," he said eventually, "we need to barricade the entrance."

"What with?" Jules demanded.

"Anything we can find," he said, running towards the inner glass doors and propping them open then bolting the left outer door. The right one pushed open; there was no key. "Shit! Without securing this we're sitting ducks." He ran back into the hall. "What are you waiting for?" he called to Vicky. "Get these women freed, we're going to need all the help we can get.

"How the hell am I supposed to do that?" Vicky yelled back.

"Bolt cutters," Saanvi said. "There are bolt cutters in one of the offices."

Mike ran into the first office and went through the desk drawers, but there was nothing. He went quickly to the second office, found the cutters, ran back to the door and lobbed them towards Vicky, who quickly sidestepped to avoid getting hit. "Hurry!" Mike said.

"Real fucking charmer, your boyfriend," Vicky said.

"He's not fucking mine," Jules replied, heading towards the office as Mike disappeared back inside.

"There you are," he said, tearing the power lead from the large screen TV bracketed to the wall. He placed the flex in his rucksack and grabbed hold of one end of the desk. "Give me a hand with this."

"Okay, ready," she said, lifting her end.

"Listen to me carefully," he said as they continued across to the entrance. "I'm going to help you block this entrance then I'm heading out of the fire exit to go find Em."

They were just about to pass the propped open internal doors when Jules dropped her end of the desk. "That's mental."

Bullets and screams continued to echo outside. "You hear that? If we get this blockaded, you're going to be safe. Em isn't, I—"

The front doors burst open and Jules screamed.

*

Emma stood watching the top level of the hotel from the carpark. There were lights on in the odd room on lower floors, presumably where a privileged few lieutenants lived, but Emma's focus was firmly fixed on the top floor. That is where she had come from; that was where she was heading to.

The screams and gunshots were of no interest to her as long as they stayed in the distance. She checked her rifle and made sure the Glock was secured in her waistband before heading towards the entrance. She immediately ducked down behind a row of shrubs as the doors swung open, banging loudly against the walls. Four men ran out, all carrying rifles. One of them was doing a radio check, and she heard Webb's voice hiss orders through the handset like the king of all the snakes. Another of the men brought the radio up to his mouth and shouted for reinforcements from the North gate.

They disappeared up a road towards the high street, and Emma sprinted across the carpark to the hotel. She navigated the dark staircase, floor after floor until she reached the top. She was about to open the fire escape door when she stopped. She remembered when Webb's henchmen had come to collect the women earlier in the evening; the door mechanism had announced their arrival long before they appeared. The stairwell was partially illuminated by the lights from the floor bleeding through the small, diamond-shaped safety glass window in the fire door. Emma looked around to see if there was anything she could prop the door open with and grabbed a sturdy, red fire extinguisher.

She opened the exit slowly and slipped through with the faintest of hinge creaks before settling the door to rest against the metal extinguisher. She quickly looked up and down the hallway; the coast was clear.

Emma advanced down the corridor; Webb stepped out of a room further down. He was talking on a handheld radio and Emma stopped dead waiting for him to lift his head in her direction, but he did not. He continued to the end room and closed the door behind him. She wasted no time, sprinting down the remainder of the hallway. She shot a glance to her left to look inside the room Webb had appeared from and skidded to a stop.

There was one woman on an examination table, sobbing, while another was in mid-operation. The parts of a helmet were laid out on a trolley.

Emma walked into the room and straight to the table. The crying girl gasped; for a split second she thought Webb had returned, but as her eyes focussed she saw it was not Webb but a wild-eyed angel who had come to free her.

"I'll unfasten your straps," Emma whispered. "You'll have to take care of your friends, I need to take care of Webb."

"Undoing her straps won't help," the girl said. "She's dead. That's why he was so angry when he left."

Emma looked across at the young woman with the mutilated face. "Sick bastard," she said, undoing the last of the restraints that were holding down the girl's arms.

"I'm Melissa," she whispered, springing up and embracing the stranger tightly.

Emma reciprocated with a one-armed hug. "Okay, Melissa, undo your leg restraints and stay quiet."

Melissa watched as the angel in black left the room. Emma charged the remainder of the way down the corridor and crashed through the door, raising the SA80 like she was a trained soldier.

Webb was stood in front of a Laptop that had four live camera feeds on. He shot round to face the door with the radio still in his hand. He began to raise it to his mouth and Emma fired, hitting him in the right shoulder. He screamed, immediately dropping the handset to the floor.

"You bitch!" he shrieked. "You'll pay for this." The second shot seemed louder than the first as the back of Webb's knee exploded, the bullet lodged into the plaster, and Webb collapsed to the floor. "Aaarrrggghhh!"

Emma walked across and loomed over him; all she was missing was the hood and the sickle. "You piece of shit," she said, raising the rifle again and shooting him in the other knee.

Webb howled with pain. "Nooo—Please! I'll give you anything…anything you want, but please stop this! Stop this, please!"

Emma grabbed hold of his hair and began to drag him like a child dragging a rag doll. "Don't worry; you're going to give me everything," she said.

"Nooo! Please, let go of me, please!" He tried to struggle, but with one arm incapacitated and both knees crippled he could do little.

Emma glanced towards the green glow of the infrared cameras on the laptop screen as she pulled him across the Honeymoon Suite's carpet. She paused as monstrous creatures in shining helmets ran towards them and the bearers of the cameras desperately raised their rifles. They fired shot after shot to no avail. The beasts pounced like a well-choreographed dance troop, and one by one the cameras jerked out of position. Two went blank while the other two lay sideways, showing the monsters feeding in gruesome detail.

"Doesn't look like anyone's coming to save you now does it?" Emma said.

The gunfire persisted in the distance, but it was becoming less frequent. "Please, you don't need to do this. You can have this place. Your people can have everything, the guns, the ammunition, everything. We've got vehicles, we've got food. Take it, it's…it's all yours. Just let me go."

"Thanks, we will take it," Emma said as she continued to drag Webb out of the room and down the hallway. They finally reached the doorway to the room where Webb had been carrying out his latest science experiment. Emma continued to drag him by the hair towards one of the examination tables. "Give me a hand," she said to Melissa.

At first, Melissa flinched like a frightened animal in the presence of a cruel owner, but as she looked at the blood pouring from Webb's knees and shoulder wound, then at the ferocious look in Emma's eyes, a nervous smile crept onto her features. She bent down and grabbed his feet while Emma yanked him by the shoulders and onto the table. He let out another pained cry. "Melissa…I've said you're all free to go, you can take everything. You don't know this woman, don't take her orders. You can get out of here before my men come back."

Emma looked at the younger woman and shook her head. "His men are dying or dead. His creations are running around on the streets killing them all."

"Creations?" Melissa asked.

Emma began to strap Webb to the table, and she gestured towards the trolley and her dead friend. "The monsters he's built. They're killing everyone outside."

"Then how are we going to get out?"

"I know a way. I can get us out of here," Webb said.

"I don't care about getting out right now," Emma said. "All I care about is a little justice."

Melissa looked at Emma then down towards Webb, then back to Emma. "What do you want me to do?"

Emma's eyes moved to the countertop that ran the length of the wall at the far end of the room. "Bring me those gloves, the pliers and oh…those pruning shears too."

"No!" screamed Webb. "No…Nooo!!!"

*

Lucy, Wren, Hughes and Prisha almost collapsed through the door of the community hall. The sheer speed and ferocity with which the entrance barged open made every head jerk towards the sound. The fearful looks dissipated quickly as familiar faces greeted them.

"The RAMs spotted us as we crossed the street," Hughes shouted.

"Shit," Mike replied, running towards the doors, pulling the hatchet from his rucksack and smashing through the two narrow vertical frosted glass panes. He snatched a glance up the road to see multiple silhouettes heading towards them, and pulled the power chord out of his bag, weaving it through the narrow slits, finally tying a tight knot. Hughes and Jules lifted the desk and placed it in front of the door as the first RAMs crashed into the thick wood, making a cacophonous bang against the frames.

"There's another desk and some more cabinets," Mike said as the growls and gnashing teeth of the beasts began to freeze the air around him.

One by one, as the captives were released from their cells, they pitched in to carry anything that could be used to help build the barricade. Two of them got hold of one of the partitions that had been the dividing wall to their respective cells. It was more weight than they could manage, considering the meagre rations they had been fed while in captivity, but when another two women joined them, the cubicle siding moved across the floor.

The bangs against the doors continued and reaching arms snaked through the narrow gaps as the barricade grew taller. Within a few minutes, there were steady processions of former captives heading to and from the blockade like worker ants. Whatever Vicky was saying to them as she freed them was working to restore their hope.

Mike looked towards Hughes and Jules, who were both busy building the blockade, then headed towards Lucy. She was cutting a pillowcase into strips to dress a nasty sore on a woman's leg where the manacle had been attached.

"Luce," he said.

"Give me a minute, Mike," she replied, as she carefully sliced through the material.

"I don't have a minute."

She looked towards him. "What is it?"

"Em's out there."

Lucy immediately stopped what she was doing. She knew what the words meant, she knew what the look on his face meant. She took two of the strips, crouched down and carefully wrapped the young woman's wound. "When we get back home, I'll get that seen to properly." She stood up and turned towards Mike. "Okay," she said, taking the Glock from the back of her jeans, "let's go find her."

"No, I meant—"

"I know what you meant, but if you're heading out there, I am too."

"I—"

"Where is she?"

"I think she went to get this Webb guy. Listen, Luce—"

"Hey Vicky," called Lucy.

Vicky emerged from a cubicle a few metres down with the bolt cutters still in her hands. "Yeah?"

"Where's Webb?"

A coldness swept over Vicky's face. "Why?"

"Where is he?"

"The hotel."

"Where's that?"

Vicky walked towards her. "Tell me why?"

"We think Em's headed there," Mike replied.

"I hope she guts the bastard," Vicky replied. "Cross the road, end of the street, turn left, keep going. You'll come to the carpark on your right. Webb has the top floor," she almost spat the words. She looked towards the barricade. "You realise those things are probably everywhere now?"

Lucy nodded. "Thanks, Vicky."

Mike and Lucy gave one glance back towards Hughes and Jules, who were busy directing the flow of workers as the barricade continued to grow, then to Wren, who was rushing from cubicle to cubicle, desperate to see if her sister was being held there.

"You ready?" Mike asked.

"I was born ready, baby," Lucy smiled.

The pair of them walked to the back of the large hall unnoticed, and Mike gently pushed against the panic bar of the emergency exit, opening the door. They stepped into the darkness, closing the door behind them. There was no going back now.

25

Emma stood over the examination table with the gleaming pair of pruning shears in her right hand. She brought the stainless-steel blades up to her face and rotated her wrist, making them glimmer in the light.

"Don't do this. Don't do this!" Webb begged and whimpered.

"Actually," Emma said turning towards Melissa, "get me those pliers as well."

Webb turned his head to watch Melissa walk across to the workbench and pick up a pair of pliers. She brought them back across and Emma held them up too, examining them under the light. Unlike the shiny blades of the shears, the gripping jaw and top of the handle were covered in dried blood.

"Looks like you've been busy with these," Emma said calmly. "Hold his head, Melissa."

A terrified look swept over Webb's face. He was about to scream, but as the pliers neared his mouth, he clamped his lips shut. He tried to shake his head loose from Melissa's grip, but to no avail. Emma pinched his nostrils together with the thumb and index finger from her free hand, and Webb resisted as long as he could. His face turned bright red and his chest and stomach heaved as he was starved of air. Eventually, he opened his mouth and greedily sucked in two lungfuls, giving Emma the time she needed to squeeze the jaws of the pliers around Webb's top two incisors. His eyes widened, and she let go of his nose, wiping her hand on his shirt. Garbled cries came from his mouth.

"Now Webb, you're going to have to talk me through some of this," she said, picking up the metal roof plate from the trolley, "is it both incisors I pull out or just one? I wouldn't want to get it wrong."

Tears rolled down Webb's cheeks and he closed his eyes as he continued to whimper. There was a mirror leant up on the bench, and Emma suddenly caught sight of herself. She backed away from Webb and dropped the pliers on the floor. "What is it?" Melissa asked.

"I can't be like him."

The stairwell door swung open and clunked heavily against the frame. "Help me! Help me!" Webb screamed.

Emma was still in shock at seeing an image of herself she thought she would never see. It wasn't until Melissa shook her that she actually woke from her moment of self-hate. Emma picked up the rifle and aimed it at the door. Had it been worth it? Putting the fear of hell and damnation into this man? If she had just killed him, she and Melissa would have been on their way now.

Mike and Lucy appeared in the doorway, but Emma did not lower the rifle at first, she wanted to make sure her eyes were not deceiving her. "Em?" Mike said.

It was then that she dropped the gun to the floor and ran to him. She wrapped her arms around him and the pair hugged tightly, before she released her grip and did the same with Lucy. "I tried to do it. I tried to do to him what he did to those poor women, but I couldn't."

Mike looked towards the trolley. He looked towards the girl standing, watching them with a bewildered look on her face. "Who's this?" Mike asked.

"This is Melissa. He was about to…"

Mike walked over to the examination table. "And this must be Webb," he said, standing over the terrified figure. "There's a good reason you couldn't do it Em. You're not a monster. It takes a monster to do that to someone." Mike picked up the pair of shears from the trolley and held them with a small smirk on his face, looking towards their captive. "Now me, on the other hand."

"No Mike," Lucy said, walking towards him and grabbing the gardening tool from his hand. "Are you seeing him?" she whispered, "Are you seeing him now?"

The words were only audible to Mike and Webb, whose look of abject terror was momentarily replaced with one of confusion. "I wasn't serious," Mike replied. "I think he's gone."

Lucy guided Mike over to a corner, briefly glancing back towards Emma, who was stood by the doorway. "I don't understand. How can he be gone just like that?"

"I was terrified of being the same man because I was prepared to do some of the same things to win. But then when I entered that hall...those women...Jesus, Luce, I would die before I would allow that kind of stuff. That's when I realised, I'll never be like him...ever. But now I know, if he comes back, if he taunts me, I'll just remember that one thing, that one hellish image, and it will remind me, yeah, I have issues, but I'll never, ever be like that piece of shit...like any of them."

Lucy smiled and took hold of Mike's hands. "That's what I was telling you all along."

"Yeah, but it wasn't until I saw it…"

The lights flickered for a few seconds before returning to normal. "What's happening?" Melissa squealed.

"Don't panic," Mike replied, "it's the generator running low on diesel."

"What's the plan?" Emma asked.

"When we made our escape from the hall, those things were massing around the entrance. We're not getting back in there any time soon," Lucy said.

"We need vehicles," Lucy said.

"There are a couple of cars out in the carpark," Emma replied.

"No, we need bigger vehicles to get everybody out of here," Lucy said.

"I thought you said the hall was a no-go."

"We might only have one chance to make all this work. We need all the pieces in place before we do. Now, the buses and vans and all the vehicles these guys transported their army around in…they've got to be around here somewhere." Mike walked over to stand by Webb once again. "So, where are they?"

Webb just looked at him. "He's not going to help us," Emma replied.

"No, he is," Mike said, looking down at him. "Y'see a monster would brutalise and torture someone for no reason, just for the sake of it. I could never do something like that," he said, looking across towards Lucy. "But if it's to get information to help my family and my friends…then that's a pretty good reason, as far as I'm concerned," he placed his hand gently on Webb's shoulder. "Now…where are your vehicles?"

"Y—you're going to kill me anyway…why should I tell you?"

"Because the pain I will put you through if you don't will make what you did to those poor women feel like a head massage."

Webb's eyes flickered. "I…I don't believe you. Your sister wouldn't do it, you won't do it."

Mike regarded Webb's bleeding knees. "I'm not my sister," he said, twisting his thumb into the bullet wound on Webb's shoulder.

"Aaarrrggghhh!!!" Webb screamed.

"The fact is, you have no idea what I'm capable of when properly motivated, and right now, getting my family and friends to safety is a huge motivational factor for me." Mike looked over to the bench and saw a length of rope next to a pile of handcuffs and manacles. "Y'see," he said, reaching down and snapping Webb's middle finger back like it was a wishbone, causing his captive to howl once more, "if you just answer my questions, you'll save yourself a lot of pain. And look, I'll sweeten the deal. You're a piece of shit, and I really want to see you dead, but the way I figure it, without your toys and your army, you'll be dead pretty soon anyway, so if you tell me where the vehicles, keys, weapons and food stash is, I promise not to kill you."

"C'mon Webb, that's a good deal," Emma said. "You offered me that just a few minutes ago." Webb gave her a disdainful look. "What? You mean you were going to renege on the deal?"

"I don't believe you."

"I'm a man of my word, Webb. I swear on my sister's life that I won't kill you, I won't let Emma or Lucy kill you, either. You tell us what we want to know, we'll verify you're telling the truth, and we'll be on our way, or…" Mike took hold of another finger.

"Wait!" he said with the pained look of a frightened child on his face. "I'll tell you."

Mike let go of Webb's finger. "There's a big public carpark that borders the back of the Fun— the community hall. The vehicles are there."

"The keys?"

"The keys are kept in the glove compartments…it…avoids confusion."

"The weapons and food?"

"There are shipping containers in the carpark too. One has weapons and ammo, the other two are filled with food."

"And how many innocent people died for those supplies?" Mike asked. Webb did not answer. "The keys…where are the keys for the shipping containers?"

The lights flickered again. "The room at the end of the hall; there's a key safe on the wall. I have the key for that in my pocket."

Mike dug into Webb's pocket and fished out the key. "Very good. Y'see how much pain you've just saved yourself?"

"I know you won't honour your deal, but I think you owe me a quick death at least."

"That's the difference between you and me, Webb. I said we wouldn't kill you and I meant it. We'll be back in a few minutes," Mike said, heading out of the room and gesturing for the others to follow.

Lucy closed the door behind them and they walked to the honeymoon suite at the end of the corridor. "We're seriously going to let him live? After everything he's done?"

"No, but we're not going to kill him."

"I don't understand," Lucy replied.

"I've got an idea," Mike said with a smile.

*

They had stacked everything they could against the entrance doors. The creatures continued to bang and smash their bodies against the wood, and two of the beasts still had their arms thrust through the glassless windows. The growls sent chills through everyone as they gathered at the front of the hall, watching the doorway for movement.

"She's not here," Wren said to Jules.

"What?" Jules replied.

"My sister, she's not here."

Vicky overheard this time and she clapped her hands to get attention. "Girls, do any of you remember seeing a lass called…" she looked towards Wren.

"Robyn!" Wren said. "She looks a lot like me. She had dyed black hair, but it's probably grown out so it will be more like my colour. She was roughly my height."

Women shook their heads. "It doesn't ring any bells, but it's hard to say for sure."

Jules put a sisterly arm around Wren's shoulder. "I'm sorry, love," she said.

Wren looked up at Jules. "I don't think I am. I wouldn't have wanted her to suffer like these women."

Jules gently rubbed Wren's shoulder and looked towards Hughes. "So what's next?"

Hughes looked around. "Where's Mike? And Lucy, for that matter?"

"Oh shite," Jules said, "They must have gone back to the hotel after Emma."

"So much for the plan," Hughes said.

"What was the plan?" one of the other women asked.

"We were going to stay put in here until morning, then fight our way out," he said, pointing to the handmade spears lying on the floor. "Right this minute, we don't know where all those things are, whether there are more of Webb's men hiding somewhere…we don't know what we'll face out there. At least in the daytime we stand a better chance of seeing anything coming towards us."

"So, what's the plan now?" Vicky asked.

"We're going to stick to our end, at least. We'll kill the lights, a couple of us will keep guard in case that barricade shifts, and we'll hunker down until morning."

"Hunkering down while a hundred pissed off zombies are battering at the door trying to get in? I don't like your plan much," one of the women said.

"Have you got a better one?" Vicky asked.

"Do what your friends did," she said, nodding towards the fire exit. "Do a runner out the back door."

"Firstly," Jules said, "They did not do a *runner*, they went to get Webb. Secondly, there's a world of difference between two people disappearing into the night and sixty people, some with injuries, disappearing into the night. I don't know how long you were out there after this shit storm started, darlin', but these things see in the dark much better than we do. They'd be on us in no time at all."

The woman looked a little embarrassed, but it was Vicky who spoke next. "Listen. These are good people. We should trust them." Mutterings went around the crowd and then the women began to nod in agreement. "Now, take a bunk for the night; it will be a long day tomorrow," she said, heading across to the light panel and waiting for the women to disperse before gradually turning the lights off a few at a time.

"So, we're good people now?" Jules said, walking across to Vicky.

Vicky dropped her head, ashamed. "I'm sorry. I'm sorry for what I said and did back in that room."

Jules looked around the community hall as women began to disappear into some of the cubicles while others pulled mattresses from the beds and set up in the aisles. "Honestly...after what you've been through...I can't say I blame you."

*

"Out of all the plans you've come up with in the past, this is one of the craziest," Lucy said.

Mike was about to say something when Emma interjected, "No, I think this is on a par. All of them have pretty much been *One Flew Over the Cuckoo's Nest* barking mad right from the start."

Lucy was about to respond when she stopped herself. "Yeah, actually, you're right."

The lights began to flicker again. "Okay, we don't have long," Mike said, placing the sturdiest chair he could find on top of the office desk he'd dragged out from the room behind reception. "I'll go get him."

Mike disappeared into the stairwell and ran back up the stairs two at a time. Webb was frantically shuffling and writhing, desperate to escape the confines of the straps that were holding him down.

Mike walked over to the bench and picked up the rope. He undid the straps that were fastened around the upper half of Webb's body and then looped the rope around his chest and underneath his armpits before tying a secure knot behind his prisoner's back.

"What are you doing? You said you'd let me go if I gave you what you wanted." Mike didn't answer him but undid another couple of straps. He proceeded to cable tie his captive's wrists together and then undid the rest of the straps before dragging him from the table onto a waiting stretcher on the floor. Webb howled with pain as his shattered knees bent nearly backward from the landing.

"Give me a hand!" Mike said to Lucy as they each took an end.

"You said—"

"I told you, I'm a man of my word," Mike said, as they carried him out of the room and made their way down the stairs. All the time, Webb was demanding to know what was happening; all the time, Mike was refusing to answer. They stepped out into the spacious foyer, and that's when Webb saw a desk with a chair standing on it. His face creased in puzzlement as he was carried across to it. Lucy and Mike placed the stretcher down next to the desk while Emma and Melissa watched on in silence. Mike took the slack from the rope that was tied around Webb's body, and climbed on top of the table. He stepped onto the chair and proceeded to lift two of the ceiling tiles.

"What is this? What are you doing?" Webb cried, looking at Mike and then towards the women. Mike looped the rope up through the gap, over a thick, stainless steel strut, and then back down through the gap where the other ceiling tile had been. "You said you were going to let me go," Webb ranted.

"No," Mike said as he began to pull the rope. "What I actually said was none of us would kill you." He continued to pull and Webb was gradually hoisted off the ground.

Webb screamed in pain as once again, his knees were forced to take the strain before they finally left the ground. "What is this? What are you doing to me?"

Mike continued to heave until Webb's feet were well above Lucy and Emma's heads. He kept the rope tense and looped the slack around the girder two more times before securing a knot. He pushed Webb and watched him swing from side to side like a pendulum before climbing back down and dragging the furniture to the wall.

Mike went to stand with Lucy, Emma and Melissa and the four of them watched for a moment while Webb hovered in the middle of the foyer. "Perfect," Mike said.

"I don't understand," Webb said again as they all walked away. "I don't understand." The four of them exited the foyer and walked outside. This wasn't the only hotel in Loch Uig, but it was certainly the most modern. The glass doors would be of no use keeping out a horde of RAMs. The walls were not much better; hastily erected plasterboard partitions which would break under too much weight. It was not a good place to put up a last stand, but it was perfect for what they intended.

Lucy threw her arms around Mike. "Be careful," she said.

"Be ready," Mike replied.

"Love you, sis," Mike said, breaking away from Lucy and embracing Emma.

"Love you too. See you soon."

"See you soon."

*

The gunshots had stopped completely now, but the town was far from silent. A hundred creatures held a morbid vigil outside what the previous inhabitants of the town had called the Fun House. Their growls raped the otherwise silent night, constantly reminding the occupants of the community hall that death was waiting for them in the darkness.

Hughes, Jules, Wren and Vicky sat in a small arc around the entrance on four plastic chairs. The creatures continued to push and thrust against the doors. The dim lights from outside made their inhuman silhouettes dance on the walls like evil shadow puppets.

"It's going to be a tough fight getting out of here tomorrow isn't it?" Vicky said.

"I won't lie to you," Hughes replied. "I'm not looking forward to it. I mean, we've faced a lot more of these things before and come out of the other side...but those metalheads. They're the big problem."

They all fell silent for a while. Eventually, it was Vicky who spoke. "I'm glad Prisha and Saanvi got to see each other again, if nothing else."

"Are they good friends?" Wren asked.

"They're sisters," Vicky replied, and the words stabbed Wren through the heart.

Even in the virtual darkness, Jules could see Wren's head drop and she reached out, taking the young girl's hand. "Just 'cos we didn't find her here, it doesn't mean she's not around somewhere. She might be in a settlement. She might be safe, living by herself or with a tall dark handsome man."

Wren let out a small laugh. "Knowing my sister, that would be her preferred option."

"How many do you think are out there?" Vicky said.

"More than a few," Hughes replied. "By the sound of it, most of the town at least."

"I hope the others are okay," Wren said.

"We'll know tomorrow morning, I sup—" An eardrum piercing crack chiselled into his words as the pressure of the RAMs against the right door caused the wood to split around the bolt. The door shifted inwards slightly and the furniture barricade juddered.

"Shite!" Jules said as they all jumped to their feet.

"Vicky, Wren, get everybody out of bed and ready," Hughes said, picking up his rifle and pointing it towards the entrance. Jules grabbed hers too and the pair of them stood side by side as the wood started to give a little more, shifting the barricade an inch at a time.

26

Mike had retraced his steps through the carpark to the corner of the street. He could hear the horde of RAMs long before he saw them, and the sound of splitting wood had echoed like a gunshot. He'd toyed with the idea of leading everyone out of the village hall through the back entrance and behind the hedge to the carpark at the rear, but it was too risky. If they got spotted or heard, nearly a hundred rabid creatures would descend on them with little warning.

He stepped out from the cover of the building he was clinging to. The street lanterns cast a dirty light, but it was enough for him to see the odd shining helmet amongst the mob of creatures throwing themselves at the door, frantically trying to get into the hall. The wood shifted again; the beasts moved forward a little more. Mike estimated there were at least sixty. Suddenly, he saw two more creatures appear at the top of the street. While the others were preoccupied with gaining access to the inhabitants of the Fun House, these newly arrived beasts centred on him as they charged down the middle of the road. For a moment he didn't understand how they could determine the difference between one of their own and someone who was living, but then he looked down to the shotgun in his hand, which he now raised into the air.

*

Some women were crying; one had actually thrown up. The fear and tension in the room were palpable as Vicky and Wren went to stand beside Hughes and Jules. The frame itself had begun to crack as the pounding fists and heaving bodies continued their relentless assault against the doors.

"Head towards the back now. When I start firing, get out of here," Hughes said.

"Where to?" Jules asked.

"I've got no idea." He turned to look at Vicky. "Is there anywhere that might be safe?"

"You're talking to me as if this is my home town. This was where I was chained for my entire stay," she said, gesturing towards the room. "Ooh, I tell a lie, for a couple of hours today, I got to be tied to a bed in the hotel too."

"The hotel. How about that?"

"I dunno…it means cutting back across that road, Jules said."

"Mike and Lucy did it," Wren said.

"There's a world of difference between two people ducking behind hedgerows and walls, and fifty or sixty doing it," Jules replied. The barricade shifted again.

"We're out of time. Get to the back door, hand the spears out, and when I fire, run. Just run." Hughes aimed his rifle, and Vicky and Wren ran back into the darkness. "You too, Jules," Hughes said.

Jules raised her rifle and aimed at the door. "Don't take this the wrong way, old man, but I'm not leaving you."

"Aww, so it's love then?"

"Yeah…like the way I used to love my grammy's British Bulldog. I've got a soft spot for ugly little fuckers with scrunched up faces."

"And the mystery as to why no man has snapped you up deepens."

"Listen…if we don't make it out of this…I—"

There was a boom from outside and, as if a wand had magicked them away, the mass of beasts attempting to force their way through the door vanished.

*

Mike stood there for a second with the shotgun still pointing towards the sky. What he envisaged and what was happening were two different things. He thought there would be fumbling and to-ing and fro-ing at the door, making the RAMs pursuit clumsy and hesitant. What was happening was something very different. They shifted like a flock of birds, like one single force, and now, he was their sole focus. They charged towards him. Mike glanced towards the pair who were coming down the street, and they converged, falling into the crowd almost as if it was preordained.

He turned and ran as the pounding feet gathered pace and rhythm behind him. Heading down the narrow alley towards the hotel carpark, the chorus of the creatures' growls rose to a malevolent roar, and as he crossed to hurdle the verge, he saw the lights in the hotel finally flicker off, leaving the building in total darkness.

Perfect. He continued to sprint, reaching around to grab the night vision goggles from his rucksack. He placed them on and everything became bathed in a green hue. He turned back and wished he hadn't. He saw the horde of marauding beasts now gaining on him, just a few metres away. In the green tinge of the goggles, they looked even more horrifying, and Mike's heart began to race faster than ever, but the entrance was in sight now, just a few more seconds. He had been here many times before; he just had to keep a cool head. He cast one final glance back, and that's when his foot hit the curb and he crashed to the ground.

*

Hughes and Jules stood there for a moment, barely able to comprehend or believe what had just happened. "Erm…" Hughes said without any follow-up.

"Yeah!" Jules replied.

"So what now?"

"You're meant to be the one with the plan."

"Opening the back door and running for your life was not one of my best, so I'm handing the mantle to you."

"Do you think it was Mike?"

"There was just one shot. It sounded close. Yeah, I'm guessing that was him drawing them away."

"So what now?" Jules asked.

"You've just asked me that. Nothing has changed in the last few seconds. I don't know."

"What's going on?" Wren asked, running across to join them with Vicky close behind.

"We think Mike's drawn them away," Jules replied.

"So what now?" Wren asked.

*

The night vision goggles went skidding across the pavement and Mike's ribs crunched against the concrete. He grunted with pain as he felt one of them crack, but he had survived worse than cracked ribs before. He sprang back to his feet, and pain shot through him from foot to neck, but he had no choice but to continue. He was down to starlight for guidance now, and he ran through the gaping, black, open entrance. He could almost feel the first creature's breath on him as he ran through the door.

"Hit the light, I can't see a thing!" he shouted as he heard the creatures storm through the narrow gap behind him. A lantern flickered on at the end of the corridor, but suddenly, the beasts became spoilt for choice as now they saw fresh meat hanging from the ceiling like a prize ham.

Most of the beasts slowed, causing the ones behind to slow, while another handful continued in pursuit of Mike. Now he could see it up ahead, the open door, and beyond that, the open window to the outside. He glanced back but the light was not strong enough to define how many moving shapes were following him. He saw two shining helmets leading the charge, and that was all he needed to see to know he was in trouble.

"Run!" he shouted as he saw Lucy stood in the doorway to the room at the end of the hall.

Lucy darted into the room, taking the lantern with her and leaving the corridor dark with just one beacon at the end lighting the way. The growls grew to fever pitch as the grabbing hands reached through the shadows towards him. He pulled the shotgun from his rucksack, still sprinting at full pace. He pumped the forend, swivelled the top half of his body, and fired. At precisely the same second, the lead creature stumbled. It lurched forward, nearly losing its balance, and there were a hundred metallic pings as the tiny lead balls buried themselves in the roof of the thick metal helmet. The creature flew back into the others, but did not fall. Others did as they collided with it. *These things are unstoppable!* Mike thought. He turned back to the direction of travel, realising if he let just one of these metalheads into the room with Lucy and his sister, it would be all over.

He had hoped to build up a bigger lead, and if he had not gone flying in the carpark then he would have done. But now he realised his plan had fallen apart.

"Shut the door!" he yelled.

"What?" Lucy screamed, holding the lantern light up higher and only then realising that there was little more than a six feet gap between Mike and the first of the beasts.

"Shut the door—Now!"

Before Lucy had a chance to respond, Mike saw Melissa rush from the corner of the room, knocking Lucy out of the way. She dropped the lantern she was carrying into the hallway, her one act of charity, before slamming the door.

Even over the sound of the creatures, Mike could hear the lock click, and that's when he knew it was all over.

He bent down, grabbing the lantern, and took the turn like a cyclist in a race. He leant over to one side, determined not to allow his momentum to knock him off balance. It worked, and instead, within a second, he heard the beasts.

Emma leapfrogged over the bed and pinned Melissa up against the wall with her thumb and forefinger closing together around the younger woman's neck.

Lucy scrambled back to her feet and rushed to the door as the thunderous volley of bodies crashed against the wood, making the very room shake. The growls of the creatures penetrated the thick door and hopelessness cloaked Lucy and Emma as they realised it was too late.

Emma unclasped her hand from around the petrified girl's neck. "You've just killed my brother," she hissed.

"You heard him," protested Melissa, "he knew—"

"Shut up!" Lucy yelled, and pressed her back against the door.

*

Mike turned to see half a dozen beasts feverishly trying to gather themselves to continue their pursuit. This time, it was an unmodified RAM leading the charge. Mike primed the forend of the shotgun and fired. Half the beast's head disintegrated, splattering the wall and some of the other pursuers.

The creature's body flew backwards, making another beast stumble. He fired another shot and a second beast went down. Mike's heart lifted a little, but that only lasted a split second as he saw the two metalheads storm to the front.

He turned back around and his heart sank further as he saw the cleaning cupboard at the end of the hall. It was a dead end.

*

"No, please," Melissa shouted as Lucy opened the door.

Lucy was not interested in her protestations. She looked down the dark hallway towards the foyer. She could not see the creatures there, but she could hear them in full voice.

She turned left and immediately saw movement at the end of the corridor. She grabbed her torch and ran out with Emma following. No sooner had they left the room than they heard the door close behind them. The two women charged forward towards the horde.

*

Mike dropped the empty shotgun and the lantern, and drew the two machetes from his rucksack. He could see light behind the beasts coming towards him, and silently cursed Lucy and Emma for putting themselves at risk. He stood there in the shadows as a rifle shot sounded. He saw a shadowy black eruption from the trailing creature's head before it collapsed to the floor. A second later, the same thing happened with another RAM, and beyond the shoulders of the two charging metalheads, Mike could just see Lucy and Emma with their rifles raised, peering down the scopes. They knew what happened was out of their hands now. They could not kill the helmeted creatures, and they could not risk shooting at them in an attempt to slow them. If a bullet passed through one of the beasts, it could hit Mike, and if the bullet didn't kill him, the blood from one of those creatures surely would.

The beasts matched each other stride for stride as they closed in, their reaching arms clawing through the darkness towards him. Mike could no longer hear the dozens of beasts in the foyer; he couldn't hear his own heavy breathing as his body cried out for more oxygen, he could not even hear the calls from Emma and Lucy as they tried to gain the attention of the metalheads. All he could hear was the pounding feet and the growl of his two immediate attackers—the growl that had haunted him from the very first time he had heard it. That growl had taken his best friend, the man who had saved him from becoming a man like Fry, his stepfather, Alex.

Mike stood there, his fists clenching ever tighter around the handles of the machetes. Six metres, five metres, four metres. He cast a final loving glance down the corridor towards Lucy and Emma, who watched on hopelessly. This was it.

27

Melissa wasted no time. The second she locked the door behind Emma and Lucy, she ran to the window and climbed out. The bottom of her trousers caught on the sill and ripped. She fell to the damp earth, dropping the torch Mike had given her, and she let out a stifled scream as she saw scuttling movement cross her field of vision at the edge of the arc of light.

Rats had always scared her, but now they were the least of her worries as she picked herself up and began running. Fear pushed her to move faster. She reached the corner and went skidding across the grass, coming to rest on the cold pavement. She felt the concrete grate the skin of her calf, but the pain was nothing compared to what she would feel if one of those things got to her. She picked herself up and started to run again. She was in the carpark when she heard two desperate shots from inside. She looked back; she knew the second she had locked that door she had sentenced Lucy and Emma to death, but it was better than all of them dying. If she had gone with them, or stayed there in that room, that's what would have happened.

Now though, still not out of the clear, she was safer than she had been since that fateful day when Fry's men had captured her and her boyfriend's family. She continued to sprint down the narrow alleyway until she emerged into the street, and there it was, cast in the dingy glow of the street lanterns, the community hall, the place that had been her prison for all these months. She thought she would never see it again, and she certainly never wanted to, but now she knew it was her one shot at salvation. No longer was fear her primary incentive, now it was hope.

*

Three metres. "Fuck this!" Mike said, throwing himself low at the creatures' legs as if they were pins and he was a bowling ball. Mike's speed and the momentum of the beasts meant there was no time for them to react. Their grabbing hands missed him and they crashed to the ground. Mike felt the blades of the machetes press against his chest as he rolled; one wrong move and he would slice himself open. His controlled tumble came to a shuddering stop as he clambered to his knees.

The beasts were flat on their fronts, violently struggling to get back to their feet to launch a second wave of attack. Not giving them the chance to gather themselves, Mike brought the machetes up over his head and whipped them down so fast that it looked like a blur to Lucy and Emma as they watched on, further down the hall. The blades crisscrossed through the air and sliced straight through the Achilles tendons of the nearest creature. It scrabbled around on the floor, shuffling to its knees, but by now the second creature had collected itself.

It turned and darted towards Mike, who sprang back to his feet then booted it using the flat of his left foot with every ounce of strength he could muster. The creature went flying into the wall and toppling over the other metalhead as they collapsed into a writhing heap once more.

Mike advanced again, this time swinging one of the machetes down on the second beast's back. The blade carved into the creature's body, severing the spine, and suddenly, everything below its shoulders stopped moving.

The RAM with the sliced heel floundered under the weight. Mike rolled the nearly paralysed beast off the first. It desperately reached for him, its mouth moved up and down, and although he could not see its eyes behind the gauze, he could feel the seething malevolence they beamed towards him. The first creature, now freed from the burdensome heft of the other, started to rise to its knees, but Mike performed a virtual replay and brought the machete down hard and fast, chopping through the creature's spine. It collapsed face down, desperately struggling to turn around and face its prey. Neither creature lost their will to attack, but now the savagery was imprisoned by their broken bodies.

Mike reached over, careful not to get caught by one of the flailing hands. He picked up the lantern and stepped back, letting out a long breath and feeling the pain in his ribs from earlier. The night was far from over, and he turned to see Emma and Lucy already heading towards him. He ran to meet them and the three flung their arms around each other.

"That little bitch locked us out of the room, and I don't really fancy going to get another key from reception, do you?" Emma said.

Mike broke the embrace and turned towards one of the hotel room doors. He glanced towards the two crippled creatures who were still growling and struggling, but they were no danger to them. Facing the door once more, he tried the handle, but it was locked. "Hold this," he said, handing the lantern to Lucy. He stepped to the other side of the corridor then ran at the door, barging it with his shoulder. The lock shattered, splintering the frame too, and the three of them entered, walking straight to the window. They opened it and speedily made their escape out of the hotel.

Emma leant against the wall. "Everything's got to be a drama with you hasn't it?" she said, and for the first time in a long time, they all laughed.

"Sorry, sis. Come on, we need to get back to the hall, then we get the hell out of this place."

"Sounds good to me," Lucy replied.

"Yeah, and just wait 'til I get my hands on that little Melissa bitch," Emma said.

*

The sound of Webb's sobbing was drowned out a hundred times over by the growls from the creatures below. He continued to dangle just out of reach. The blonde-haired American woman who had arrived with that psychotic who lynched him up here had tied tourniquets around his bullet wounds, but the occasional drop of blood continued to drip onto the crowd below, sending them into a heightened frenzy.

In the dark interior of the foyer, he could only make out shifting silhouettes. When rifle shots had sounded earlier, he had hoped the throng of monsters, some of his own creation, would be tempted away, but they were not. He hoped whoever had fired the shots had come to a sticky end. The thought of his enemy's bloody demise gave him comfort for a short time, but as something hit the tip of his toe and he began to swing, he let out a renewed cry of fear. Up until now, he had felt sure he was out of reach of the creatures, but now he realised there was one, at least, that was tall enough to make contact with him.

"Help me! Help me!" he screamed through his tears, but the only thing his pleas achieved was to rally the beasts beneath him into a flurry of even greater excitement. His tears continued to flow as his shouting turned to whimpers. "Help me…help me!"

*

Several of the women held lanterns up while Hughes covered the emergency fire exit as Jules hit the panic bar. The frantic knocking had demonstrated more control than that of a RAM, and when the shouts for help had started it had become obvious. The voice was muffled through the thick wood and they had expected to see Emma or Lucy at the door, but instead, it was a younger woman.

"Melissa," Vicky said, as Jules closed the door behind her.

"Thank god! He had me over there. He wanted to—" she burst out crying and buried her head into Vicky's shoulder for comfort. The other woman embraced her.

"It's okay, it's okay," Vicky said, stroking her back.

"You were across at the hotel?" Jules said.

Melissa brought her head up. Her eyes were still full of tears. "Yes," she nodded.

"Our friends? Our friends went over there," Jules said.

"They...they saved me...but they didn't make it. I'm sorry," she said.

Hughes and Jules looked at each other in shock. Wren had been covering the front door just in case any of the creatures had reappeared, but now she joined the growing crowd at the rear of the hall.

"Melissa?" she said with an incredulous look on her face.

"You know her?" Jules asked.

Melissa looked up again. "Wren?"

"Was Bobbi here? Did my sister ever get brought here?" Wren demanded, foregoing all pleasantries.

Melissa shook her head. "No, I never saw her. What are—"

"How the hell do you know this girl?" Jules interrupted.

"Her group left us in the middle of nowhere and then—"

A frantic banging sounded at the door once again, killing all conversations dead. Hughes raised his rifle. "Who the fuck is that going to be?" he asked.

"Who is it?" shouted Jules.

"Who the hell do you think it is? Fucking Jehovah's Witnesses. Let us in," Mike shouted.

Jules looked back towards Hughes and she could see the same confusion on his face that she was experiencing. They both looked towards Melissa, who began to shrink into the gathered crowd of women.

Jules opened the door and Lucy, Emma and Mike piled in. The door closed behind them and they stood, hunched over, catching their breath.

"We...we thought you were dead," Jules said.

"We came pretty close to it," Emma said, straightening up and beginning to look around the assembled faces. "It was sheer luck—" She caught sight of Melissa and lurched towards her, grabbing her by the scruff of her neck and throwing her down onto the floor. "You bitch!" she shouted.

Hughes, Jules and the rest of the women were taken aback, all apart from Wren, who scowled. She knew what treachery Melissa was capable of. Even in the subdued light of the lanterns, everybody could see the anger bubbling in Emma's face as she stood over the woman.

Vicky stepped in. "Melissa, you told us they were dead. What happened?"

"I'll tell you what happened. The little bitch slammed the door shut on Mike then locked us out of the room in a hallway full of those things," Emma replied.

Melissa curled up into a ball on the floor and started crying. "I'm sorry. I was so scared! I'm sorry."

"I'll give you something to be sorry about," Emma said, stepping forward.

"Hey, look, whatever happened, we can sort it out later. I'm just happy to see you standing here," Jules said. "In case you hadn't noticed, we're stuck in a town full of RAMs; I think getting out of it should be our main concern."

Lucy walked up to Emma and placed a reassuring hand on her shoulder. Emma looked towards her and then down at the pathetic figure curled up in front of them, and the rage dissipated.

Mike dug into his pocket and fished out the keys to the containers. "There's a carpark behind here somewhere. It's where they keep the guns and ammo and the food supply. It's also where all the vehicles are parked. They keep the keys in the vehicles."

"Okay," Hughes said, "what are we waiting for?"

Within minutes, the makeshift spears had been handed out, and everyone was lined up at the fire exit. Jules opened it one final time and Hughes, with his rifle raised, stepped out into the darkness with Wren by his side. They led the procession of women into the night in virtual silence. Mike, Lucy, Emma and Jules brought up the rear, constantly checking behind them to make sure there were no pursuers.

They were not walking long before they came to the carpark. There were all sorts of vehicles there, but two coaches with armoured sidings and snowploughs attached to the front were what Hughes and Mike homed in on.

"They've got a kind of *Mad Max* feel to them, haven't they?" Mike said, smiling.

"Erm...I was thinking more about the fact that these would fit everybody on," Hughes replied.

"Well, yeah, that as well."

Lucy, Emma, Jules and Wren opened up the shipping containers and everyone started loading the supplies into the luggage compartments of the coaches.

"I think we should worry less about the supplies and more about getting out of here," Hughes said, as he watched the women form lines, passing boxes of food and arms to one another.

"Those things are all in the hotel," Mike replied, "You don't need to worry about that."

"We don't know if all of them are in there," Hughes said, "and for that matter, we don't know if all the men have been taken care of. They could be watching us right now."

Mike looked beyond the lines of lanterns to the edges of the carpark. "This won't take much longer with all these people working on it. We've got a lot more mouths to feed now, mate. We'll need the extra food."

"I suppose you're right." Hughes paused for a moment, looking at the women.

Vicky walked up to join the two men. "Is this what it's like back at your place? The women do all the work and the men just stand around?"

"Pretty much," Mike replied.

Vicky smiled as she watched the work continue. "I still don't think I can believe all this."

"We're not out of the woods yet, love," Hughes said.

"No, but we're free now."

"You were free before," Mike said. "You and Prisha and the others."

"No, we weren't. We were just dying slower."

"I can't even imagine what it was like for you, Vicky, but it's over now. You'll come back with us to Safe Haven and if you like it you can stay; if you don't, you can move on. If you stay, everybody contributes, but nobody goes hungry and nobody takes from others," Mike said.

"It sounds perfect," Vicky replied.

"Well, it's not perfect by a long shot, but it's getting better day by day."

"We're not going to get all this stuff and all the people into the buses," Lucy said, walking across to join them.

"Okay," Hughes replied, "we'll use some of the vans too."

Mike and Vicky got back to work with the others while Hughes and Lucy kept a watchful eye on the perimeter to make sure that there was no danger of attack from anyone or anything.

Eventually, the trucks and coaches were loaded with everyone on board except for Mike, Hughes, Emma, Lucy, Jules, Wren and Vicky. "I'm going to drive the lead bus. Mike's going to bring up the rear. The vans are going to be in the centre. Once we're through the North Gate, we just keep going, all the way to Inverness. That's when we might need to break out the guns."

"What's in Inverness?" Vicky asked.

"A combine harvester," Emma replied.

"What?"

"Long story."

"Yeah," continued Hughes, "anyway, that's going to take a while to get out of the way, but then it's homeward bound."

"Get out of the way? What are you talking about?" Vicky asked again.

"It's blocking the route out of the city to where we need to go. The battery will be long dead, so we're going to have to budge it off the road or dismantle it somehow," Hughes replied.

"In a city full of the dead?"

"In fairness, it's on the outskirts of the city, and Inverness is nowhere near as full of the dead as it used to be," Mike said.

"Oh great. That makes me feel much better," Vicky replied.

"Right then," Hughes said, clapping his hands together. "Let's get this show on the road."

They all climbed on board their respective vehicles. The engines started with roars and the wheels slowly began to move. Hughes led them out of the carpark, turning right up to the main street, which had seen so much devastation earlier. Now though, he turned the vehicle left, in the opposite direction to the pub. Northbound they continued, scouring the edge of the headlight beams for movement. He kept checking the mirror, nervously expecting to see figures emerging from the shadows, throwing themselves at the vehicles, but his anxiety was unfounded.

Hughes brought the coach to a stop at the North gate. At some point during the night, it had been abandoned, and now it stood, closed and bolted, with a single lantern knocked on its side—the only evidence remaining of a hasty departure. Jules accompanied him. There was a sliding peephole which they moved across. It was dark on the other side, and Hughes pulled a torch out of his pocket. He flicked it on and placed it through the hole, panning it left and right looking for danger, but all he saw was road and forest.

Hughes moved the bolts across and swung the heavy gate open. He and Jules climbed back onto the coach, casting several more glances into the darkness before retaking their seats. The convoy began to crawl forward once again.

"Funny, isn't it?" Jules said.

"What's funny?" Hughes asked.

"You get so used to shitty stuff happening, that when it doesn't, it makes you paranoid."

Hughes let out a small chuckle. "I suppose you're right there."

The convoy moved through the gates, gradually picking up speed, and when they went around the first bend, the women who had been held captive in that place for so long started to cry, and laugh, and cheer. They hugged and they shouted and whooped. Their nightmare had finally come to an end. Whatever happened to them now, happened to them as free women.

28

Webb had no idea what time it was. It felt like he had been there for hours, which he probably had. What seemed like an age ago now, he'd heard engines roaring to life. He had hoped the rest of the town had perished. He did not like the thought of someone winning, other than him. He feared more than anything, though, that it was those people who had strung him up here.

The crowd below continued their growling dirge, jostling for position, but whatever had touched the tip of his toe before had not managed to do it again. The tourniquets had been well tied, and the blood flow had stemmed considerably, but not stopped; surely it would not be much longer before he passed out. His angry shouts and screams had ended some time ago. His voice was hoarse and he was in enough pain without exacerbating it further by making his throat raw.

A little more time passed, and now his eyes were beginning to feel heavy. They kept shutting, and there were longer and longer gaps before they reopened. A calm smile slowly crept onto his face. Death was coming for him and it would not be violent and vicious and bloody; it would be warm and gentle. He let his eyes close again, and this time did not fight, he kept them closed. He blocked out the sound of the creatures, he blocked out the smell of death, and—his eyes sprang open again.

Whatever creature had managed to reach his toe earlier, had hit it again. His body swung gently and he desperately tried to raise his feet, but was in too much pain from the wounds in his knees.

"Noo!!!" he screamed for the first time in a long time as whatever had nudged him, now had the tips of his toes in a vice-like grip. He stopped swinging; now he felt like he was being stretched. The rope tied around his chest and woven underneath his arms tightened as not just gravity, but the grasp of one of these beasts tried to drag him down. He screamed again, but this time he could not hear his own voice over the excited growls of the creatures. Whereas he could only see shadows and outlines, their night vision was perfect, and for the first time since they had held their hungry vigil, they saw the prey was in reach. As much as he tried to struggle, he could not break free from the tall creature's fingers.

The rope, which had adjusted to the movement and weight of Webb over the last few hours, now possessed new elasticity as another force influenced it. Webb felt his body slip, maybe just a couple of inches, but it was all the flesh-hungry monsters needed. One hand became two, two became three, as he felt the cold fingers of death wrap around his foot. He screamed again. Nails sank into his flesh as more beasts took hold and desperately sought to drag him down to the floor. "Nooo!!! Nooo!!! Nooo!!!"

His left shoulder dislocated and he slipped through the safe clench of the rope like he was a wet bar of soap. For a split second, the creatures released their grip and he fell through the air unencumbered before crashing to the floor. "Aaarrrggghhh!!!" he cried, landing on his coccyx with pain that he thought impossible up until that second. It was pitch black as the bodies of the creatures crowded around him. He felt the bites in choreographed synchronicity. His legs, his torso, his arms. He screamed as loud as he could until the bite to his neck silenced him forever. His blood continued to pump for a while; all the time he felt colder and colder. He did not think the darkness that surrounded him could get any blacker, but it did. It did get blacker, because to join the darkness on the outside, there was a darkness rising within him now. He had done untold evil in this life, but what was rising from the depths within him now went beyond evil. It went beyond Hell. This was a darkness from another place entirely, and as he sucked in his final, bloody, gurgling breath and smelt the foul stench of rot and decay coat his lungs like an aerosol, he realised this would be his eternity. A final tear left his eye, then Webb never cried again.

*

The A9 north had been cleared of vehicles. They passed many that were either burnt out or just pushed to the side of the road. This had obviously been the main route for Webb and his raiding parties and to their credit, they had kept it clear. The convoy made great time, and it came as no surprise when Hughes brought the lead coach to a standstill in Inverness. This had, after all, been a part of the plan from the beginning. He put the full beam of the headlights on and they lit up the bridge. He and Jules climbed out of the vehicle, and they were soon joined by Emma, Lucy, Mike and Vicky, as well as a few of the other women who were driving the vans.

"Erm…" Mike said.

"Yeah," Hughes replied.

"What…erm…" Emma said as they all looked across the clear bridge.

"So, somebody has cleared the pileup and got rid of the harvester?" Mike said.

"Pileup?" Vicky said.

"Long story. Some of Fry's men…. Point is, there was a big, rusty pileup, and beyond that, there was a big fuck-off combine harvester, and none of it's here anymore," Mike said.

"Well, that's good, isn't it?" Vicky asked.

"Yes and no," Hughes said. "Whoever did this was organised and they had resources. If they're on our side, that's great. If they're not, it's not so great."

The group continued looking for a moment. "The bodies," Emma said.

"What?" Hughes replied.

"The bodies are gone too. Remember? There were dozens of them on the bridge, now they're all gone," Emma said.

"There's movement," Lucy shouted, looking down towards the starlit city streets. "The engines and the lights must have roused the hungry masses."

They all peered into the darkness. "Bloody 'ell, you've got eyes like a rat in a brick shithouse," Hughes said, squinting into the distance. "Come on, let's mount up."

They all ran back to their vehicles and sped off once again, disappearing out of the city long before the first of the RAMs managed to reach the bridge.

"Who do you think did all that?" Jules asked once they were clear of Inverness.

"I have no idea, but sooner or later, we'll find out."

*

It was starting to get light when Mary roused Don from his sleep. They had been the lookouts at the North Ridge countless times together, and more often than not, they had just played cards and board games with nothing of note ever arising. Today would not be one of those days.

"Don," Mary said, shaking him.

"What? What is it?" he demanded, immediately seeing the concerned look on her face.

"I can hear engines."

He jumped out of bed and ran to the window of the small cabin. He grabbed the binoculars, but for the time being, could not see a vehicle. Mary was not mistaken, though; there were engines, and a good number of them, by the sound of it. He opened the door and they both walked out into the cold, leaving the warmth and comfort of the log stove behind them.

"I see someone—a man," he said, focussing the binoculars. The man had a torch, and started to flash a signal in Morse code.

"What's he saying?" Mary asked.

"I keep telling you that you should learn to bloody read."

"Why do I need to learn code while you're around?"

"It never harms."

"Meh. So what are they saying?"

"If you'd give me a bloody minute I'll tell you."

"It's Hughes. They've got vehicles and food. They're going straight to the village. Go get me the torch."

"Yes, sir."

She returned a moment later with the torch in her hand. Don grabbed it and started to signal back. Hughes disappeared again and a few seconds later, the lead vehicle in the convoy came into view. "That's some haul," Don said as they watched all the vehicles go by. "Better let Shaw know."

The two lookouts went inside and Mary picked up the radio. "Shaw, it's North Ridge. Over." There was no response, so she repeated the message.

"This is Shaw. Go ahead. Over."

"They're back. Over."

"They who? Over."

"Hughes is back. They're heading straight to the village. Over."

There was a long pause, but finally, the radio crackled again. "Okay, thanks. Over and out."

*

The sun began its climb on the horizon and the women who had been held captive in Loch Uig for so long just gawped at the image. It glistened against the rippling waves. They had all seen sunrises before, but never had they seen one so beautiful. Hughes and Jules looked at each other and smiled. He gradually applied the brakes as they began the final descent into the village, and by the time they pulled into the campsite carpark, there was a small congregation waiting for them.

Before they even climbed from the vehicles, the Safe Haven residents knew something was wrong. There were patched up bullet holes; obviously, a firefight had taken place. Not waiting to park in line, Mike pulled on the handbrake, opened the door and ran up to Shaw, who was waiting there with Jenny, Raj, Talikha, and a few nurses.

"What happened?" Mike demanded.

"We got attacked," Shaw replied.

"Attacked? By who?"

"They're taken care of." Shaw locked eyes with Mike and the younger man immediately understood. "Mike, Sarah's dead."

"*What?*"

"She got shot. George did too, but he's going to make it."

Mike looked towards Raj, who, in turn, looked to the ground. "I did everything I could," he said quietly.

"Fuck!" was all Mike could manage. He turned to look at the other vehicles just as Emma stepped down from the van she was driving. She began to walk across to join them. "Okay," he said quietly, "I'll tell her."

"What the hell happened?" Emma asked, looking around at the damage.

"Em. We were attacked," Mike said.

"Attacked by who?"

"Em," he said, taking hold of her hand. Mike started to cry. "Sarah's dead."

Emma just looked towards him, not able to speak. For a few seconds, she thought it was part of some terrible joke, but then as she saw Mike's tears glistening in the rising sun, she realised it was real. She gripped her stomach and turned her face away as tears threatened. She wrenched her hand free from his. "Where is she? I want to see her."

"Em—" Mike said.

"Where is she?" Emma screamed.

"She's still in the operating room," Raj said. Emma turned and ran towards the hospital.

"What the hell's going on?" Lucy asked as she, Jules and Wren all ran across. They looked startled as they saw the tears in Mike's eyes.

"Sarah's dead," his voice croaked.

Lucy put her hand up to her mouth and Jules began to cry too.

Shaw put a hand on Wren's shoulder. "Your grandad got hurt too, Wren, but he's doing fine. He's a tough old fella."

Wren's eyes widened and she ran towards the hospital without a word.

*

Emma ignored the nurse on duty, walked straight past the beds with the sleeping women, and switched the light on. Nobody had thought to turn the generator off with the events of the day, and the bright fluorescent tubes flickered on. The figure on the operating table was covered in a blue sheet, and as Emma approached, she hoped it was all some big mistake, that it wasn't her Sarah lying there. As she peeled the sheet back, though, a silent cry left her mouth and the tears she had fended off until now began to flow. "Oh Sarah! My sweet girl. Oh Sarah," she said over and over as she looked at her love's white face.

She put her hand up to her cheek and the shock of feeling the icy skin beneath her fingertips made her recoil and cry out louder. It was real, it was happening; Sarah really was dead. She peeled the sheet back and found Sarah's hand,

and, clutching it tightly in her own, she stepped forward and held it up to her heart.

"Oh god, Sarah. I'm not ready to say goodbye. I didn't get to say sorry! I didn't get to say a lot of things. There was so much I needed to tell you and now I'll never get the chance. I wish I could say I love you one last time. Just once." Emma let go of her hand and lifted her already stiffening body to her own. She felt the cold flesh of Sarah's cheek against hers and cried, and cried, and cried.

*

Lucy had given Emma a sedative to help her sleep. The day had been a long one. Shaw, Hughes, Jules, Beth, Barnes and Jenny took charge of dealing with the logistics of getting the new arrivals settled and fed. It was important that Mike and Lucy were with their family.

Emma and the children had been inconsolable all day, and the house seemed empty without Sarah. Everywhere they looked there was a memory.

Lucy and Mike sat in the kitchen with two candles burning. They each had a stiff drink in their hands and occasionally took a sip in the hope they could dull even part of the pain.

"I don't think I've ever seen Em like that. Even after Mum died," Mike said.

"They were in love. I mean, hell, if something happened to you, I'd be broken. Losing a parent is horrible, painful, devastating, but losing someone you share your life with, have planned your future with, that's...that's beyond painful."

Mike took another long drink and refilled his glass, then Lucy's. "Sammy and Jake were in a real state too."

"Sarah was like a sister to them...to all of us."

"If I hadn't gone off on one the other night, none of this would have happened."

Lucy leaned forward in her chair and put her hand over his. "We don't know that, Mike. It might still have happened and who knows? You could be dead, I could be dead, Em could be dead. We have no way of predicting what could or could not have happened. All we can do is deal with it. We saved all those women from a day to day horror I don't even want to think about. Wren found out that her sister hadn't been captured. We brought a shit load of food, meds and weapons back that will make Safe Haven stronger. It was right that we went. It was right we did what we did. There are no crystal balls, Mike. Nobody can see into the future. It was right to go."

"I love you," Mike said, squeezing her hand.

"I love you too. Now, come on, we should get some sleep. It's been a tough couple of days, and who knows what tomorrow will bring?

EPILOGUE

Mike was the first to wake the following morning. He looked towards Lucy, who was still fast asleep, then quietly climbed out of bed and went downstairs. He walked into the kitchen and saw an envelope leant up against one of the empty glasses from the previous evening. In printed capital letters it read: MIKE.

He opened it nervously and began to read.

Dear Mike,
There's no easy way to say this so I'm just going to come out and say it. I don't want to be around you anymore. I had happiness with Sarah, true happiness, and we had so many plans.
It's not enough just to be right. It's not enough to always look to take the moral high ground. Not everything is black and white, Mike. I gave in to you the other night. You made me feel guilty, and I gave in, and now I'll never spend another day with the woman I loved.

Don't get me wrong. You are my brother and I will always love you, but I realise now that while ever I'm around you, I'll never find peace.

I thought for a while I might, but I'm only deceiving myself. I'm going to be alone. What I know now in my heart is not something I would want Sammy and Jake to learn at such a young age, so they are better off without me there.

I'm sure they will flourish, and I know you will not let anything happen to them. I am taking Sarah's body and I am going to lay her to rest myself.

Don't worry about me, and don't come looking for me. The way I'm feeling at the moment, I'll probably shoot you.

Who knows, one day I might show up at the door to say hi, but Safe Haven is the last place I want to be at the moment—way too many memories.

Give my love to Lucy and tell Raj none of this was his fault. I don't doubt for a second that he did all he could to save her.

I hope you have a happy and long life.

I love you.

Emma

THE END.

A NOTE FROM THE AUTHOR

I really hope you enjoyed this book and would be very grateful if you took a minute to leave a review on Amazon and Goodreads.

If you would like to stay informed about what I'm doing, including current writing projects, and all the latest news and release information; these are the places to go:

Join the fan club on Facebook
https://www.facebook.com/groups/127693634504226

Like the Christopher Artinian author page
https://www.facebook.com/safehaventrilogy/

Buy exclusive and signed books and merchandise, subscribe to the newsletter and follow the blog:
https://www.christopherartinian.com/

Follow me on Twitter
https://twitter.com/Christo71635959

Follow me on Amazon
https://amzn.to/2I1llU6

Follow me on Goodreads
https://bit.ly/2P7iDzX

Other books by Christopher Artinian:

Safe Haven: Rise of the RAMs
Safe Haven: Realm of the Raiders
Safe Haven: Reap of the Righteous
Safe Haven: Ice
Before Safe Haven: Lucy
Before Safe Haven: Alex
Before Safe Haven: Mike
The End of Everything: Book 1
The End of Everything: Book 2
The End of Everything: Book 3

Anthologies featuring short stories by Christopher Artinian

Undead Worlds: A Reanimated Writers Anthology

Featuring: Before Safe Haven: Losing the Battle by Christopher Artinian

Tales from Zombie Road: The Long-Haul Anthology
Featuring: Condemned by Christopher Artinian

Treasured Chests: A Zombie Anthology for Breast Cancer Care
Featuring: Last Light by Christopher Artinian

Trick or Treat Thrillers (Best Paranormal 2018) Featuring: The Akkadian Vessel.

CHRISTOPHER ARTINIAN

Christopher Artinian was born and raised in Leeds, West Yorkshire. Wanting to escape life in a big city and concentrate more on working to live than living to work, he and his family moved to the Outer Hebrides in the northwest of Scotland in 2004, where he now works as a full-time author.

Chris is a huge music fan, a cinephile, an avid reader and a supporter of Yorkshire county cricket club. When he's not sat in front of his laptop living out his next post-apocalyptic/dystopian/horror adventure, he will be passionately immersed in one of his other interests.

Printed in Great Britain
by Amazon